JOE DEATH
AND THE GRAVEN IMAGE

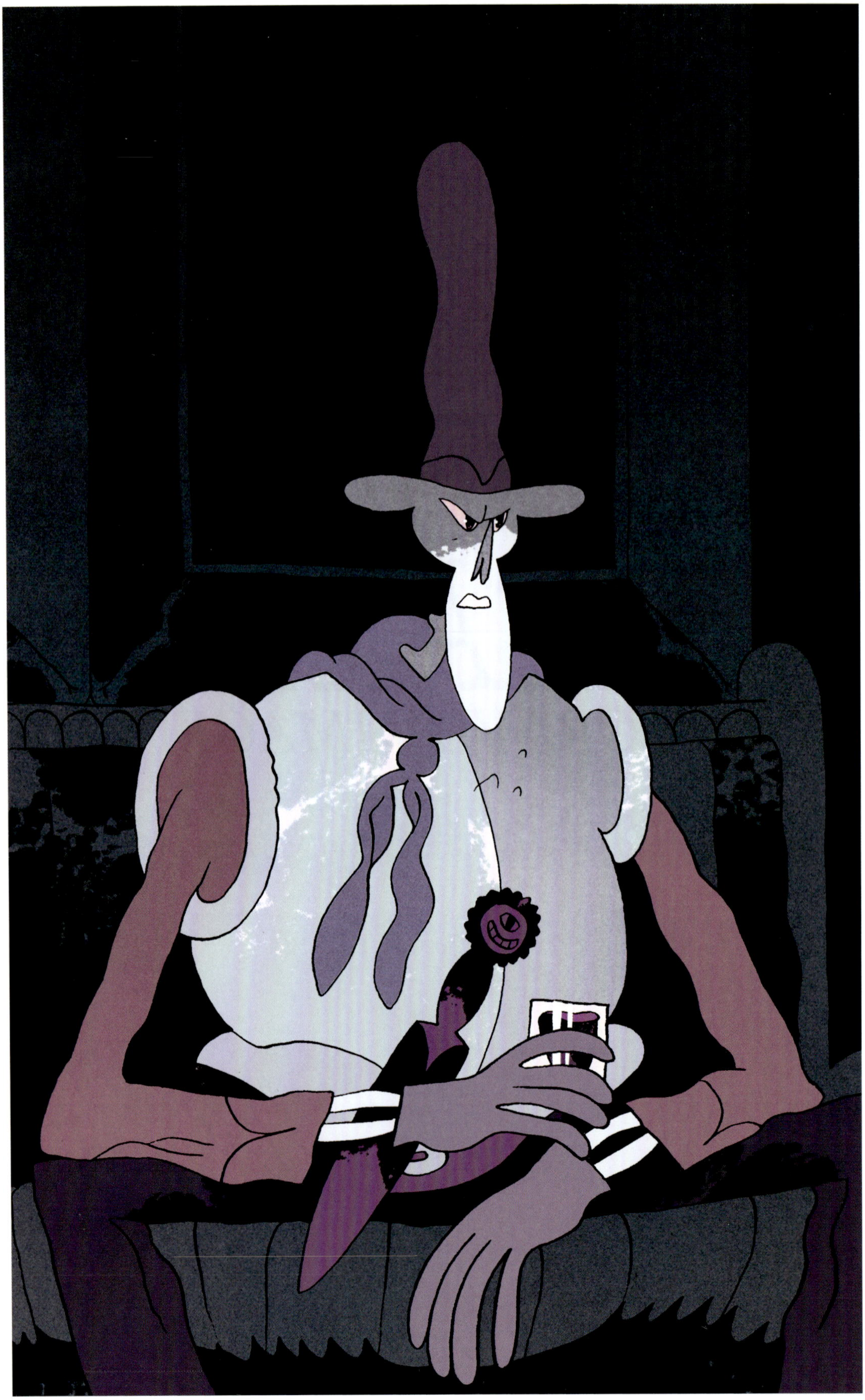

JOE DEATH
AND THE GRAVEN IMAGE

by
BENJAMIN SCHIPPER

DARK HORSE BOOKS

publisher
MIKE RICHARDSON

editor
SPENCER CUSHING

assistant editor
KONNER KNUDSEN

designer
PATRICK SATTERFIELD

digital art technician
ANN GRAY

JOE DEATH AND THE GRAVEN IMAGE, January 2023. Published by Dark Horse Comics LLC, 10956 SE Main Street, Milwaukie, Oregon 97222. Joe Death and the Graven Image © 2023 Benjamin Schipper. All rights reserved. Dark Horse Comics® and the Dark Horse logo are trademarks of Dark Horse Comics LLC, registered in various categories and countries. All rights reserved. No portion of this publication may be reproduced or transmitted, in any form or by any means, without the express written permission of Dark Horse Comics LLC.

Published by Dark Horse Books
A division of Dark Horse Comics LLC
10956 SE Main Street
Milwaukie, OR 97222

DarkHorse.com

First edition: January 2023
Ebook ISBN 978-1-50671-708-1
ISBN 978-1-50671-707-4

1 3 5 7 9 10 8 6 4 2
Printed in China

NEIL HANKERSON *executive vice president* • TOM WEDDLE *chief financial officer* • DALE LaFOUNTAIN *chief information officer* • TIM WIESCH *vice president of licensing* • MATT PARKINSON *vice president of marketing* VANESSA TODD-HOLMES *vice president of production and scheduling* • MARK BERNARDI *vice president of book trade and digital sales* • KEN LIZZI *general counsel* • DAVE MARSHALL *editor in chief* • DAVEY ESTRADA *editorial director* • CHRIS WARNER *senior books editor* • CARY GRAZZINI *director of specialty projects* • LIA RIBACCHI *art director* • MATT DRYER *director of digital art and prepress* • MICHAEL GOMBOS *senior director of licensed publications* • KARI YADRO *director of custom programs* • KARI TORSON *director of international licensing* • SEAN BRICE *director of trade sales* • RANDY LAHRMAN *director of product sales*

Library of Congress Cataloging-in-Publication Data

Names: Schipper, Benjamin, author, artist.
Title: Joe Death and the graven image / Benjamin Schipper.
Description: First edition. | Milwaukie, OR : Dark Horse Books, 2022. | Summary: "After surviving a brutal massacre, the last surviving heir of the town of Hard Hollow is kidnapped by the bloodthirsty bandit, Scary Harry. The spirit of Hard Hollow enlists Joe Death--a six-shooter-totin' grim reaper--to rescue the child"-- Provided by publisher.
Identifiers: LCCN 2020043198 | ISBN 9781506717074 (trade paperback)
Subjects: LCSH: Graphic novels.
Classification: LCC PN6727.S283 J64 2021 | DDC 741.5/973--dc23
LC record available at https://lccn.loc.gov/2020043198

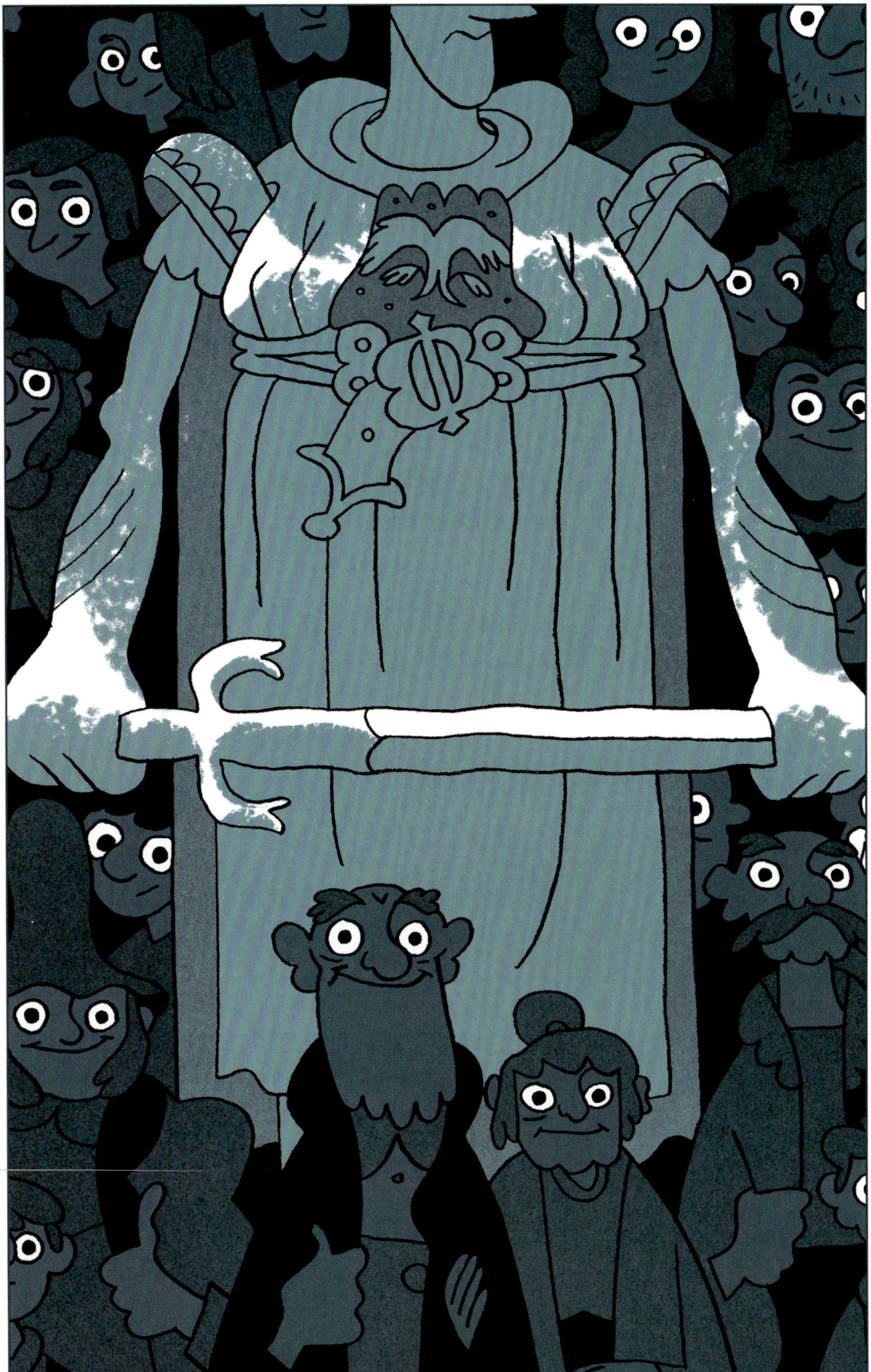

JOE DEATH
AND THE GRAVEN IMAGE

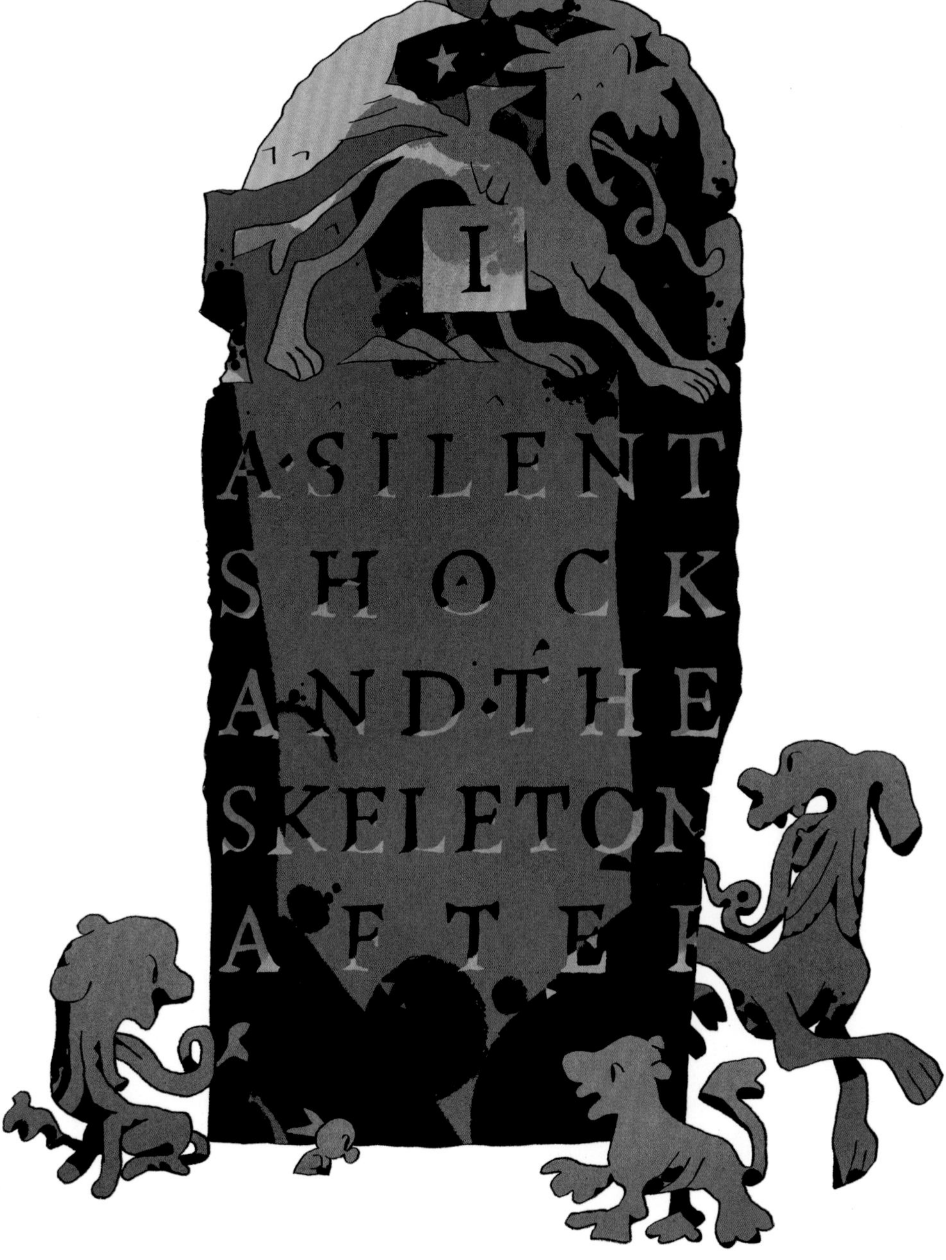
I
A SILENT
SHOCK
AND THE
SKELETON
AFTER

Wings inside that tummy / Flutter, flutter. Flutter, flutter.
Wind all through that body / Gusty, guster. Gusty, guster.
Rain down cheeks forever? / Never, never. Oh, not ever.

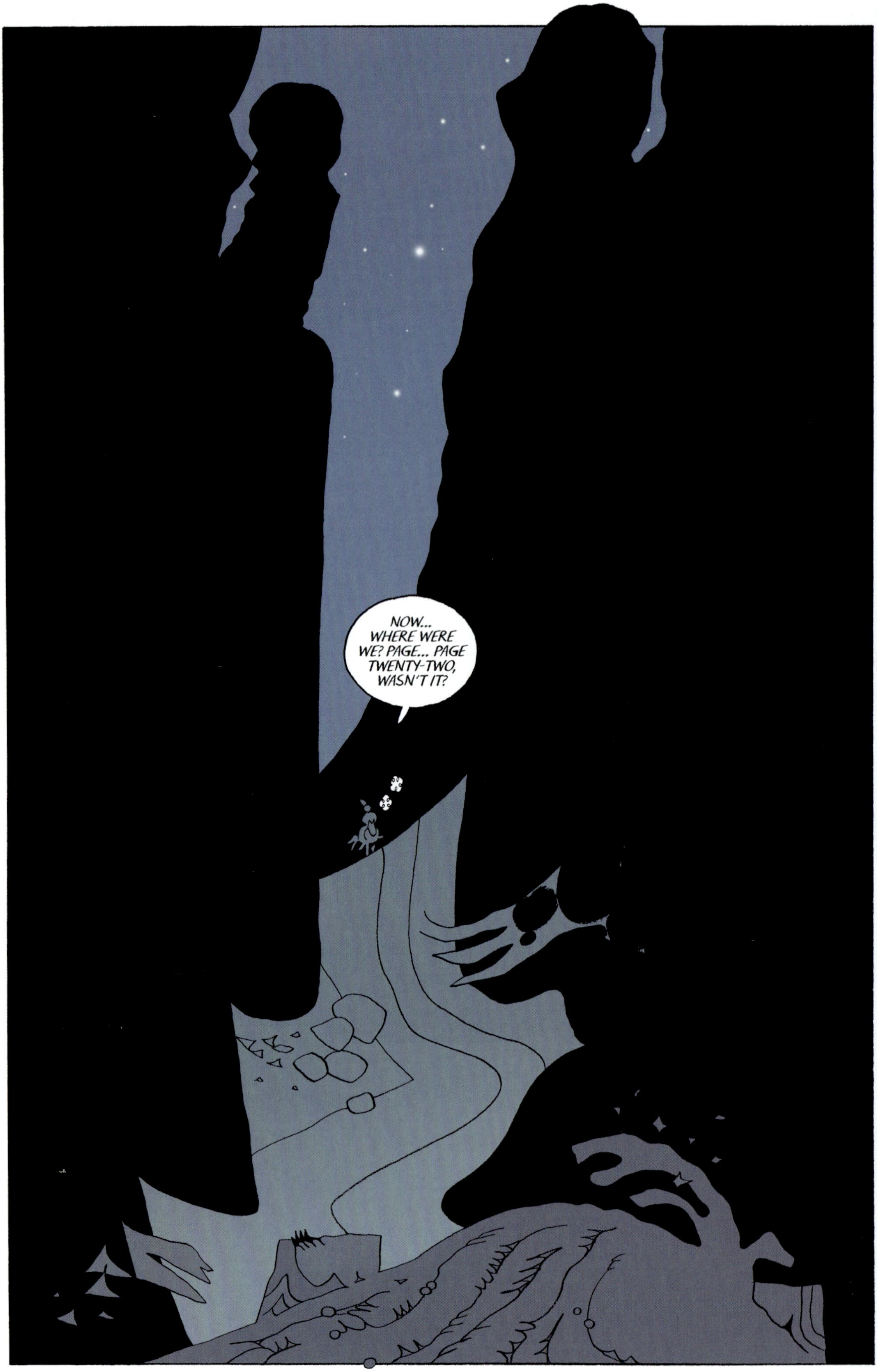
NOW... WHERE WERE WE? PAGE... PAGE TWENTY-TWO, WASN'T IT?

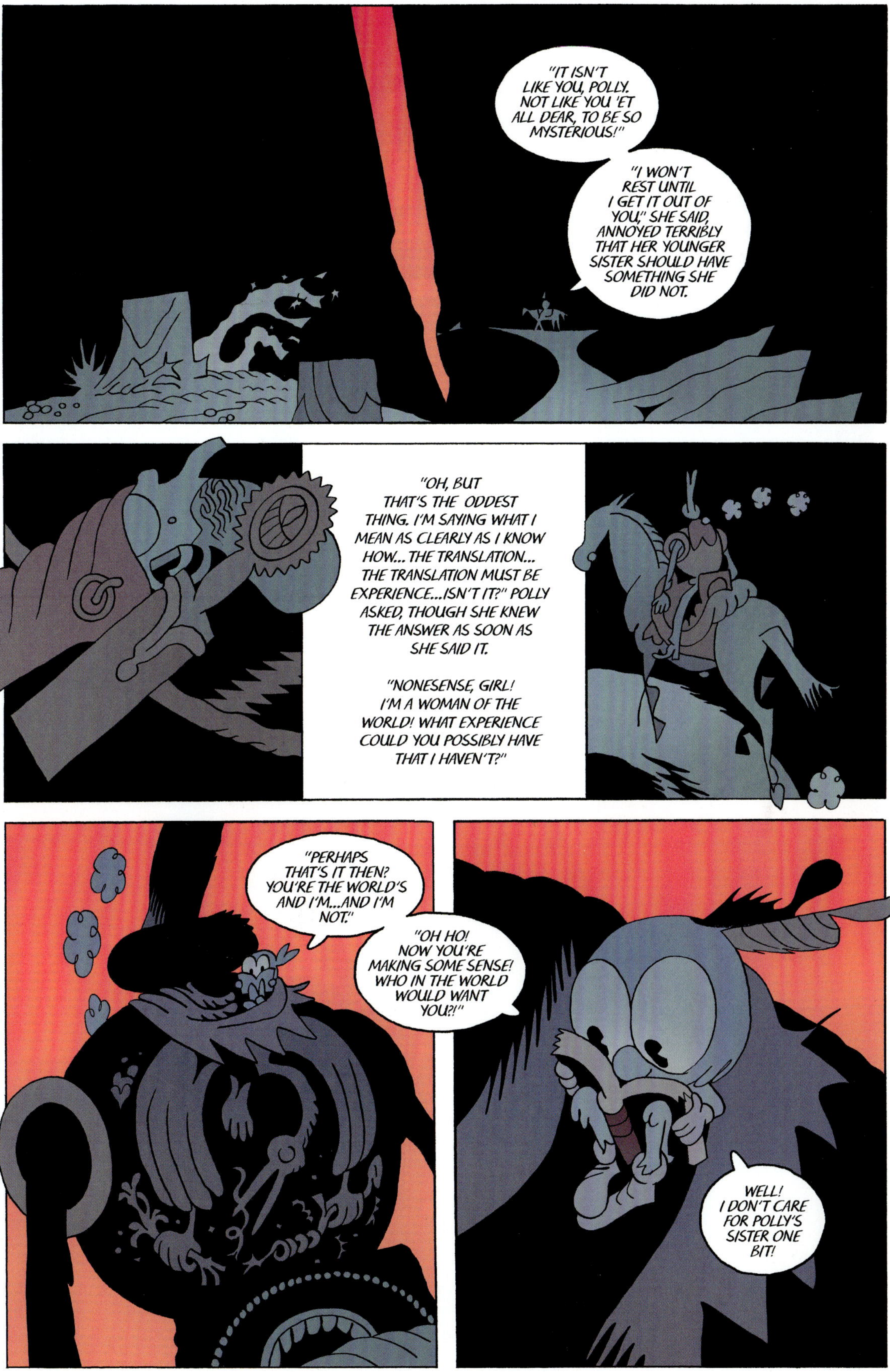
"IT ISN'T LIKE YOU, POLLY. NOT LIKE YOU 'ET ALL DEAR, TO BE SO MYSTERIOUS!"
"I WON'T REST UNTIL I GET IT OUT OF YOU," SHE SAID, ANNOYED TERRIBLY THAT HER YOUNGER SISTER SHOULD HAVE SOMETHING SHE DID NOT.
"OH, BUT THAT'S THE ODDEST THING. I'M SAYING WHAT I MEAN AS CLEARLY AS I KNOW HOW... THE TRANSLATION... THE TRANSLATION MUST BE EXPERIENCE...ISN'T IT?" POLLY ASKED, THOUGH SHE KNEW THE ANSWER AS SOON AS SHE SAID IT.
"NONESENSE, GIRL! I'M A WOMAN OF THE WORLD! WHAT EXPERIENCE COULD YOU POSSIBLY HAVE THAT I HAVEN'T?"
"PERHAPS THAT'S IT THEN? YOU'RE THE WORLD'S AND I'M...AND I'M NOT."
"OH HO! NOW YOU'RE MAKING SOME SENSE! WHO IN THE WORLD WOULD WANT YOU?!"
WELL! I DON'T CARE FOR POLLY'S SISTER ONE BIT!

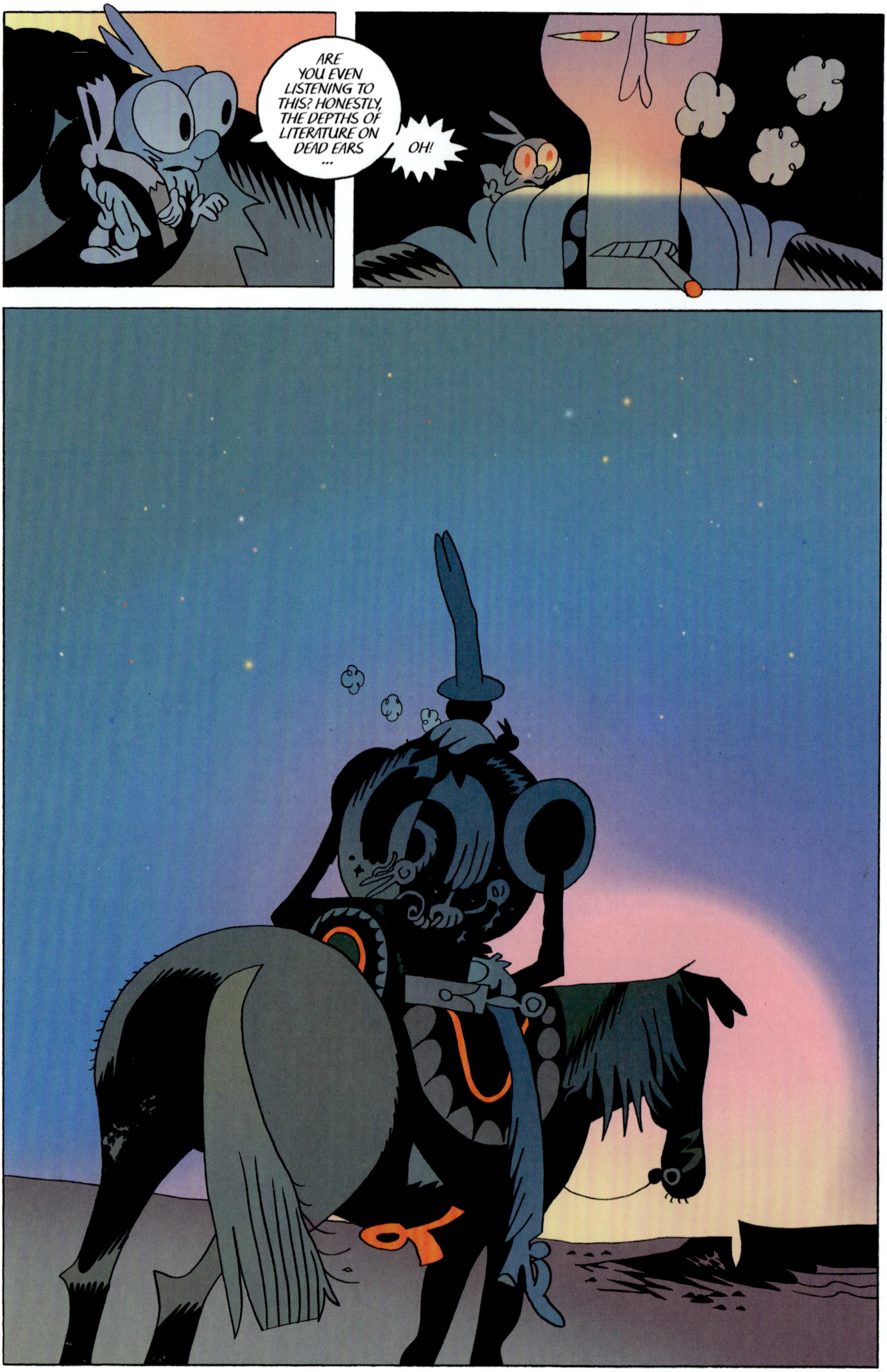
ARE YOU EVEN LISTENING TO THIS? HONESTLY, THE DEPTHS OF LITERATURE ON DEAD EARS ...
OH!

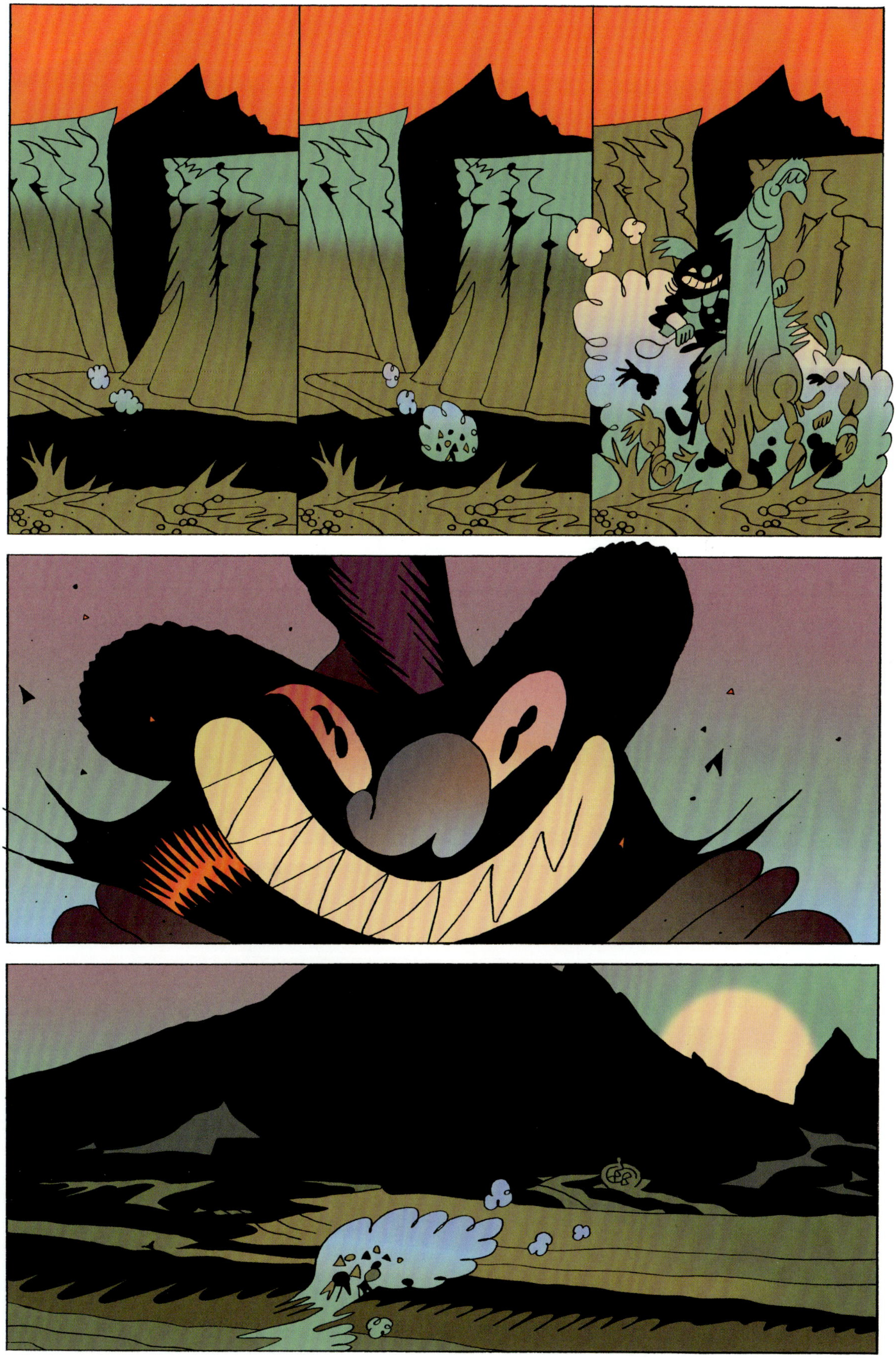

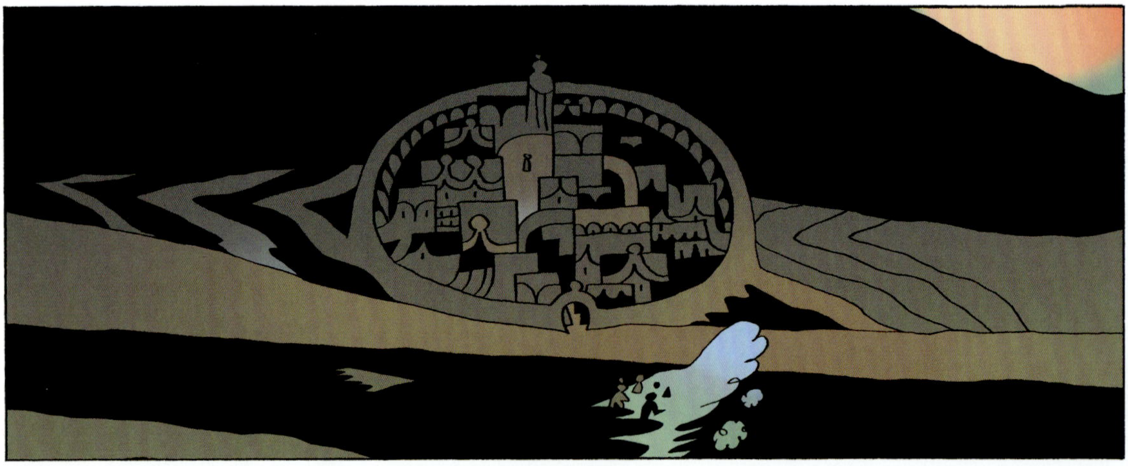

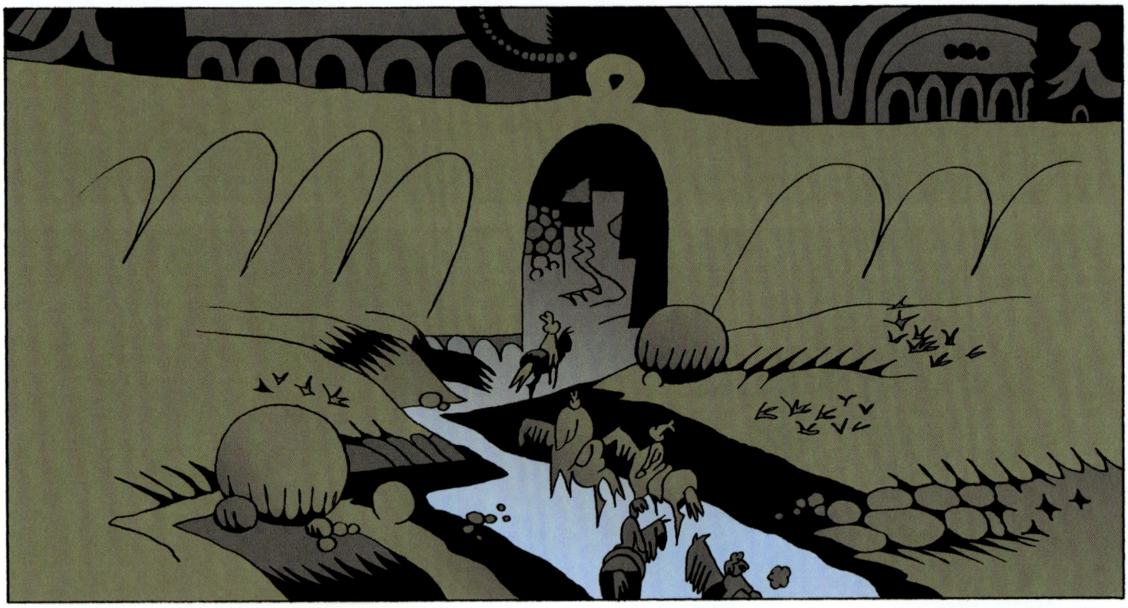

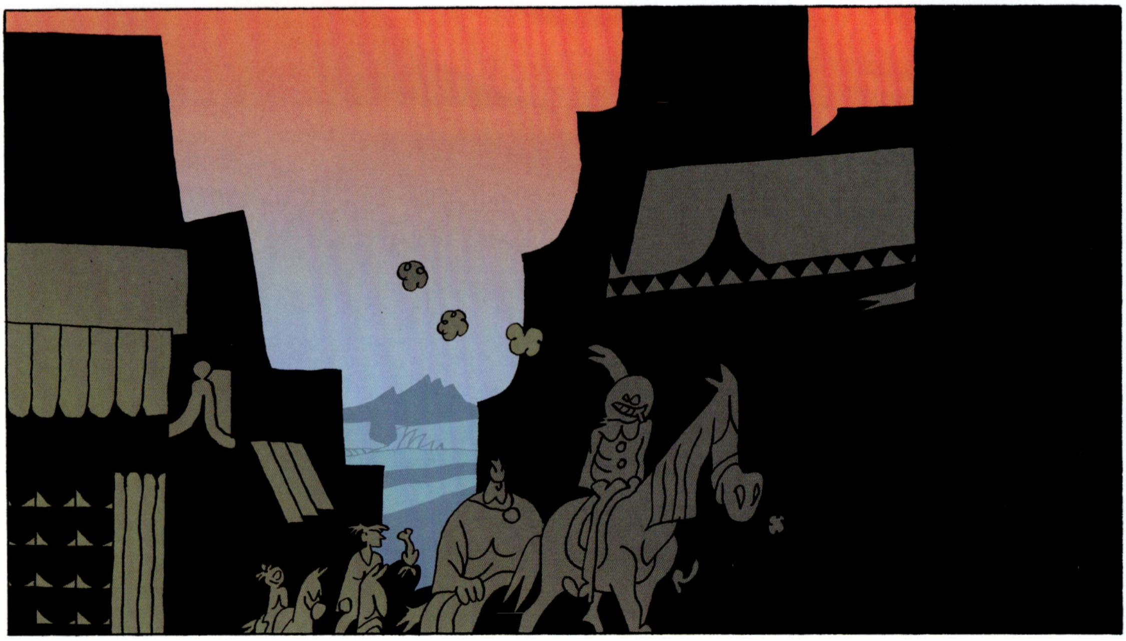

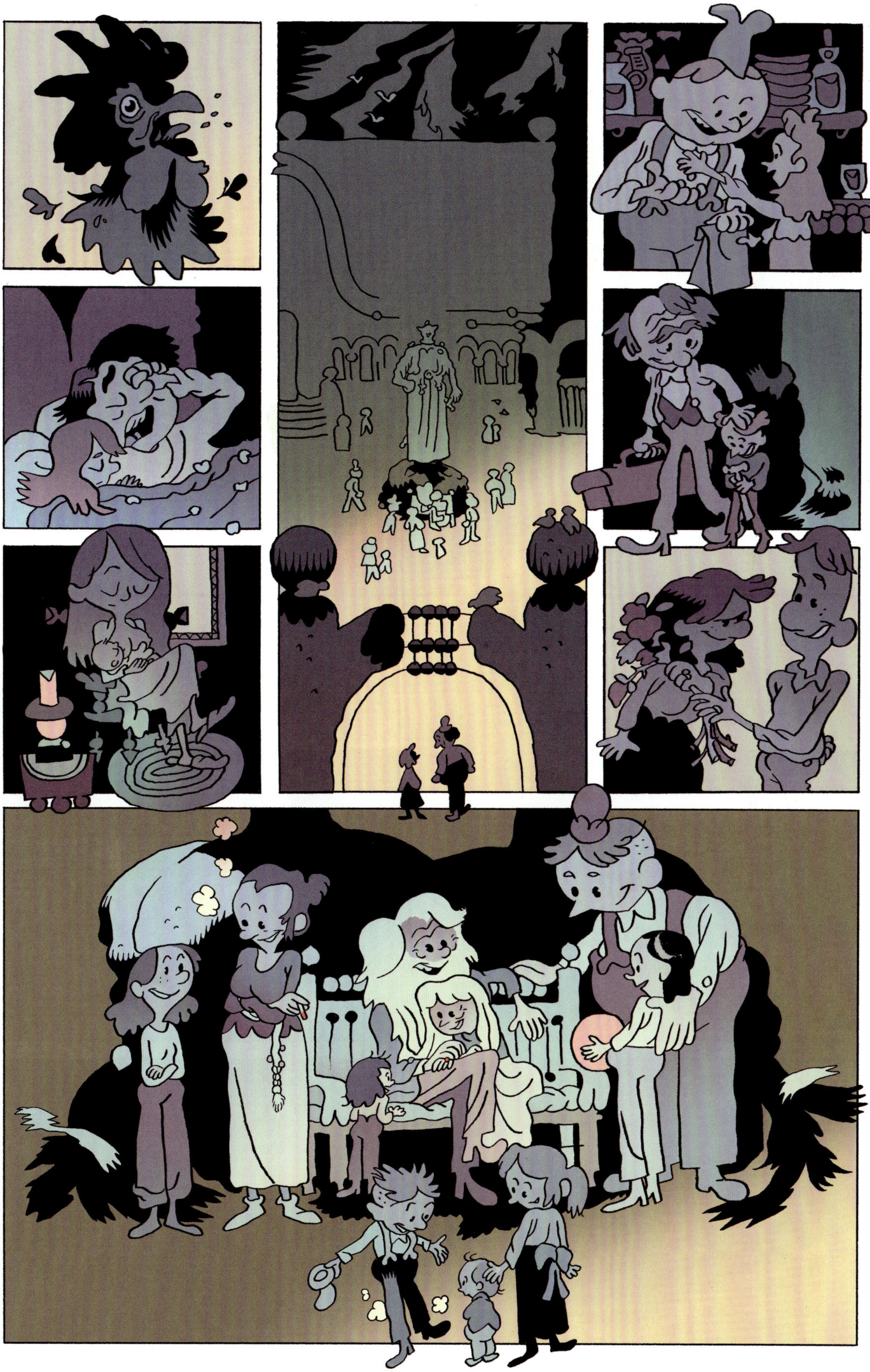

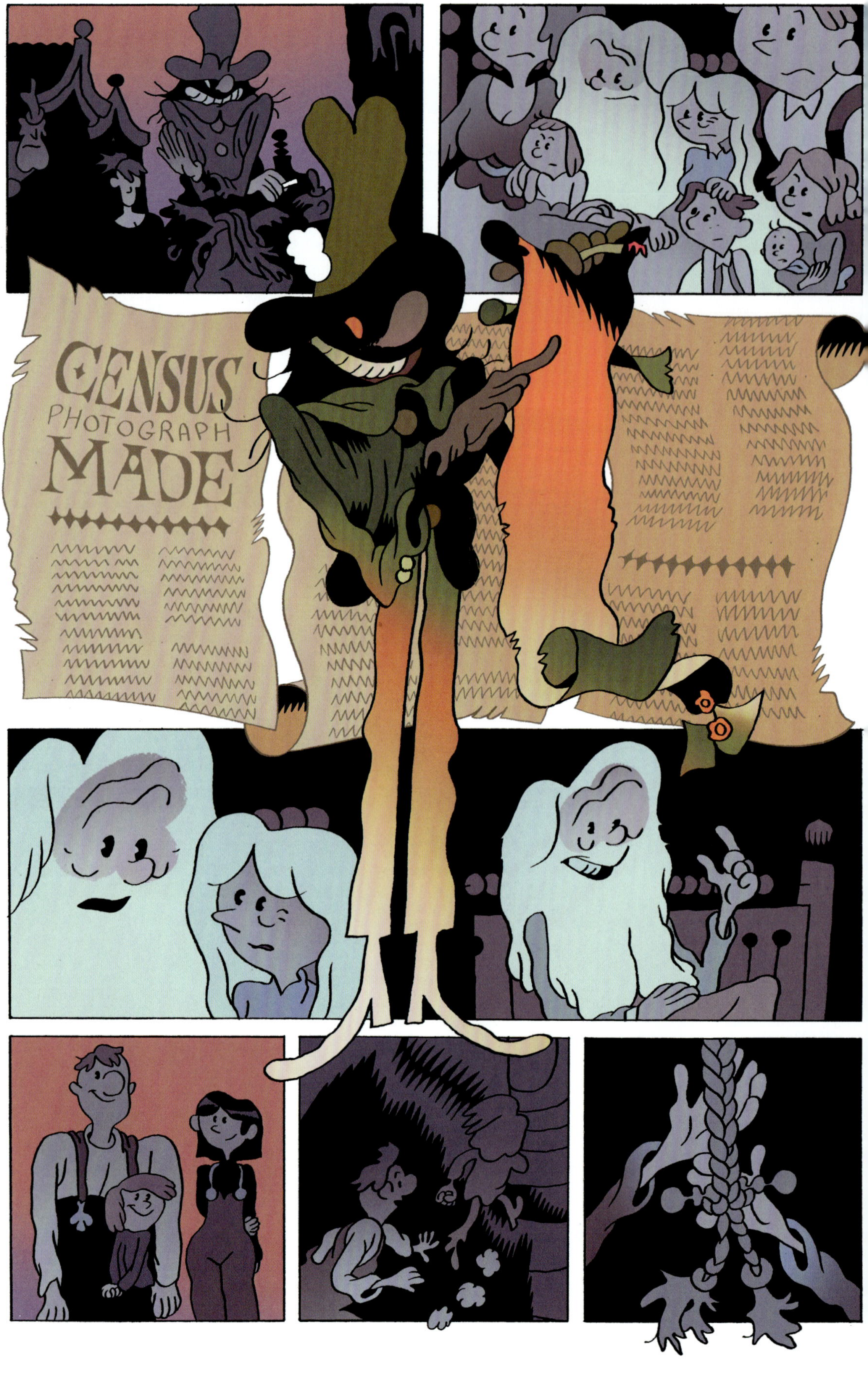
CENSUS
PHOTOGRAPH
MADE

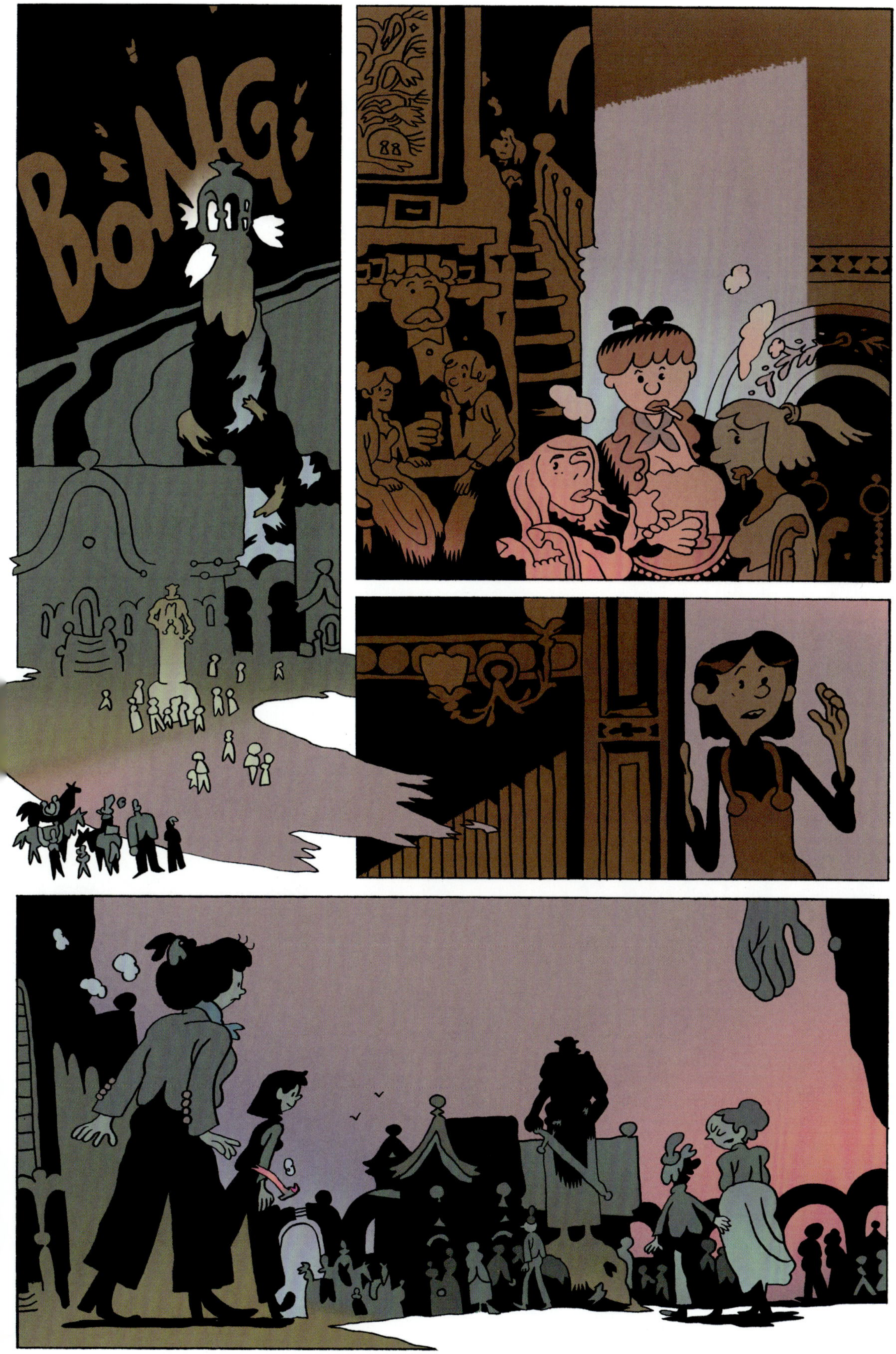
BONG

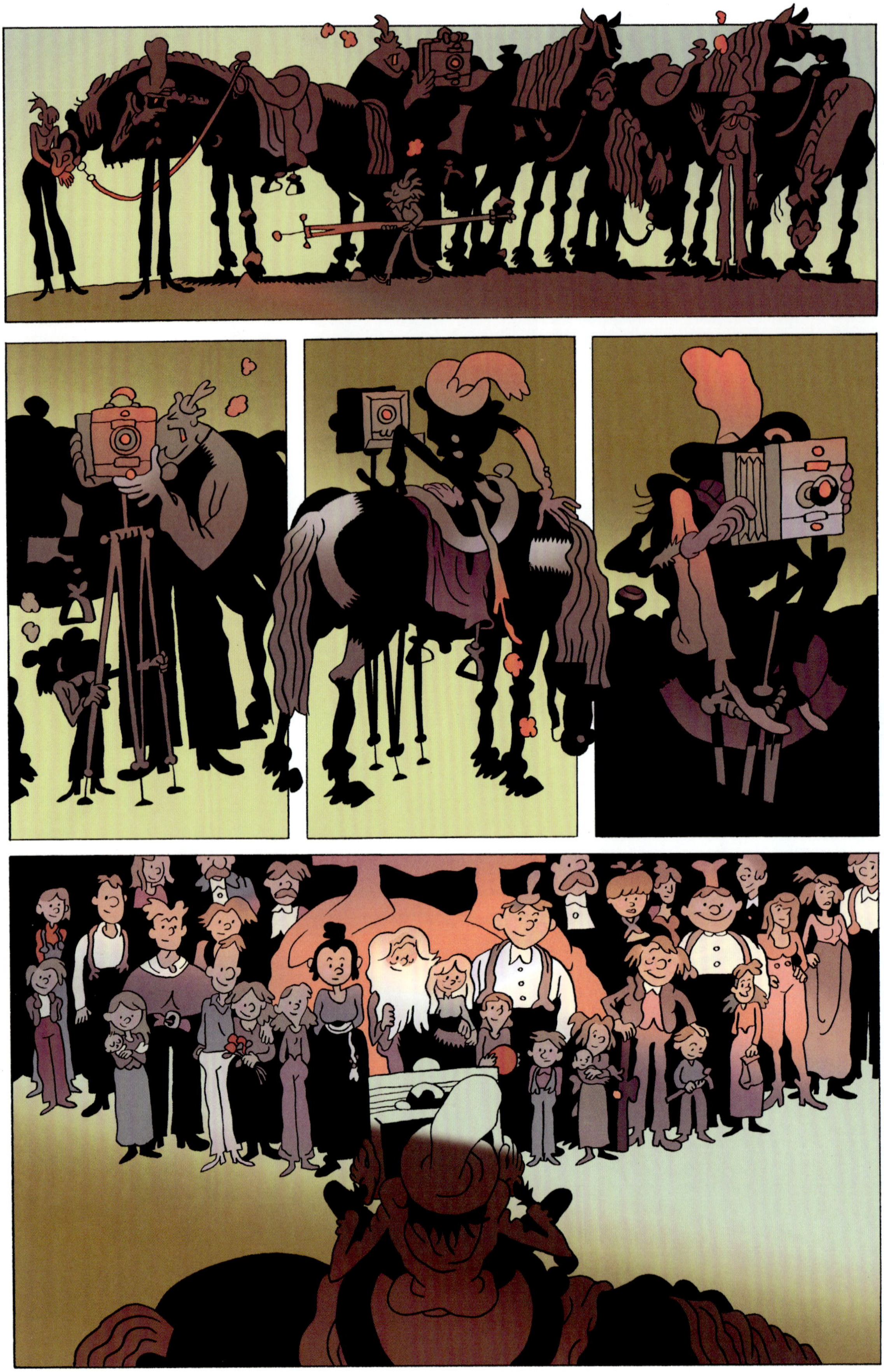

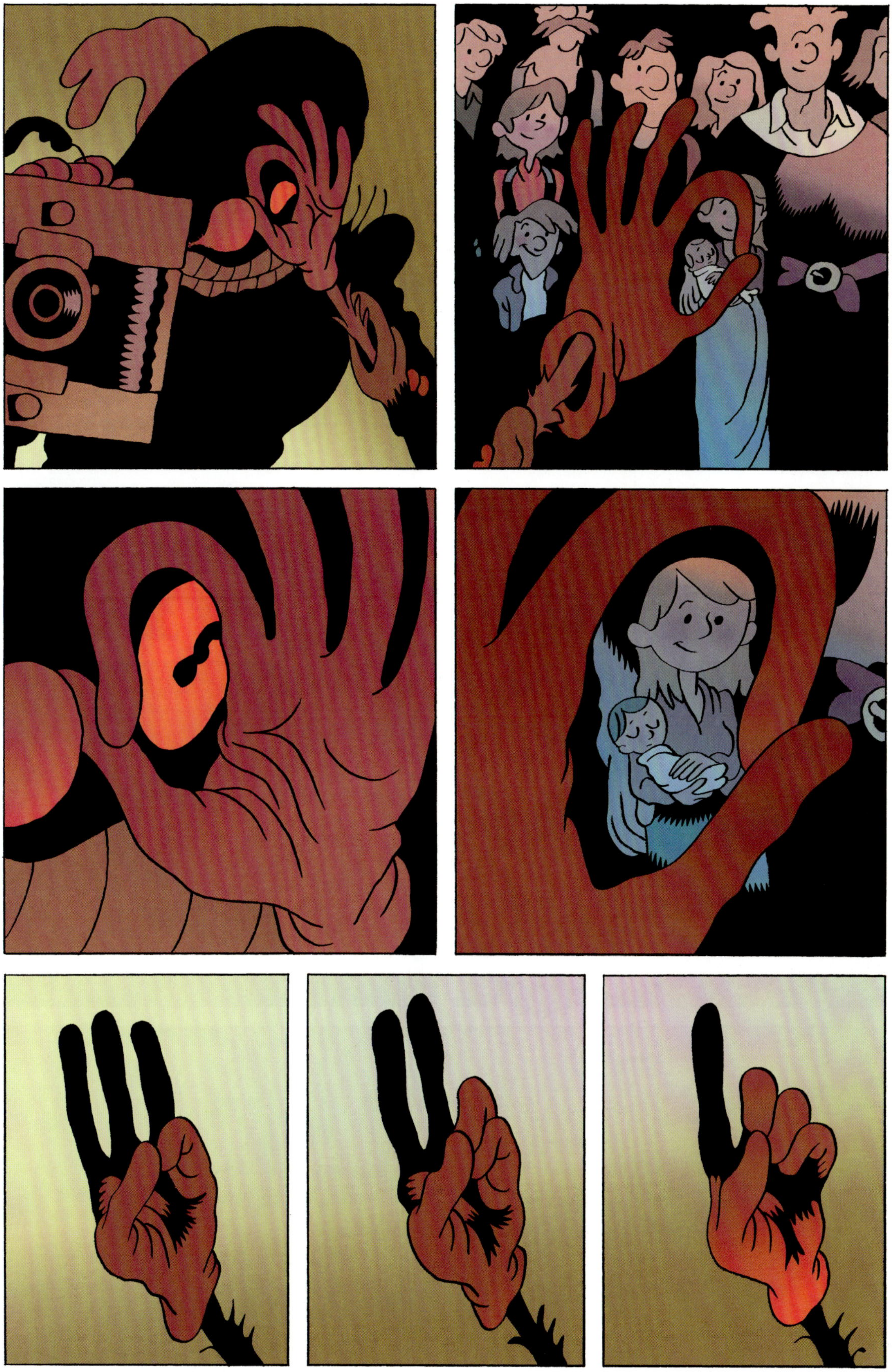

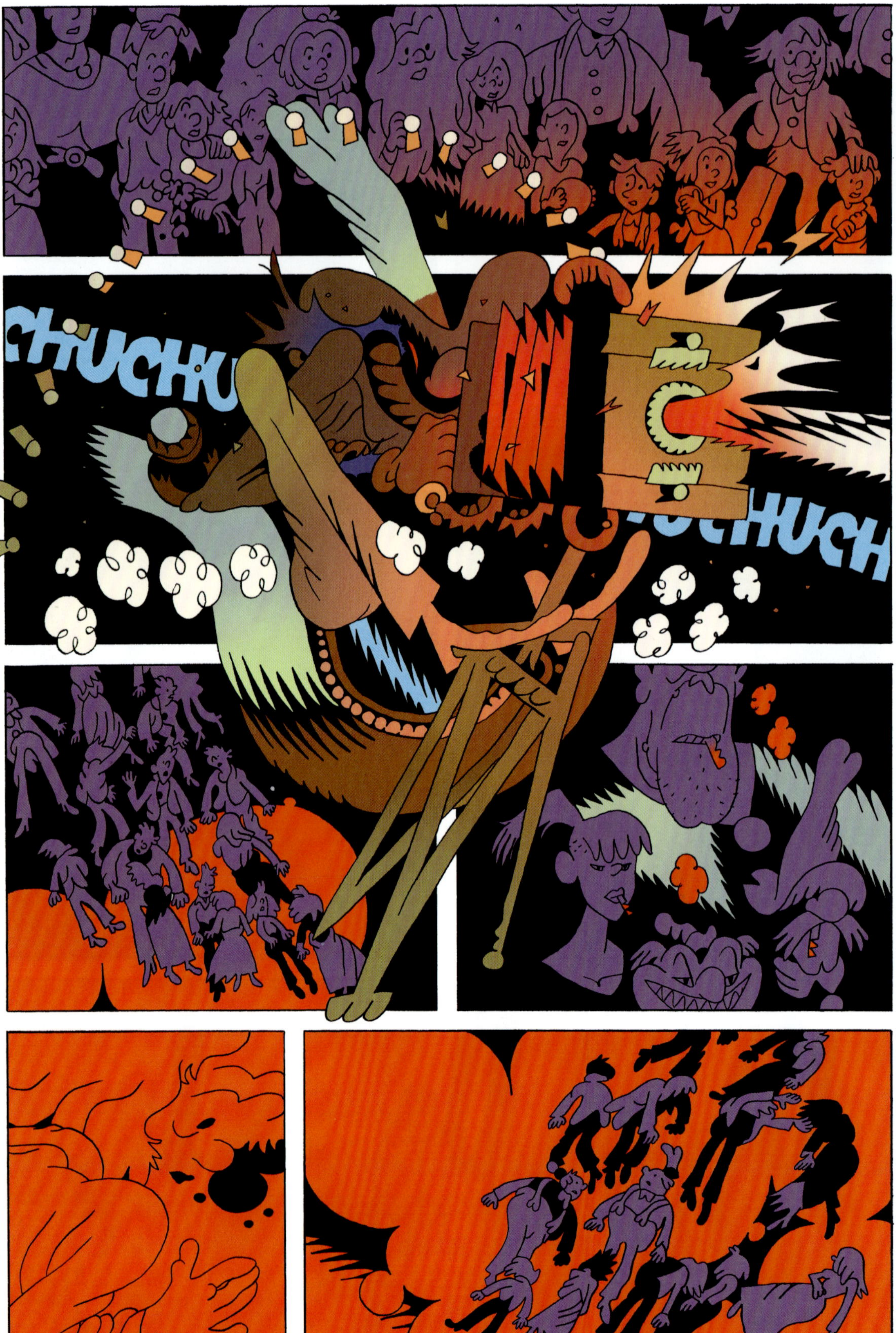
CHUCHU
CHUCH

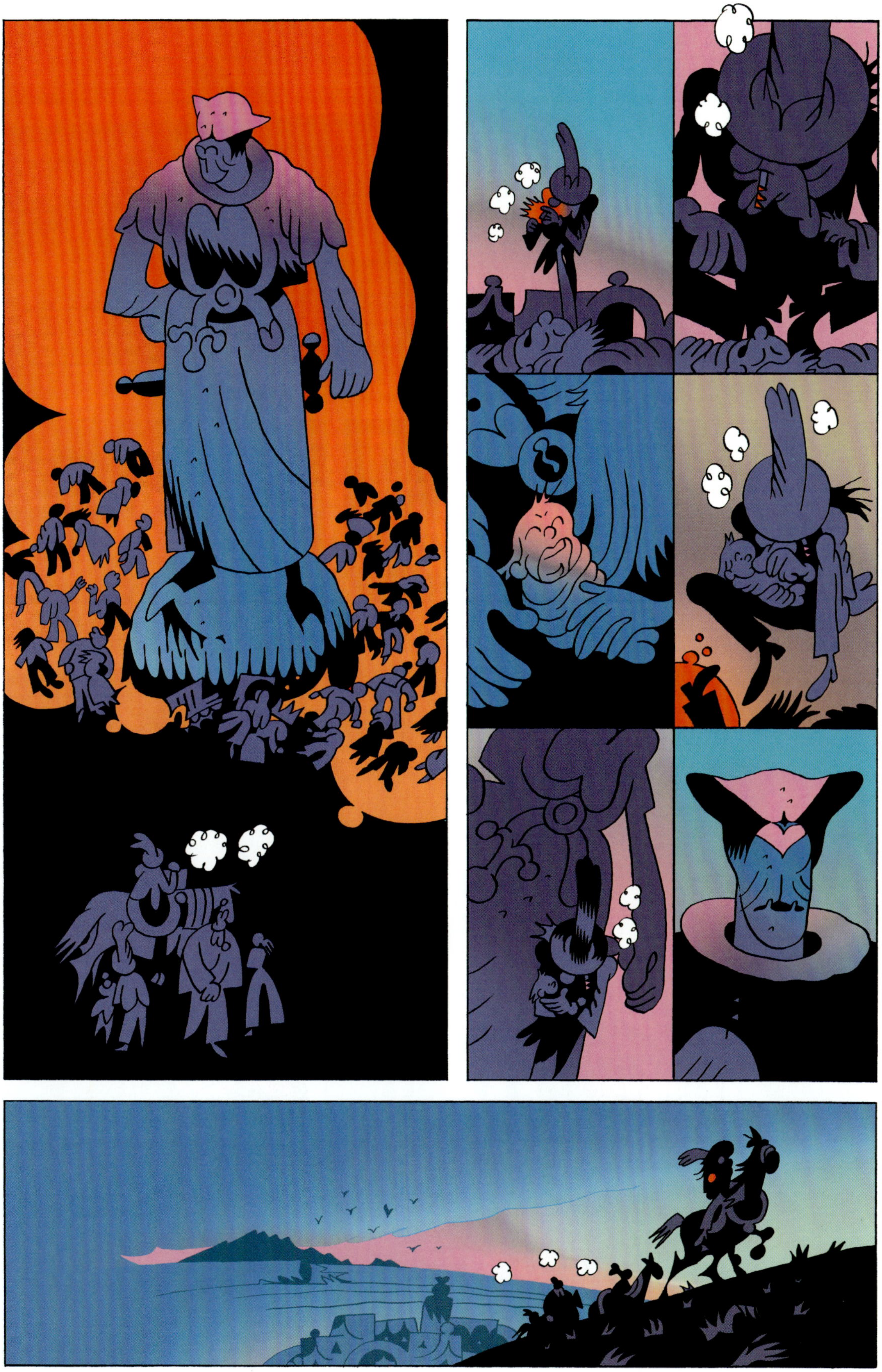

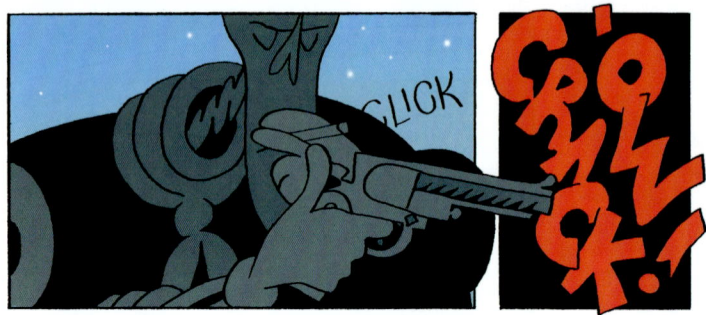

CLICK

CR-O-ACK!

WHAT A MESS.

OH NO...

WHERE ARE WE?

SÄUHER-DOUGH IDWAY. WESTERN FOOTHILLS OF THE GORECKI LINE.

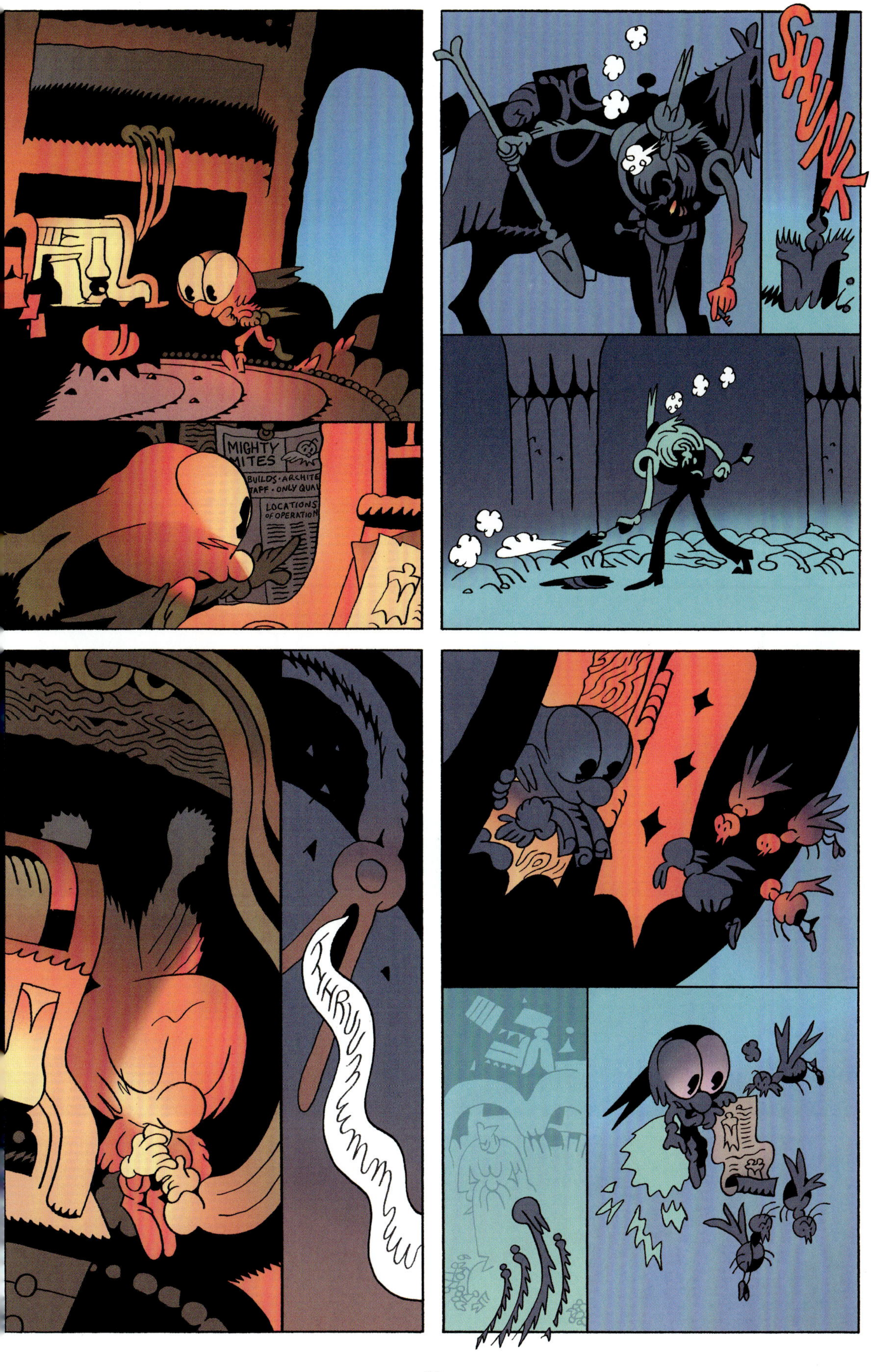
SHUNK
MIGHTY MITES
BUILDS • ARCHITE
TAFF • ONLY QUA
LOCATIONS OF OPERATION

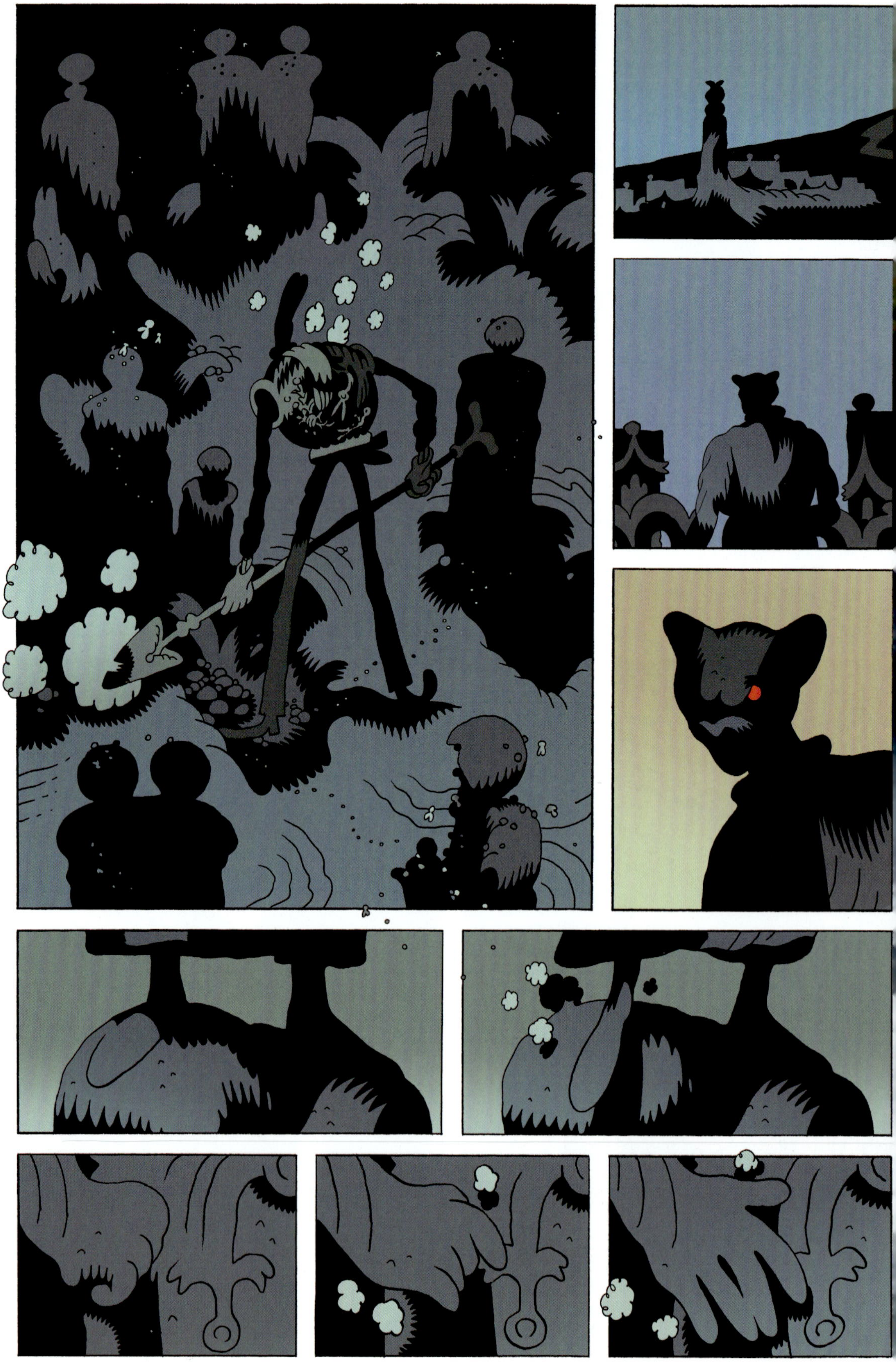

YOOOOWWW
OWWW
STAY YOUR HAND, KINSMAN. PUT BACK THY KEY. MY TIME HERE ISN'T OVER. YEA, THE NEWEST CHILD IS NOT HERE... THE SMALL BABE.
HE ALONE REMAINS IN THE VALLEY, BUT WAS TAKEN.
BY WHO?

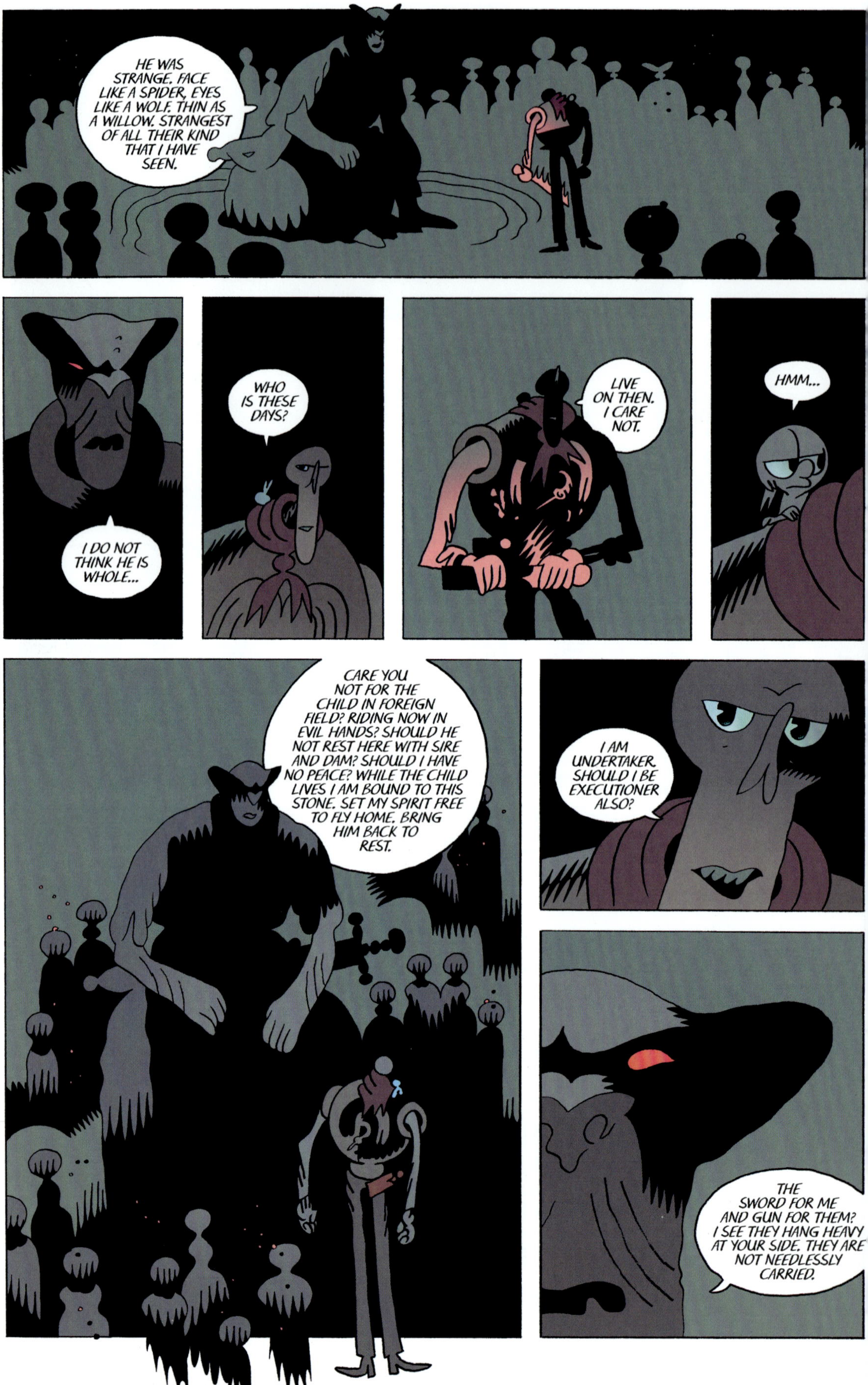
HE WAS STRANGE. FACE LIKE A SPIDER, EYES LIKE A WOLF. THIN AS A WILLOW. STRANGEST OF ALL THEIR KIND THAT I HAVE SEEN.
I DO NOT THINK HE IS WHOLE...
WHO IS THESE DAYS?
LIVE ON THEN. I CARE NOT.
HMM...
CARE YOU NOT FOR THE CHILD IN FOREIGN FIELD? RIDING NOW IN EVIL HANDS? SHOULD HE NOT REST HERE WITH SIRE AND DAM? SHOULD I HAVE NO PEACE? WHILE THE CHILD LIVES I AM BOUND TO THIS STONE. SET MY SPIRIT FREE TO FLY HOME. BRING HIM BACK TO REST.
I AM UNDERTAKER. SHOULD I BE EXECUTIONER ALSO?
THE SWORD FOR ME AND GUN FOR THEM? I SEE THEY HANG HEAVY AT YOUR SIDE. THEY ARE NOT NEEDLESSLY CARRIED.

IN THE LIGHT OF THE MOON, I CHARGE YOU NOW.

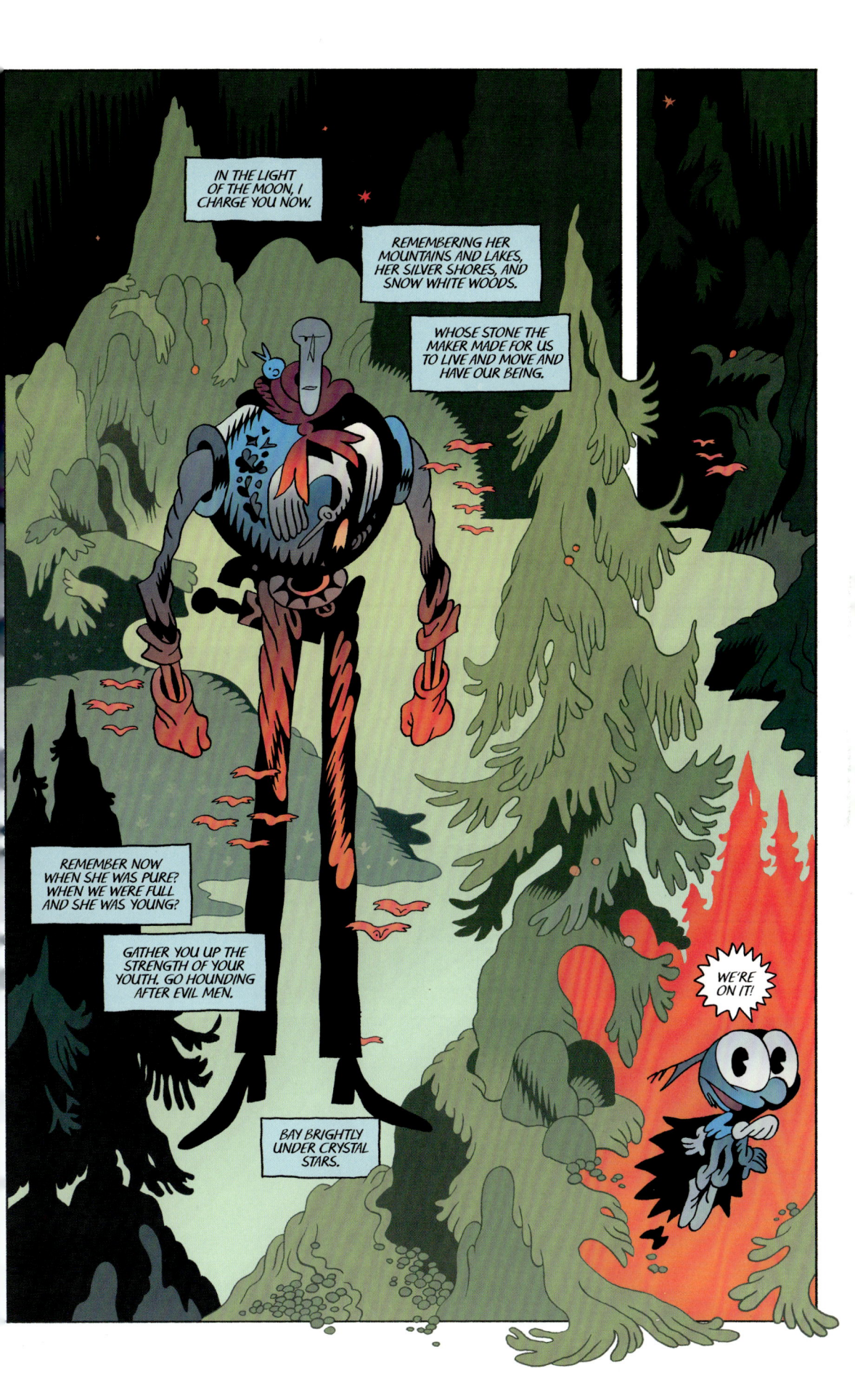

REMEMBERING HER MOUNTAINS AND LAKES, HER SILVER SHORES, AND SNOW WHITE WOODS.

WHOSE STONE THE MAKER MADE FOR US TO LIVE AND MOVE AND HAVE OUR BEING.

REMEMBER NOW WHEN SHE WAS PURE? WHEN WE WERE FULL AND SHE WAS YOUNG?

GATHER YOU UP THE STRENGTH OF YOUR YOUTH. GO HOUNDING AFTER EVIL MEN.

BAY BRIGHTLY UNDER CRYSTAL STARS.

WE'RE ON IT!

"MY HUNTING DAYS ARE OVER."

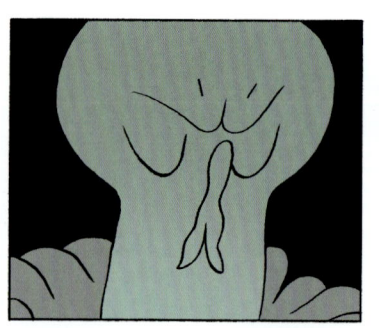

"HMPHF!"

"I'LL SEE WHAT I CAN DO."

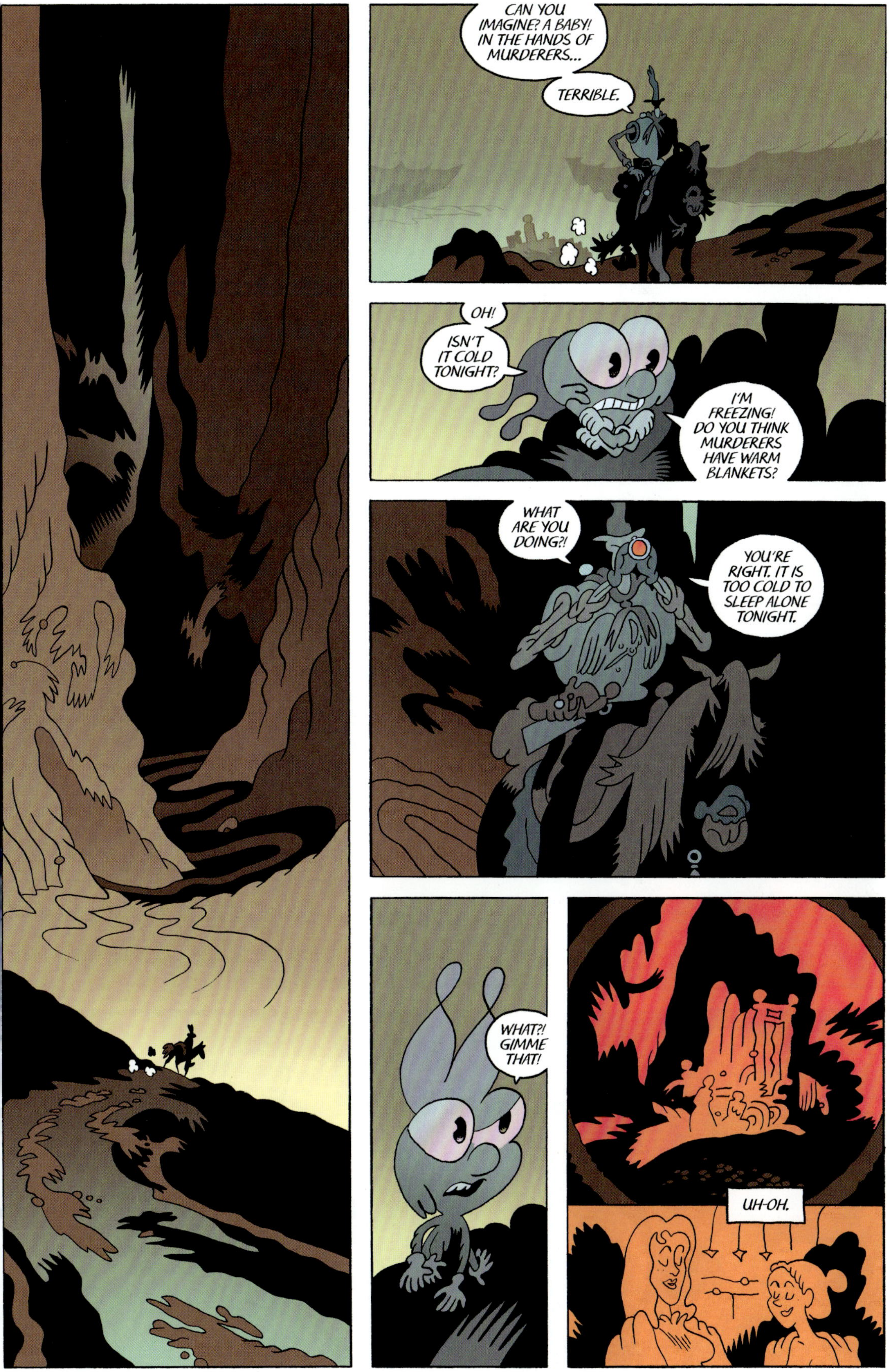
CAN YOU IMAGINE? A BABY! IN THE HANDS OF MURDERERS...
TERRIBLE.
OH!
ISN'T IT COLD TONIGHT?
I'M FREEZING! DO YOU THINK MURDERERS HAVE WARM BLANKETS?
WHAT ARE YOU DOING?!
YOU'RE RIGHT. IT IS TOO COLD TO SLEEP ALONE TONIGHT.
WHAT?! GIMME THAT!
UH-OH.

GOOD WOMEN, BE CALM. YOU HAVE NO NEED OF FEAR. IN TRUTH, I AM YOUR BEST HOPE FOR SAFETY TONIGHT. NOT FAR FROM HERE AND NOT LONG AGO A TOWN OF LITTLE PEOPLE WAS RAVAGED. AN AWFUL SIGHT. THE KILLERS ARE NEAR, YOU HAVEN'T SEEN ANYTHING-
-STRANGE, HAVE YOU?
NOTHING SO STRANGE AS YOURSELF, SIR!
GOODNESS! HOW ARE WE TO KNOW YOU AREN'T THE KILLER?
HUSH, BEATRICE. DON'T YOU SEE HE'S RUSH-LEEDO? THEY MAY BE RARE BUT HONORABLE.
RUSH-LEEDO?
THE TALKING BEAST?
MOON MEN?
LEGENDS!
BUT SISTER, I REMEMBER DARK RUMORS OF THEIR KIND ALONG WITH THE GOOD.
INDEED, A TEST OF YOUR FIBER IS REQUIRED...
WHO FILLED THE BIG EMPTY AND CHANNELED THIS VALLEY?
WHO STRUNG THE NIGHT LIGHTS AND WEDGED OUT THE DARKNESS?

HIS NAMES ARE MANY, AND WHO CAN KNOW HIM? TO ME HE IS MAGIC AND...
AND ONCE UPON A TIME HIS BIG BOOTS STEPPED INTO SHAGGY TIME. HE ROVED BLACK WILDERNESS AND WROUGHT IT BEAUTIFUL. HE DUG THE FLOOR AND LEVELED THE FIELD. HE RAISED THE CANOPY AND PINHOLED THE ABYSS WITH SIGIL AND SIGN AND WE ENTERED WITH HIM. THE PARTY BEGAN, THE DANCE WAS WILD, AND WE WERE GLAD TO REST IN THE RIBBONS OF TIME.
BUT THE TIMES GREW ILL, AND DANGEROUS. NO?
VERY...
REJOICE, SISTER. WE ARE IN LUCK, THIS ONE IS NEITHER SO BAD THAT WE SHOULD RUN, NOR SO GOOD WE SHAN'T HAVE FUN TO- -NIGHT. AND HE SPINS YARNS! FINE ONES TOO, I THINK.
DO! JUST SO LONG AS THEY ARE YARNS, AND NOT WEBS TO CATCH US IN! HEHE.
I WAS CAUGHT, THE NOOSE AROUND ME.
THE CORI-OI SURROUNDING. EYELSS IN THE DEEPS, SIGHTLESS EXCEPT FOR SMELL. THE FEAR LEAKED OUT OF ME, A STRONG SCENT, SO I REPLACED IT WITH BOLDNESS AND A LITTLE WRATH BESIDES.
WELL, THEIR NOSES GOT TO WORKING AND THEY DIDN'T WANT ANY PIECE OF THAT.
THEY POOFED! LIKE SMOKE ON THE BREEZE.
MAGNIFICENT, MR. JOE! I'LL SLEEP WELL WITH YOU ON WATCH!
MAGNIFICENT, MR. JOE...
SLEEP SWEETLY, FAIR PEOPLE, MY EYES ARE PEELED AND THE SAFETY'S OFF.
SAFELY PEELED AND EYES ARE OFF!

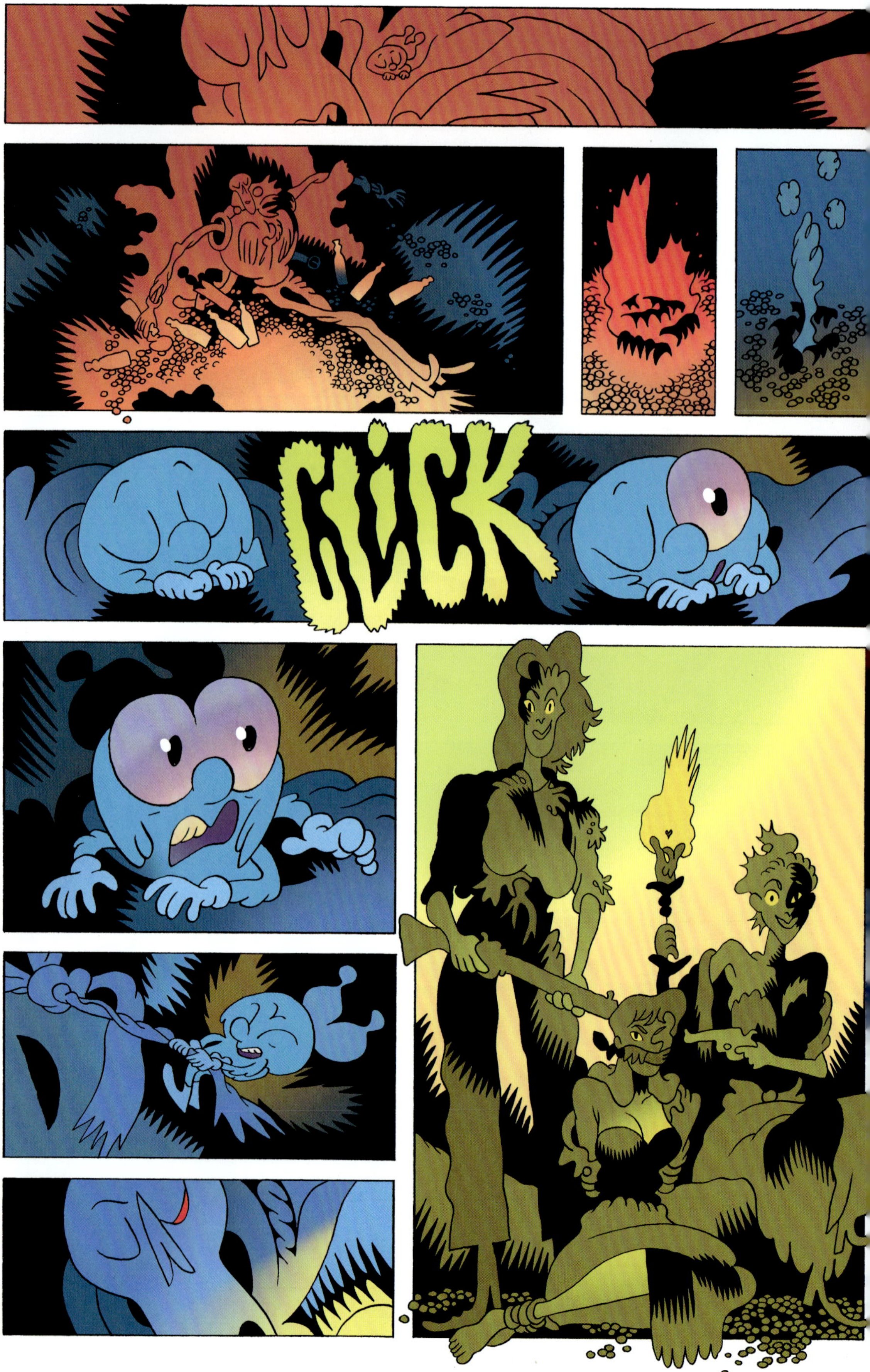
CLICK

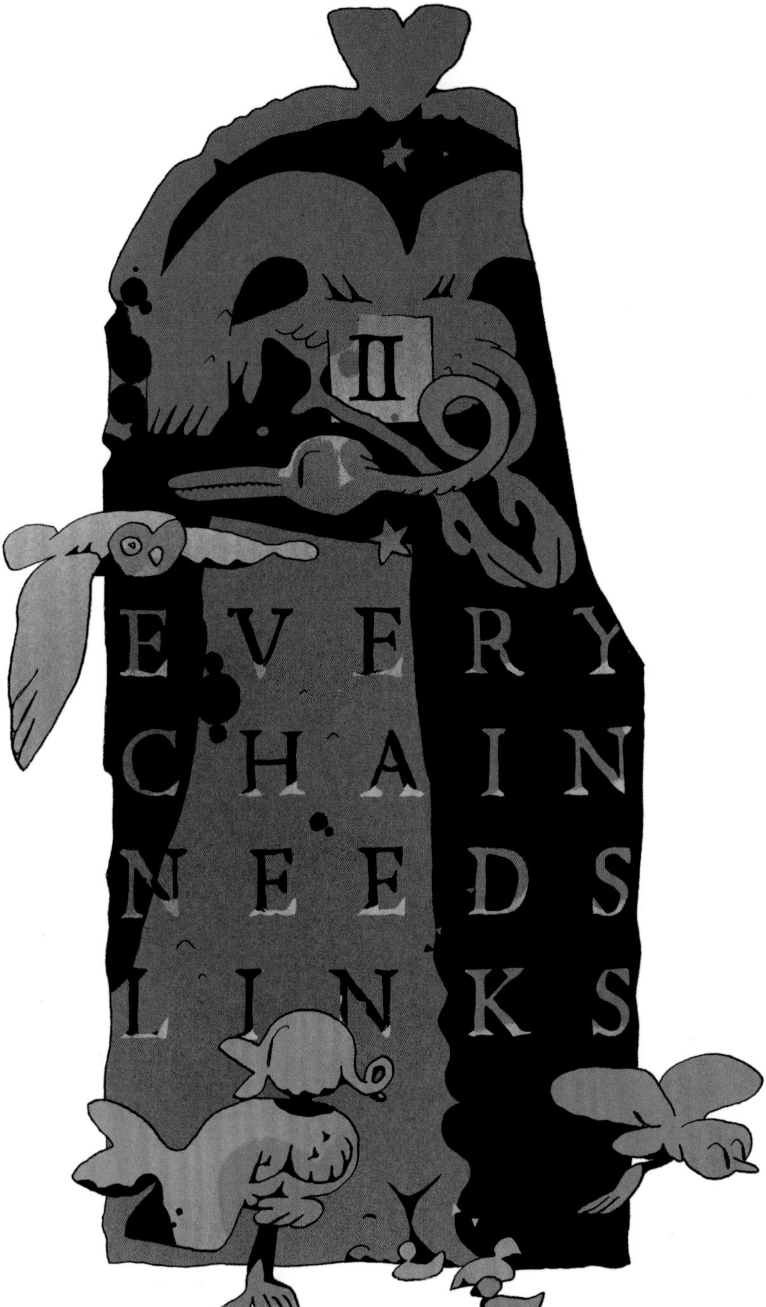
II
EVERY
CHAIN
NEEDS
LINKS

Golden ring in piggy's snout,
That's what they thought of her.
But silver tongue in cotton mouth,
A truth unmasked that year.

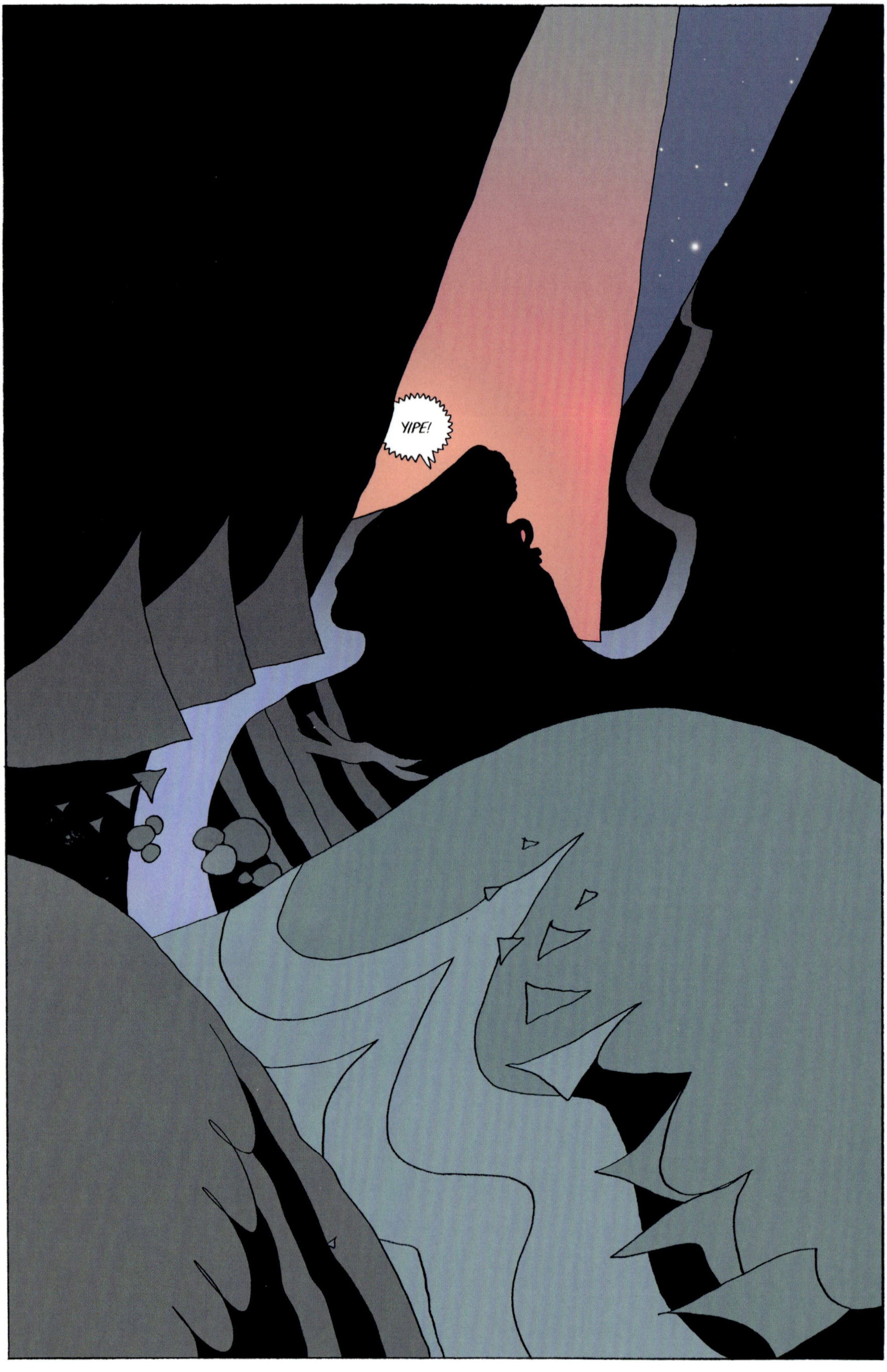
YIPE!

NOW IT'S YOUR TURN TO STAY CALM, GOOD SLAVE AND BEAST THAT YOU ARE, UNWILLING TO SHAKE THE CHAINS THAT BIND YOU TO US.
LOOK NOW ON FREE WOMEN AND DO AS COMMANDED.
IS IT THE MARK OF FREEDOM TO BIND AND GAG OTHERS?
WHO IS THAT BETWEEN YOU?
SHE IS NOT FOULED BY WITCH'S STINK.
DOG! YOUR KIND WAS MADE FOR LICKING OUR BOOTS! YOU HAVE NO STOMACH FOR FREEDOM.
AND THAT STORY! MY, MY HOW YOU DO PUT ON AIRS!
OUR CORI FRIENDS HAVE SPOKEN OF YOU BEFORE.
IN AN ALTOGETHER DIFFERENT FASHION.
THEY SAY YOU TURNED TAIL SO FAST YOU LEFT THEM CHICKEN FEATHERS IN THE BREEZE!
HAHA HA!

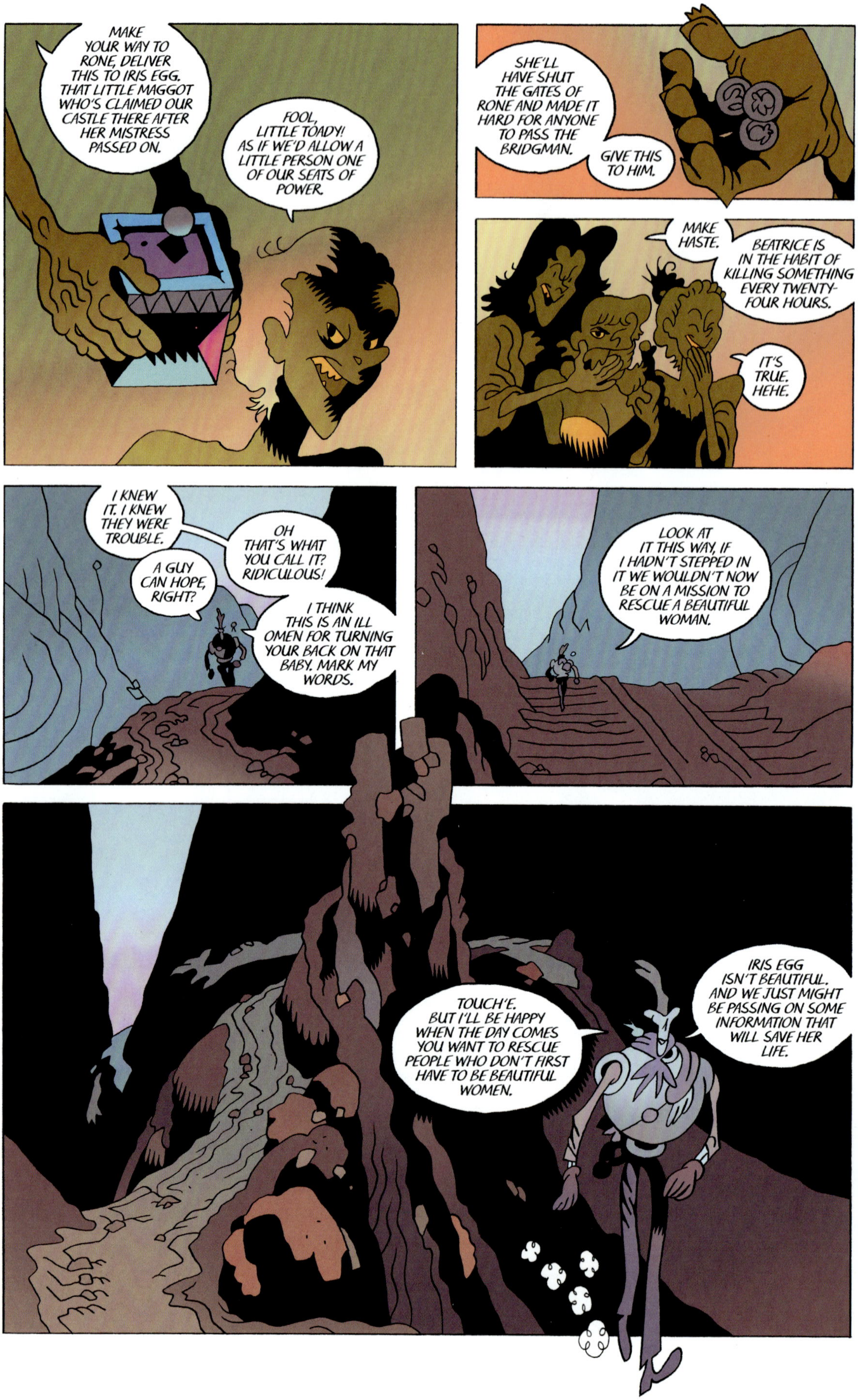
MAKE YOUR WAY TO RONE, DELIVER THIS TO IRIS EGG. THAT LITTLE MAGGOT WHO'S CLAIMED OUR CASTLE THERE AFTER HER MISTRESS PASSED ON.
FOOL, LITTLE TOADY! AS IF WE'D ALLOW A LITTLE PERSON ONE OF OUR SEATS OF POWER.
SHE'LL HAVE SHUT THE GATES OF RONE AND MADE IT HARD FOR ANYONE TO PASS THE BRIDGMAN.
GIVE THIS TO HIM.
MAKE HASTE.
BEATRICE IS IN THE HABIT OF KILLING SOMETHING EVERY TWENTY-FOUR HOURS.
IT'S TRUE. HEHE.
I KNEW IT. I KNEW THEY WERE TROUBLE.
OH THAT'S WHAT YOU CALL IT? RIDICULOUS!
A GUY CAN HOPE, RIGHT?
I THINK THIS IS AN ILL OMEN FOR TURNING YOUR BACK ON THAT BABY. MARK MY WORDS.
LOOK AT IT THIS WAY, IF I HADN'T STEPPED IN IT WE WOULDN'T NOW BE ON A MISSION TO RESCUE A BEAUTIFUL WOMAN.
IRIS EGG ISN'T BEAUTIFUL, AND WE JUST MIGHT BE PASSING ON SOME INFORMATION THAT WILL SAVE HER LIFE.
TOUCH'E. BUT I'LL BE HAPPY WHEN THE DAY COMES YOU WANT TO RESCUE PEOPLE WHO DON'T FIRST HAVE TO BE BEAUTIFUL WOMEN.

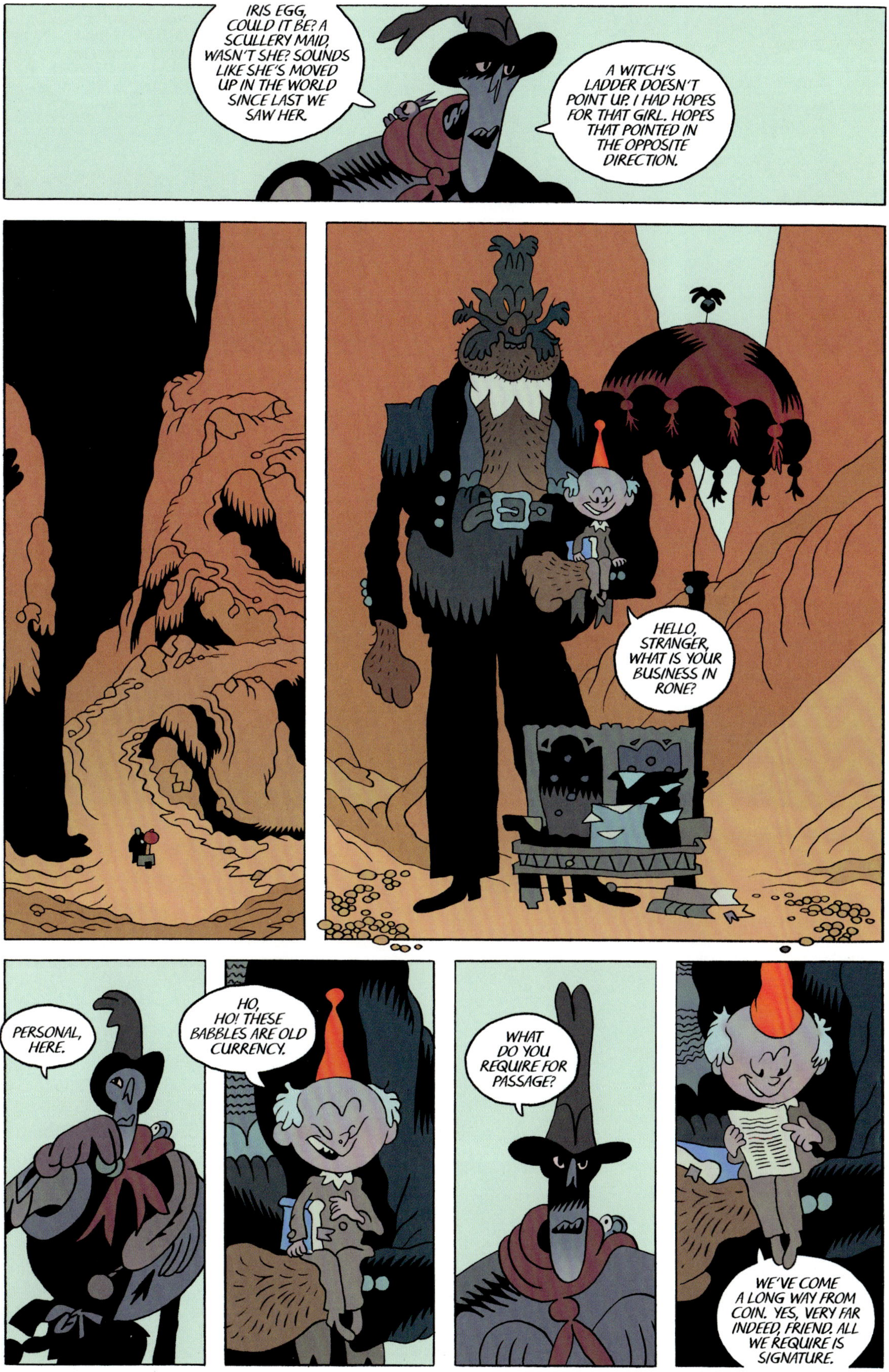
IRIS EGG, COULD IT BE? A SCULLERY MAID, WASN'T SHE? SOUNDS LIKE SHE'S MOVED UP IN THE WORLD SINCE LAST WE SAW HER.
A WITCH'S LADDER DOESN'T POINT UP. I HAD HOPES FOR THAT GIRL. HOPES THAT POINTED IN THE OPPOSITE DIRECTION.
HELLO, STRANGER, WHAT IS YOUR BUSINESS IN RONE?
PERSONAL, HERE.
HO, HO! THESE BABBLES ARE OLD CURRENCY.
WHAT DO YOU REQUIRE FOR PASSAGE?
WE'VE COME A LONG WAY FROM COIN. YES, VERY FAR INDEED, FRIEND. ALL WE REQUIRE IS SIGNATURE.

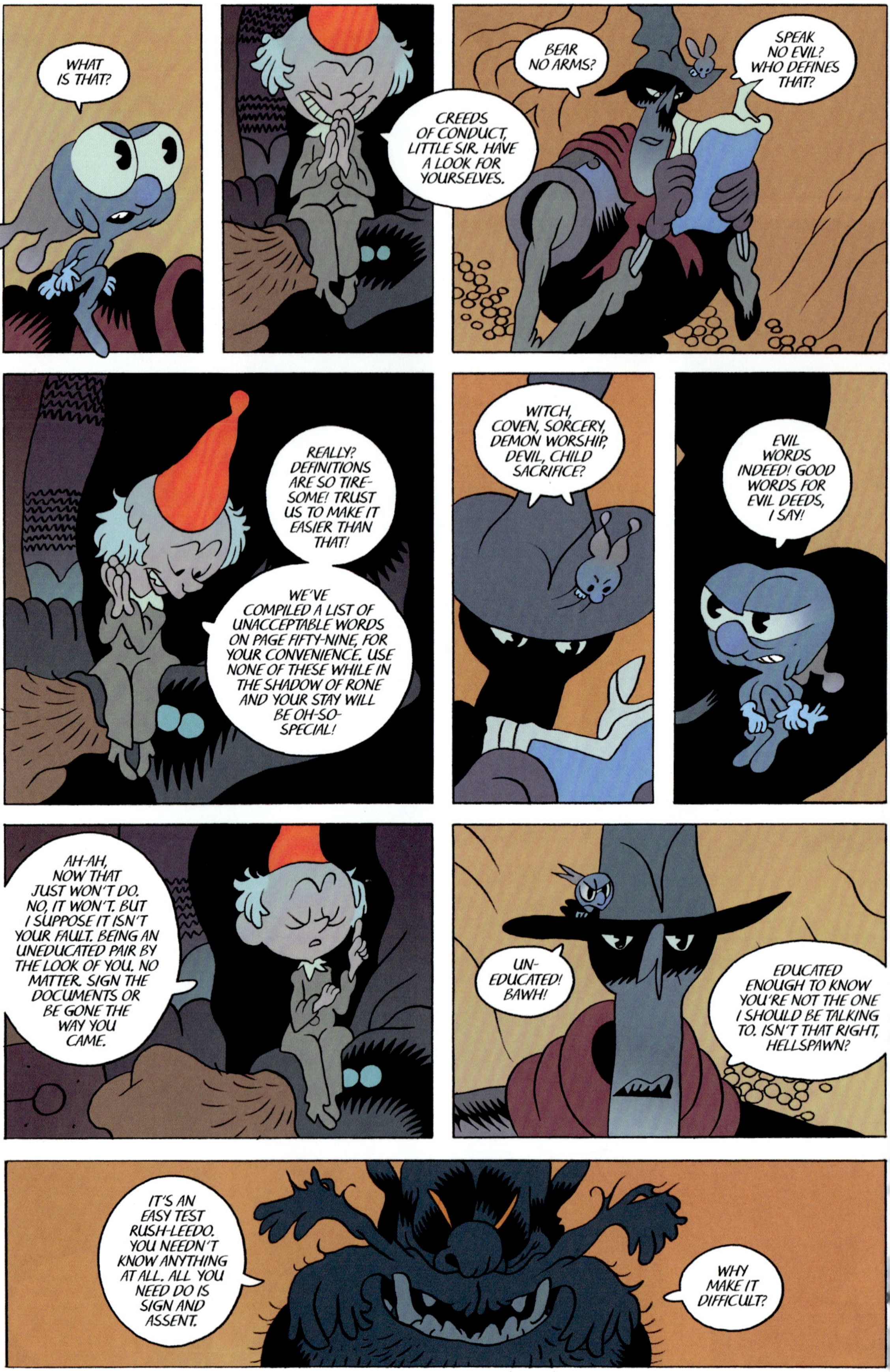
WHAT IS THAT?
CREEDS OF CONDUCT, LITTLE SIR. HAVE A LOOK FOR YOURSELVES.
BEAR NO ARMS?
SPEAK NO EVIL? WHO DEFINES THAT?
REALLY? DEFINITIONS ARE SO TIRESOME! TRUST US TO MAKE IT EASIER THAN THAT!
WE'VE COMPILED A LIST OF UNACCEPTABLE WORDS ON PAGE FIFTY-NINE, FOR YOUR CONVENIENCE. USE NONE OF THESE WHILE IN THE SHADOW OF RONE AND YOUR STAY WILL BE OH-SO-SPECIAL!
WITCH, COVEN, SORCERY, DEMON WORSHIP, DEVIL, CHILD SACRIFICE?
EVIL WORDS INDEED! GOOD WORDS FOR EVIL DEEDS, I SAY!
AH-AH, NOW THAT JUST WON'T DO. NO, IT WON'T. BUT I SUPPOSE IT ISN'T YOUR FAULT. BEING AN UNEDUCATED PAIR BY THE LOOK OF YOU. NO MATTER. SIGN THE DOCUMENTS OR BE GONE THE WAY YOU CAME.
UN-EDUCATED! BAWH!
EDUCATED ENOUGH TO KNOW YOU'RE NOT THE ONE I SHOULD BE TALKING TO. ISN'T THAT RIGHT, HELLSPAWN?
IT'S AN EASY TEST RUSH-LEEDO. YOU NEEDN'T KNOW ANYTHING AT ALL. ALL YOU NEED DO IS SIGN AND ASSENT.
WHY MAKE IT DIFFICULT?

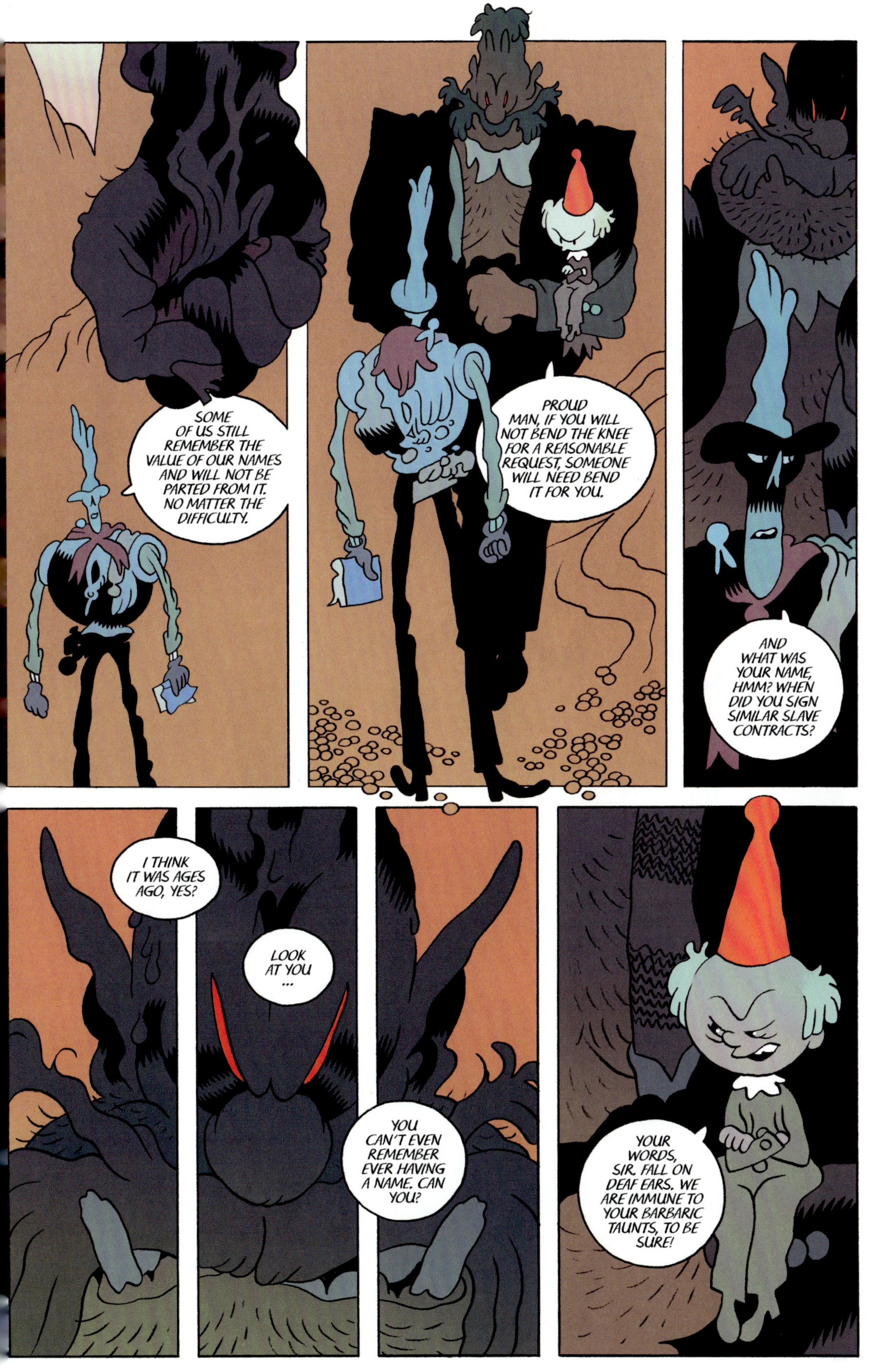
SOME OF US STILL REMEMBER THE VALUE OF OUR NAMES AND WILL NOT BE PARTED FROM IT. NO MATTER THE DIFFICULTY.
PROUD MAN, IF YOU WILL NOT BEND THE KNEE FOR A REASONABLE REQUEST, SOMEONE WILL NEED BEND IT FOR YOU.
AND WHAT WAS YOUR NAME, HMM? WHEN DID YOU SIGN SIMILAR SLAVE CONTRACTS?
I THINK IT WAS AGES AGO, YES?
LOOK AT YOU ...
YOU CAN'T EVEN REMEMBER EVER HAVING A NAME. CAN YOU?
YOUR WORDS, SIR. FALL ON DEAF EARS. WE ARE IMMUNE TO YOUR BARBARIC TAUNTS, TO BE SURE!

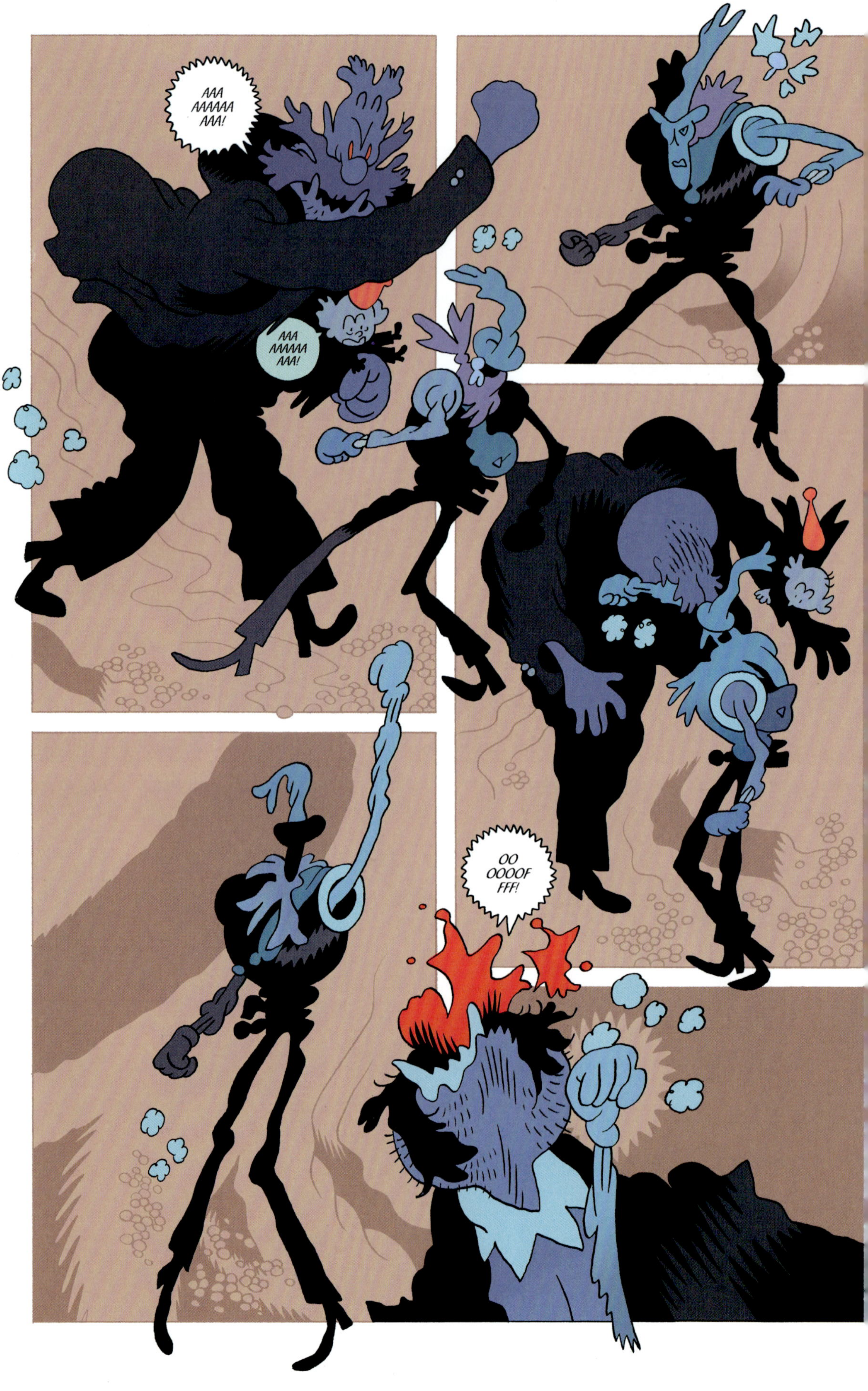
AAA AAAAAA AAA!
AAA AAAAAA AAA!
OO OOOOF FFF!

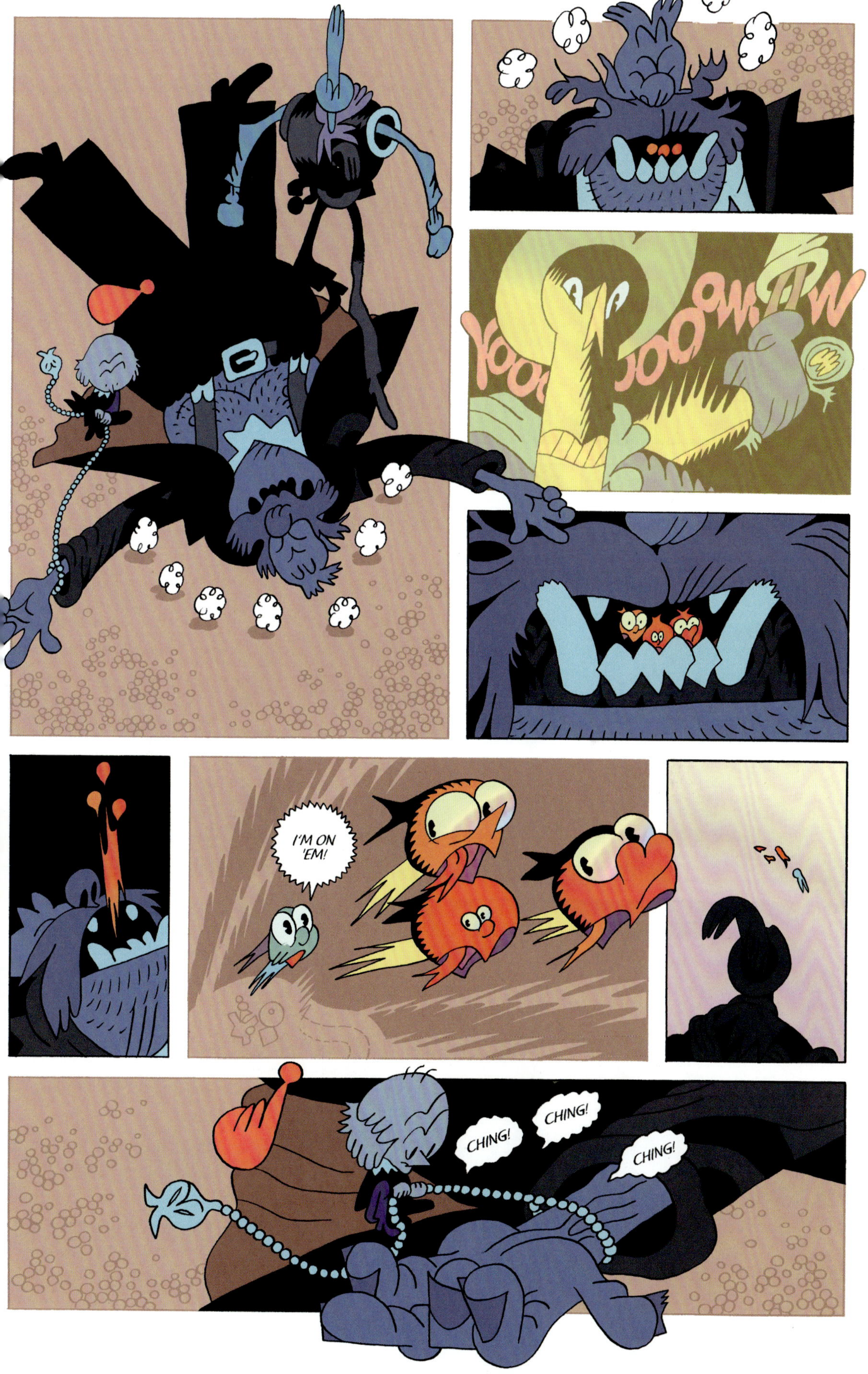
YOOOOOOOWWW
I'M ON 'EM!
CHING!
CHING!
CHING!

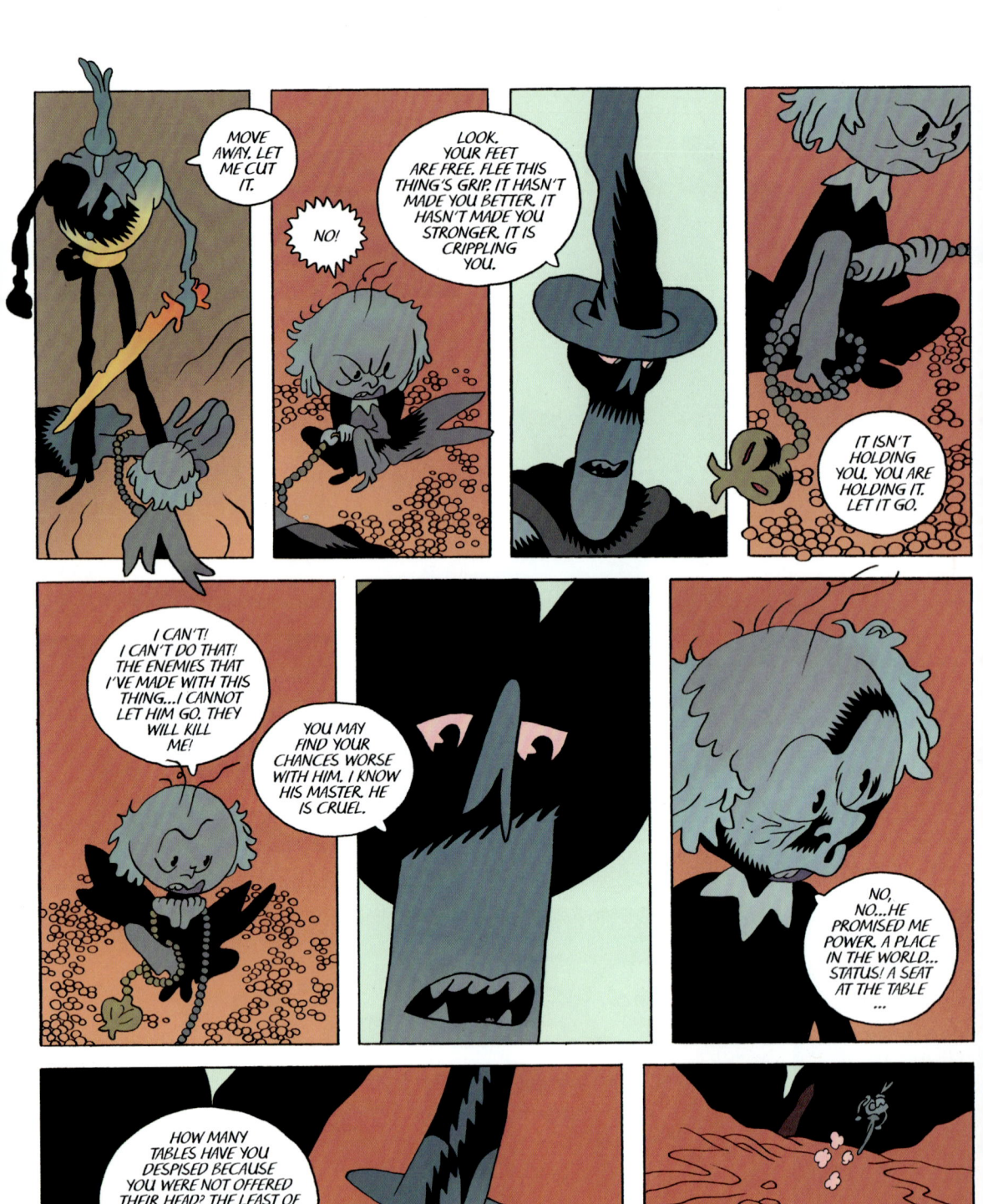

MOVE AWAY. LET ME CUT IT.

NO!

LOOK. YOUR FEET ARE FREE. FLEE THIS THING'S GRIP. IT HASN'T MADE YOU BETTER. IT HASN'T MADE YOU STRONGER. IT IS CRIPPLING YOU.

IT ISN'T HOLDING YOU. YOU ARE HOLDING IT. LET IT GO.

I CAN'T! I CAN'T DO THAT! THE ENEMIES THAT I'VE MADE WITH THIS THING...I CANNOT LET HIM GO. THEY WILL KILL ME!

YOU MAY FIND YOUR CHANCES WORSE WITH HIM. I KNOW HIS MASTER. HE IS CRUEL.

NO, NO...HE PROMISED ME POWER. A PLACE IN THE WORLD... STATUS! A SEAT AT THE TABLE...

HOW MANY TABLES HAVE YOU DESPISED BECAUSE YOU WERE NOT OFFERED THEIR HEAD? THE LEAST OF SEATS AT A GOOD TABLE IS BETTER THAN THE HEAD OF AN EVIL ONE.

FARE WELL.

CHING!
CHING!
CHING!

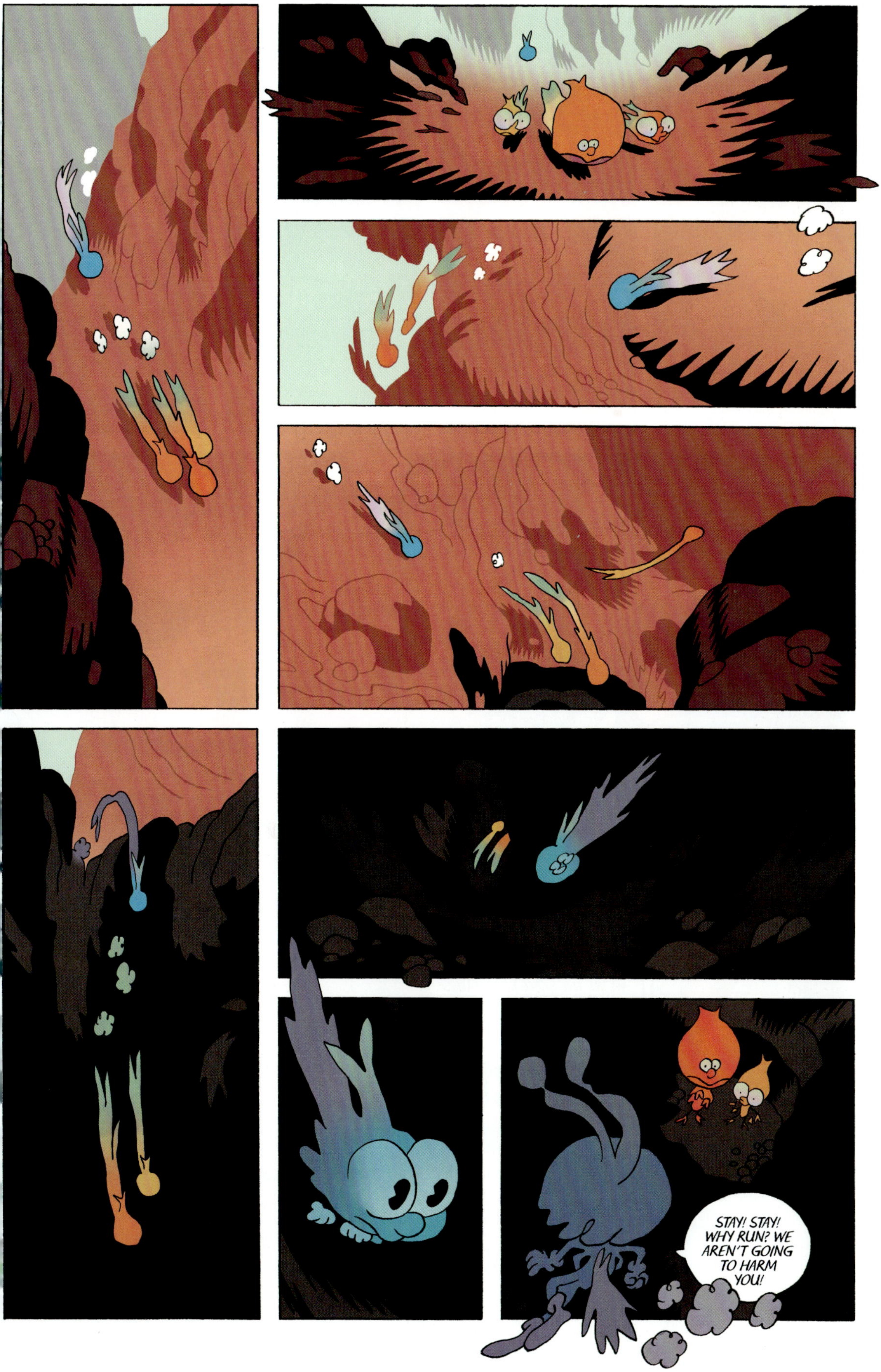
STAY! STAY! WHY RUN? WE AREN'T GOING TO HARM YOU!

THE SWORD! A GHOST LIGHT! A NEEDLE TO PIERCE THE HEART OF THE OUTER DARKNESS. SAKKENGABLE, HE CALLS IT!
JOE'S SWORD?
WHAT DO YOU MEAN?
NO! DON'T SAY NO MORE MORKY!
THE RIMHORN! HE WILL KNOW!
THE RIMHORN? WHO IS THAT? I'VE HEARD THIS NAME BEFORE.
NOW WAIT A MINUTE! JUST WAIT A MINUTE! WHAT'S HAPPENING HERE? WE'RE THE SAME KIND! BUGS OUGHT NOT TO FIGHT THIS WAY! LAY YOUR CASE OUT AND MAYBE THEN WE'LL GET INTO IT!
BUT I DON'T SEE THE TROUBLE HERE. THE WARS BETWEEN BEASTS AND BIG PEOPLES HAVE ALWAYS BLOWN OVER US. WHY DO YOU SIDE WITH A CREATURE LIKE THAT BRIDGEMAN AND HIS LITTLE FOOL?
HAS BEAST OR BIGMAN EVER BEFORE STOOPED TO OFFER US A PLACE OF POWER?

POWER? WHAT ARE YOU TALKING ABOUT? WHAT DO WE NEED IT FOR?
PAH! POWER IS EVERYTHING! COMMAND, THE RULE OF LAW, THE ORDERING OF OUR AFFAIRS, THE CREATION OF CIVILIZATION! WHAT COULDN'T WE DO WITH POWER?
I'VE NEVER HAD ANY PROBLEM ORDERING MY OWN AFFAIRS ...
WELL, LUCKY YOU! BUT TAKE INTO ACCOUNT THE IMPOVERISHED! HAVEN'T YOU NOTICED ALL THE THINGS THEY HAVE THAT WE DON'T? THE BIGMEN, I MEAN. THEY RIDE AROUND ON HORSES WITH FANCY HATS, THEY SMOKE LEAVES, AND PAY FOR THINGS WITH GOLDEN COINS!
SILLY ANT! WE ARE DIFFERENT THAN THEY! WHAT DO YOU NEED WITH HORSES? WE HAVE WINGS! AS FOR HATS, WHY NOT MAKE THEM YOURSELF? THE ART OF WEAVING IS KNOWN TO US.
SMOKING LEAVES AND GOLDEN COINS? BAH!
I'M GUESSING YOU NEVER WANTED THEM BEFORE THEY WERE PROMISED YOU? PROMISED BY THIS RIM-HORN CHARACTER, AM I RIGHT?
YOU SPOKE OF THE RIMHORN! FOOLS, HE WILL KILL US!
STUFF IT SICKLE, YOU AIN'T NO LORD OF US. THOUGH I RECKON YOU WANT 'TER BE.
THIS FUZZY GUY ISN'T CRAZY. I COULDN'T NEVER UNDERSTAND WHY OUR HIVE TOOK TO THIS GOLD COIN IDEA THE WAY THEY DONE...ALL 'A SUDDEN LIKE, THE MOMENT THE RIMHORN CAME IN...
WAS LIKE SOMEONE SAYS TO THE MOON IT NEEDED TO HAVE STARS! WHAT THE 'ELL WOULD THE MOON DO WITH STARS? IT'S THE MOON!

FOOL! IF THE MOON HAD STARS IT WOULD BE A MOON WITH STARS INSTEAD OF A MOON WITHOUT STARS! IT'D BE RICHER! AND RICHERNESS IS A VERY POWERFUL THING!
LOOKS LIKE YOU BOYS CHOSE THE BOTTOM OF THE TOTEM POLE!
LET 'IM GO MORKY, DON'T GO WITH 'IM. OUR CHANCES IS FAIRER OUTSIDE THE HIVE THAN INSIDE, IF HE'S THE TYPE THE MOTHER FAVORS!
OUTSIDE THE HIVE? HOW WILL WE LIVE?
BUT I GUESS I KNOW ABOUT LIVING OUTSIDE THEM IN THAT CASE...WELL NOW...I'M NOT SURE I KNOW FROM PERSONAL EXPERIENCE ABOUT HIVES. I'VE NEVER BEEN IN ONE. YOU MUST BERESOURCE-FUL AND NOT PROUD SEEKING HELP AND KNOWLEDGE FROM THOSE LIKE AND UNLIKE YOUR-SELVES. THE WORLD IS LARGE AND THERE ARE MANY PLACES TO BUILD A GOOD HOME. YOU WILL FIND FRIENDS ON THE ROAD IF YOU LOOK.
MAYHAPS WE HAVE FOUND ONE ALREADY. MY NAME IS GILLIS AND THIS IS MORKY.
IF YOU'RE HEADED TO RONE LOOK FOR MORE PEOPLE LIKE SICKLE. POWER-MAD, I SAY!
I DON'T LOOK FORWARD TO THAT, BUT IT IS OUR ROAD. DO YOU KNOW HOW WE MIGHT GET IN UNNOTICED?
THE OLD STABLE GATE, BENEATH THE RAILROAD TRACKS, HASN'T BEEN USED IN YEARS.
THANK YOU MORKY. GOODBYE!

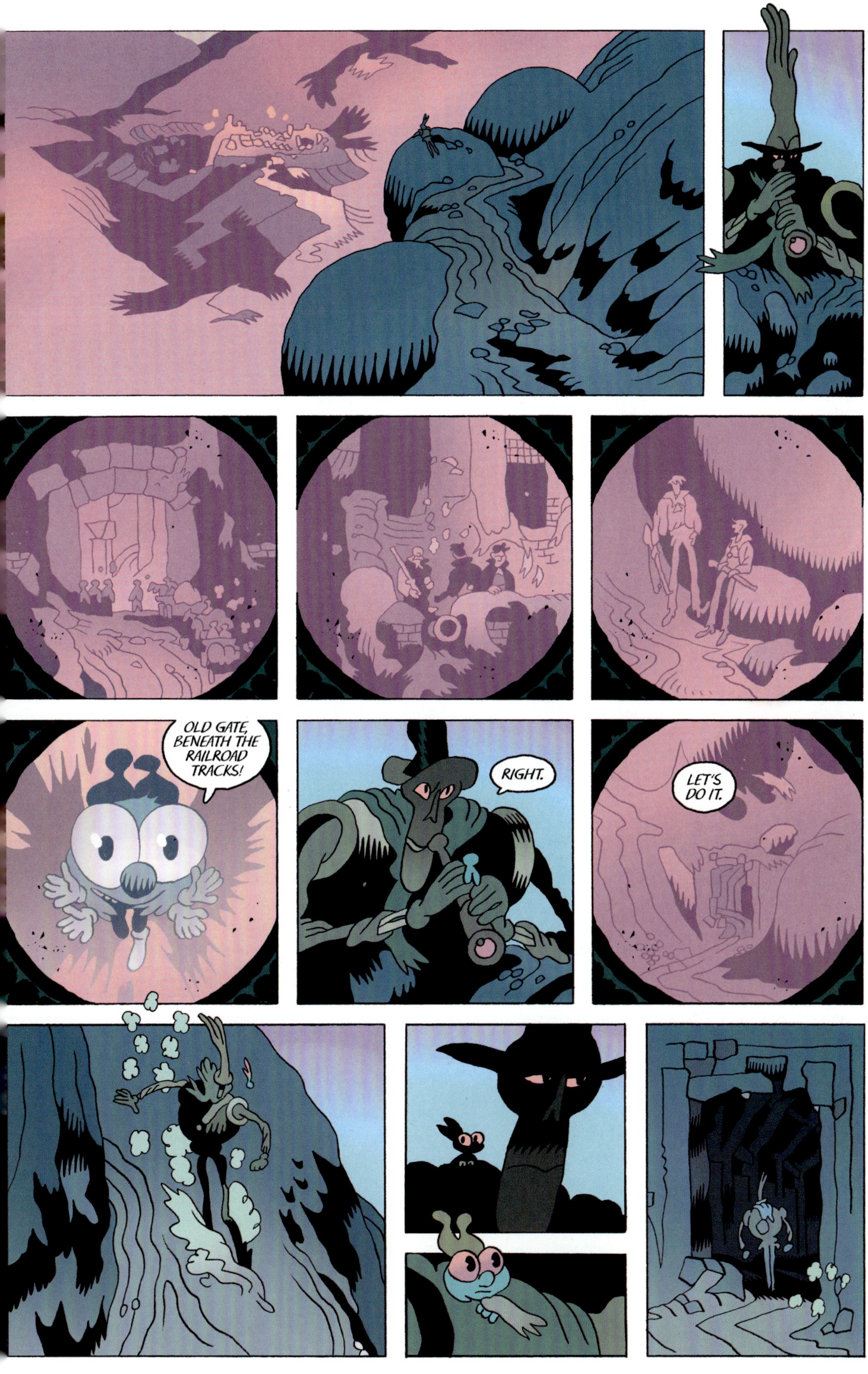
OLD GATE, BENEATH THE RAILROAD TRACKS!
RIGHT.
LET'S DO IT.

OY, PATCHICK, HERE THEY COME.
WE'RE SET CAPTAIN.
HELLO HAIRY!
GOLD.
GOLD HE SAYS!
SMILES HERE AIN'T UP TO SPEED. WE'RE A POST-CAPITAL OUTFIT HERE FRIENDS!
HA!
HA!
HA HAHA HA!
HA HAHA HA!
HA!

I DON'T LIKE IT.
THERE'S UNITY AND THEN THERE'S USURY.
SOME-THING TELLS ME THAT PARTICULAR COLLECTION OF INDIVIDUALS WERE ONLY TOGETHER FOR BAD REASONS... RUNNING UP RATES THEY CAN NEVER PAY OFF.
EVERY CHAIN NEEDS LINKS...
SO MUCH THE BETTER IF THEY CAN'T THINK FOR THEMSELVE--
HA HAHA HA!
I CAN'T MAKE OUT WHAT THEY'RE SAYING...
SHH..
CLAY MIRED TITRON. HARDLY DO I BIDE THEE.
GOLD ME NOW. THERE WILL BE NO LATER.
HOLD YER HORSES MATE. WE'LL BRING YOU UP TO HER LORD-SHIP, BUT SHE AIN'T THE LAW IN RONE.
NO SHE AIN'T. NOT WHILE THE GOVNER'S STILL KICKIN'. HE WANTS TO KNOW HER BUSINESS. WHAT'S SHE NEED THIS BABE FOR?
IS IT MAGIC?
MAGIC! HAHAHAHA! HA HA HA. MAGIC...
AIN'T IT SO BOYS? AIN'T IT SO?
THE BABY!
MAGIC?

CRACK
HUH?
TRAP!
CLUNK
WHAT A COCKUP!
WHAT'LL WE TELL HER LORDSHIP? SHE MAY NOT BE THE LAW, BUT THAT HASN'T STOPPED HER BEING THE EXECUTIONER!
GIVE HER THIS THING HERE! TELL HER HE MESSED IT UP.
AND WHAT IS IT?! 'E LOOKS LIKE DEATH!
DAMNED IF I KNOW! JUST GET HIM OUTTA HERE. AND FIND THAT DAMN CLOWN!
HE'LL BE HEADED FOR THE TRAIN.

I...
...WOULDN'T OPEN THAT IF I WERE YOU.
NO, I SHOULD THINK NOT. WELL MY FRIEND, IT'S BEEN AGES SINCE WE LAST SPOKE. TOO LONG.
BUT PERHAPS TOO SHORT FOR YOU TO NOW BE SITTING IN THAT SEAT? HOW DID THIS HAPPEN?
SWEEPING STONE FLOORS NEVER AGREED WITH ME. MY SIGHTS HAVE ALWAYS BEEN HIGHER THAN MY STATURE.
IT WAS NOT SO WHEN LAST WE TALKED.
YOU OLD THING! WHY SHOULD PEOPLE AND PLACES STAY THE SAME? I HAVE IMPROVED MY LOT.
BE HAPPY FOR ME!
I CAN-NOT BE. THE CONSORTIUM OWNS THAT CHAIR AND BY SITTING ON IT THE SITTER ALSO IS OWNED.
WHAT MARKS HAVE THEY LAIN UPON YOU?
NO ONE HAS LAID ANYTHING UPON ME THAT I HAVE NOT ASKED FOR. I GREW IN FAVOR WITH MY LORD AND SHE GAVE ME ASCCESS TO HER SECRET WISDOM. I AM HER SUCCESSOR BY RITES KNOWN TO THE CONSORTIUM.
I HAVE ACCESSED EQUALITY BY DIVORCING MYSELF FROM SERVITUDE.
THIS ROAD IS DANGEROUS AND SEEMS FAR TWISTED FROM WHEN YOU FIRST BEGAN YOUR STUDY.
MY WAY IS MY OWN, AND TO ME IT IS STRAIGHT. LOOK AT ME, BONES, WHEN HAVE YOU SEEN LITTLE OVER BIG, HMM? WHATEVER I AM DOING, IT'S WORKING FOR ME.

THIS WAS NOT THE WORK YOU BEGAN. YOU ASKED ME YEARS AGO THE COSMIC HISTORY... WASN'T THAT ENOUGH TO WARN YOU AWAY FROM SUCH PERILOUS GAIN AND EVIL FRIENDS? THE CONSORTIUM IS DOOMED TO EAT ITSELF, OVER AND OVER AGAIN. THE WAY OF THE DEVIL HASN'T CHANGED. NO MATTER WHAT NEW WORDS HE FAVORS TODAY.
AND YOU REALLY BELIEVE YOU REPRESENT HISTORY IN THE ROUND? NO, MY STUDIES HAVE NOT BEEN IN VAIN. I HAVE LEARNED THE LESSON OF TWO SIDES TO EVERY COIN.
YOU ARE RUSHLEEDO, AN ANCIENT PEOPLE, BUT NOT OF ONE DOCTRINE. THERE ARE HISTORIES OTHER THAN YOURS.
SO SAID THE WINGED SERPENT WHO BEGAN THIS DAY OF RUIN YOU NOW BELIEVE INDOMITABLE.
YOUR FAIRY-TALES CONDEMN THEMSELVES. THEIR KINGDOM IS A TYRANNY BY ALL ACCOUNTS.
I WILL LEAVE THIS HOUSE, BEFORE IT CRUMBLES ON YOUR HEAD.
COME, LOOK AND SEE AN ALTERNATIVE TO CRUMBLING.
YOUR HISTORY SAYS THE WORLD IS BEAUTIFUL. FLOWER CROWN OF THE COSMOS. OASIS IN THE WILDERNESS. MEANINGFULLY MADE BY THE MAGIC MAN. LOOK OUT THIS WINDOW. IS THAT WHAT YOU SEE OUT THERE?
I ONLY SEE THE CHAOS SCULPTURE. THE JAGGED MAZE, DOORLESS AND UNENDING. FULL OF TERRORS. IF THE GOD YOU SAY MADE THIS PLACE, DOESN'T HE DESERVE REBELLION?

SEE YOU NOW WHAT FREE MAGIC CAN DO? LAUGH NO MORE AT THE CONSORTIUM. THEY CAN RESTORE YOU IF YOU LET THEM.
YOUR COSMIKA IS A VISION OF THE FUTURE, NOT THE PAST.
A GARDEN THERE WILL BE, BUT ONLY IF WE MAKE IT. ONLY IF WE'RE BRAVE ENOUGH TO DO WHAT MUST BE DONE.
EASY ROADS ARE FULL OF THIEVES BECAUSE SOFT PEOPLE CHOOSE THEM.
YOU PREFER THE WAY OF THE VULTURE AND CROW? I'VE HEARD ABOUT YOUR TOMBSTONED ROAD. WHY KEEP BURYING THE BONES? WHY KEEP SWEEPING THE BROKEN PIECES UNDER THE MAT? PLAYING THE CHARADE THAT LIFE AND DEATH HAVE ANY MEANING?
TELL ME WHAT YOU KNOW OF SAUGHERDOUGH IDWAY? WHY DOES THE SOLDIERY TRADE WITH HER MURDERERS? WHAT PURPOSE DO YOU HAVE WITH THE CHILD?
I'VE ONLY JUST HEARD OF THIS MYSELF.
IT SEEMS THE MURDERERS THOUGHT ME LIKE OTHER WITCHES WHO PRIZE SUCH DEEDS AND BLOOD BOUGHT CHILDREN. DON'T BE SO SURPRISED, WITCHES COME IN EVERY SHADE ...
OR AT LEAST FIVE... YOU MAY BE PLEASED TO KNOW I AM TURNING RONE STATION AWAY FROM RING AND OVER TO PINK.
THE FIVE FINGERS MAY NOT BE THE SAME, BUT THEY ARE ALL PART OF THE SAME HAND. THE CONSORTIUM OWNS YOU ALL.
A GAMBLE FOR US BOTH THEN. FIND THIS CHILD, BRING IT BACK HOME AND YOU'LL SEE. I SHALL MAKE SAUHERDOUGH A PARADISE GARDEN. A GOOD HOME FOR YOU BOTH PERHAPS?

YOU'VE GAMBLED TOO MUCH ALREADY.
THAT'S LIFE.
NOT MINE.
WE'LL SEE.
HERE. TAKE TWO FOR YOUR TROUBLE.
DON'T BE AFRAID OF THE FUTURE.
NECROMANCERS FINEST
EXTRA STRENGTH PATCH
GRAB IT WITH BOTH HANDS AND LET GO OF THE PAST.
IT'S SUCKING YOU DRY.

NECROMANCERS FINEST
LITTLE BLACKS
BIG LIFE
ULTRA STRENGTH PATCH
JOE!
THE MURDERER'S HOPPED THE GORECKI ABOUT TWO HOURS AGO. THERE ARE A NUMBRER OF STOPS BEFORE IT REACHES MIDDING, CONNECTIONS AVAILABLE THERE TO OTHER LINES.
RIGHT. THEY'LL BE GOING TO STACY.
I RECKON THERE'S AT LEAST A DOZEN WITCHES AT THE ALLWEATHER WHO'D LOVE TO GET THEIR HANDS ON A NEWBORN.
THE RETREAT?
AND UNDERGROUND AUCTION HOUSE.
CIRCLE BACK AROUND TO THE CAMPSITE, TELL THOSE WITCHES THE BOX IS DELIVERED. AND TELL THE GIRL TO TAKE MY HORSE.
YOU SHOULD BE ABLE TO MAKE IT BACK BEFORE THE TRAIN PULLS OUT.
IF YOU DON'T, YOU'LL KNOW WHERE I AM.
RIGHT!

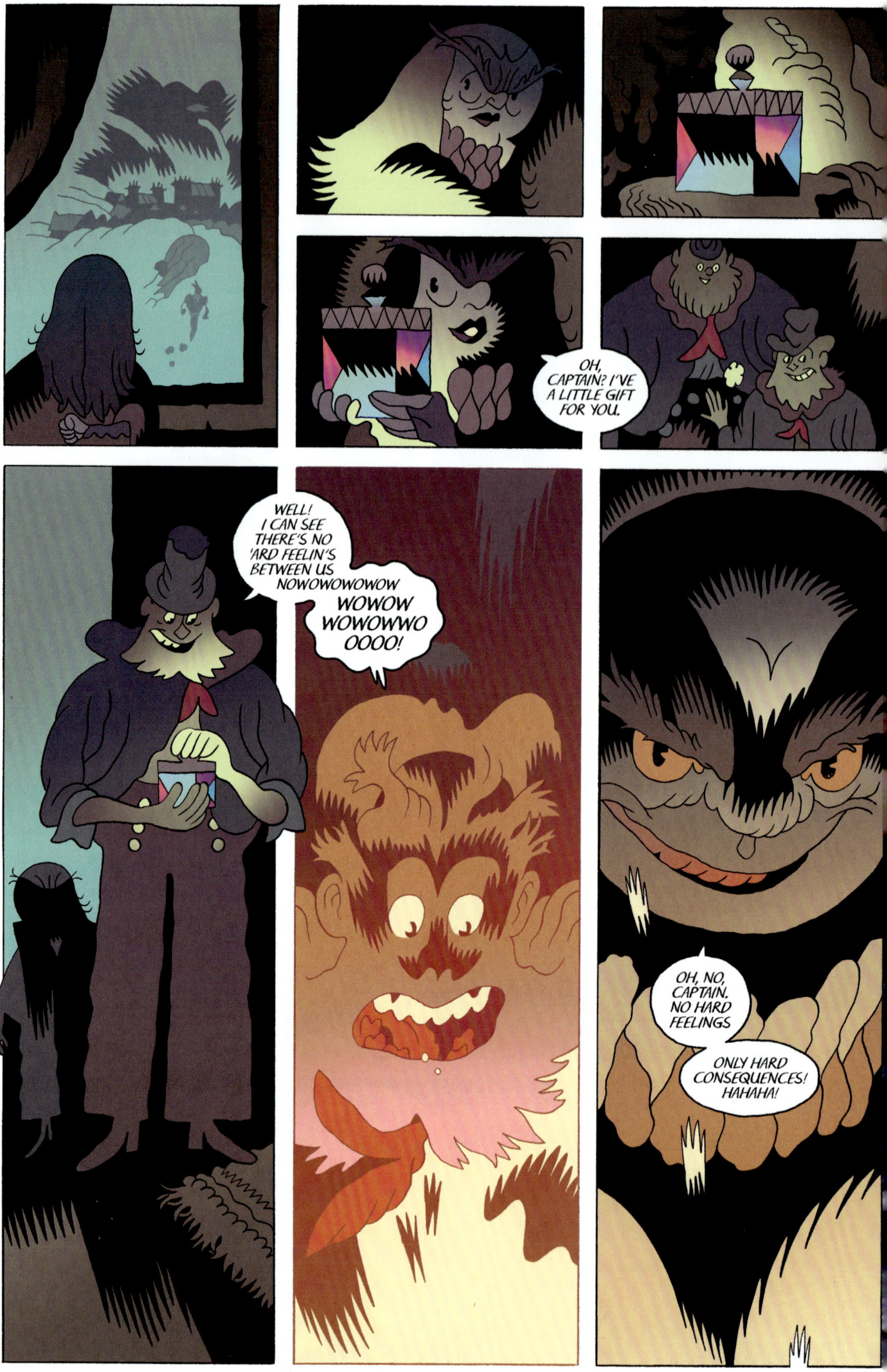
OH, CAPTAIN? I'VE A LITTLE GIFT FOR YOU.
WELL! I CAN SEE THERE'S NO 'ARD FEELIN'S BETWEEN US NOWOWOWOWOW WOWOW WOWOWWO OOOO!
OH, NO, CAPTAIN. NO HARD FEELINGS
ONLY HARD CONSEQUENCES! HAHAHA!

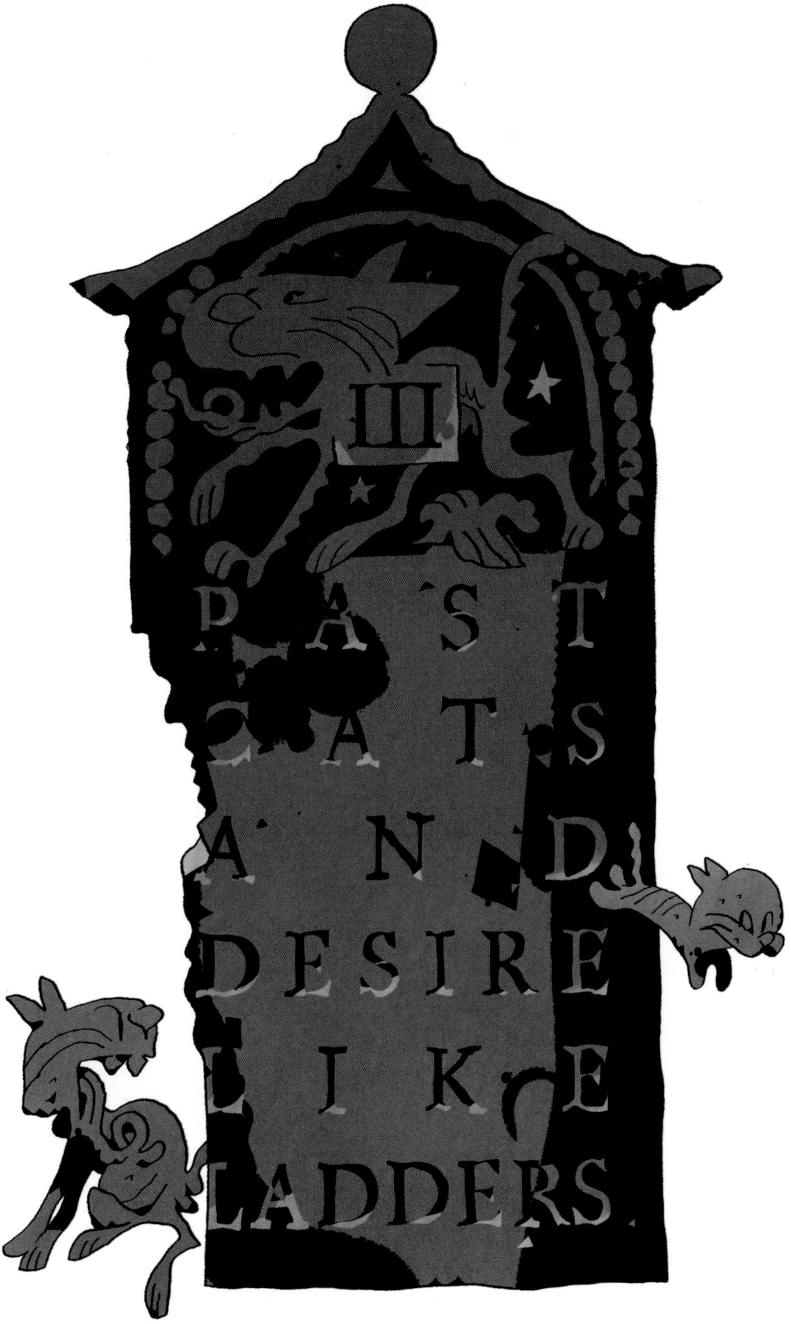
III
PAST
CATS
AND
DESIRE
LIKE
LADDERS

Every night it's tears / And every bedtime crying.
I think he knows the sleeping / Is a kind of dying.
I think he does, but also / In the morning singing,
In the waking, living / And in the living / Dreaming.

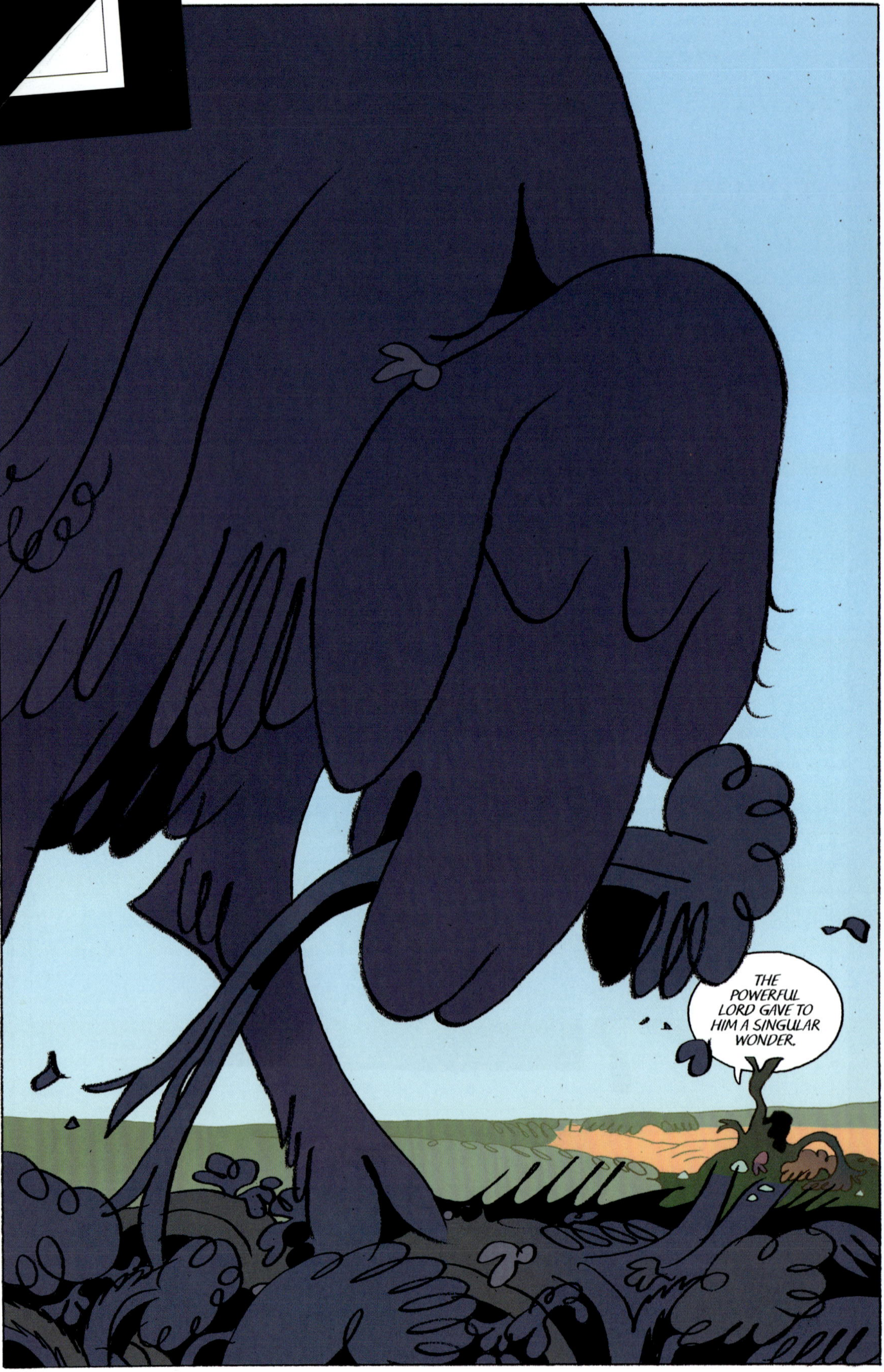
THE POWERFUL LORD GAVE TO HIM A SINGULAR WONDER.

A KEY OF PIERCING BEAUTY. IT SHONE BEFORE HIM UNDER THE GOLD RED SUN.
THIS, HIS PASSAGE THROUGH EVERY GATE IN THE DAY OF TROUBLE, HELD HE CLOSE TO HIS HEART.
BUT CURSES UPON THE KEY WERE LAIN, SUCH THAT IT ONLY SEEMED TO FIT EVERY LOCK ...

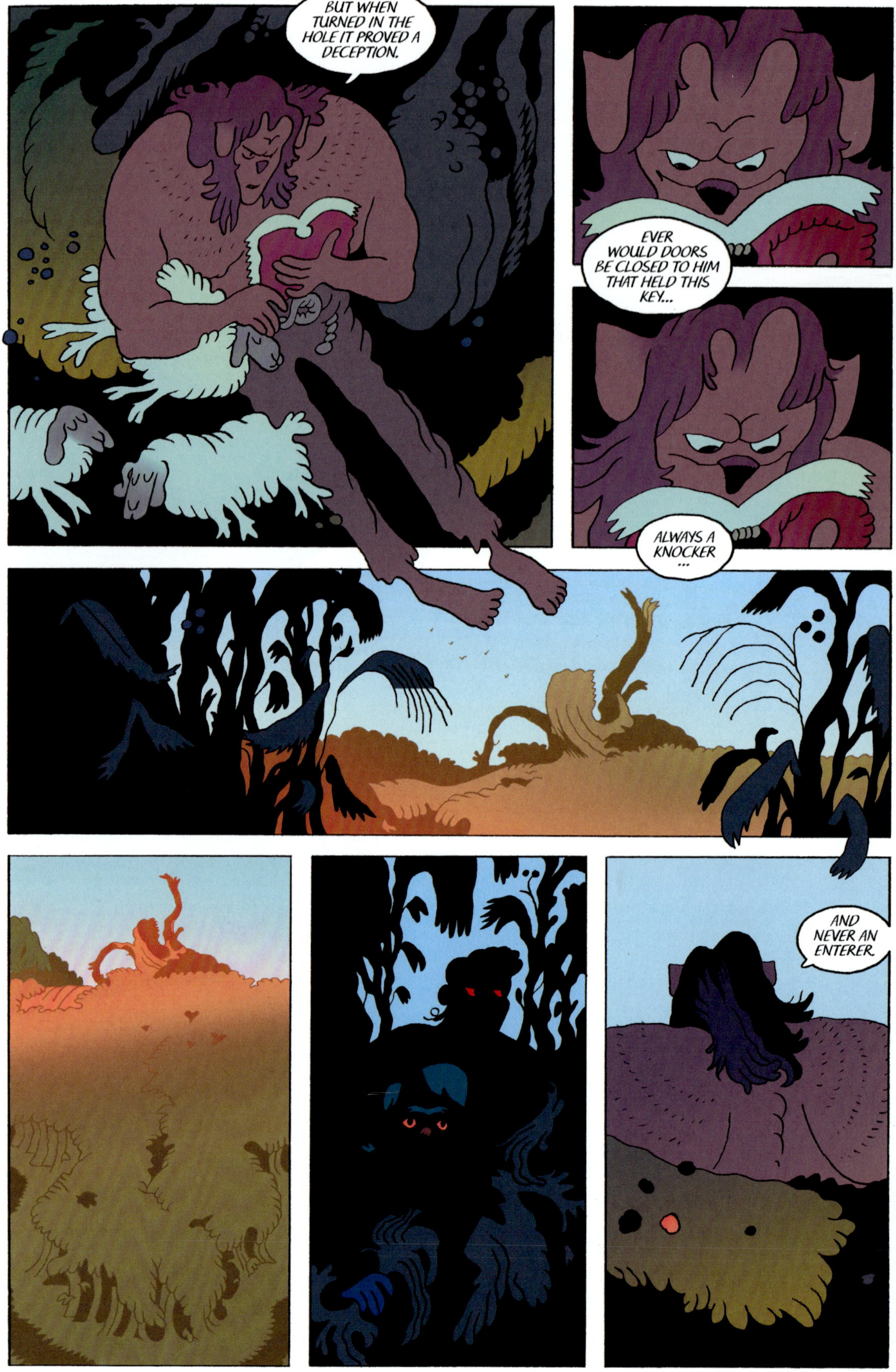
BUT WHEN TURNED IN THE HOLE IT PROVED A DECEPTION.
EVER WOULD DOORS BE CLOSED TO HIM THAT HELD THIS KEY...
ALWAYS A KNOCKER ...
AND NEVER AN ENTERER.

HO!
YAWP!
BAW AH AH AH!
AAAA!
BAWH!
BAA AAAA!
MAA AAAAA AAW!
HA! I KNEW I'D FIND YOU HERE!
WHAT DO YOU READ TODAY?!
HOY, YIGGLE! WHY TORMENT THE POOR THING SO? YOU SEE HE'S ONLY A BEAST. WHY TEACH HIM WORDS?
BECAUSE I WANT TO. AND SO DOES HE. BUT, ASK HIM. NOT ME.
BAH! DO THE SONS OF GOD POUR WATER INTO NETS? A SERVANT SHOULD BE CONTENT WITH SERVICE. I WILL NOT ENCOURAGE THIS THING TO THINK IT CAN BE MORE THAN WHAT IT IS.
THEN DO NOT DISCOURAGE HIM. OUR FATHER HASN'T. WHY SHOULD WE?

YOU THINK ALL OUR FATHER'S WAYS BEST? YES, I CAN SEE THAT YOU DO. PLAINLY YOU ARE STILL A CHILD.
I WILL LEAVE YOU WITH YOUR TOYS.
WHAT SAY YOU, JOSHONAAN? DOES MY YOKE WEIGH HEAVY ON YOU? DO THESE WORDS CATCH IN THY THROAT?
I WILL NOT SAY THEY ARE EASY.
HA!
YOU SHOULDN'T BECAUSE THEY ARE NOT.
BUT FREEDOM IS HERE ...
AND HERE.
COMMUNE WITH ME.

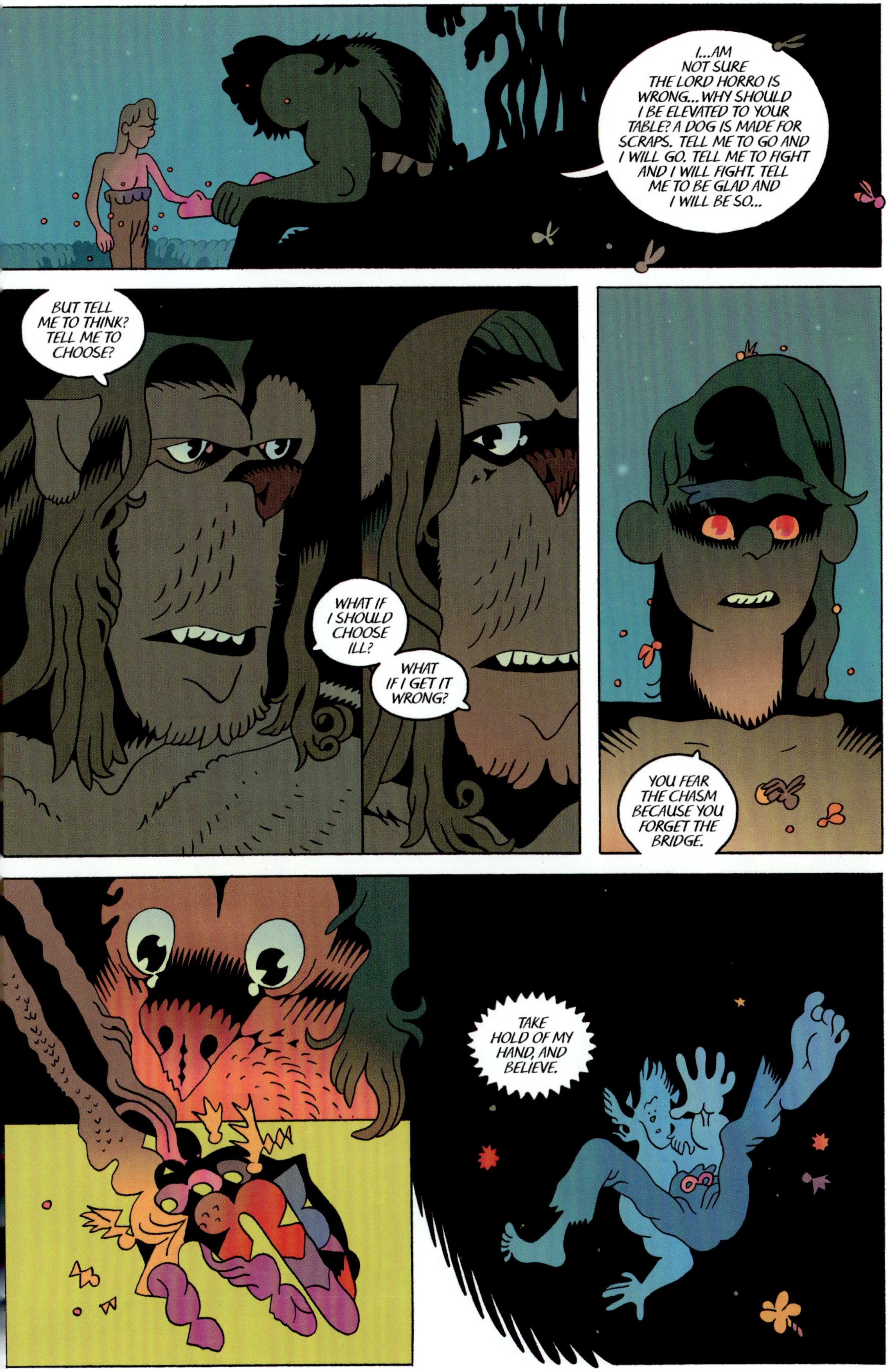
I...AM NOT SURE THE LORD HORRO IS WRONG... WHY SHOULD I BE ELEVATED TO YOUR TABLE? A DOG IS MADE FOR SCRAPS. TELL ME TO GO AND I WILL GO. TELL ME TO FIGHT AND I WILL FIGHT. TELL ME TO BE GLAD AND I WILL BE SO...
BUT TELL ME TO THINK? TELL ME TO CHOOSE?
WHAT IF I SHOULD CHOOSE ILL?
WHAT IF I GET IT WRONG?
YOU FEAR THE CHASM BECAUSE YOU FORGET THE BRIDGE.
TAKE HOLD OF MY HAND, AND BELIEVE.

AH!
UH?
DO YOU SMELL THAT?
SMELLS LIKE...
THE PAST
TOM BOOSE!
WELL!
JOE BONES!
HA! WHAT LUCK!

AND DON'T YOU LOOK LIKE A REGULAR OL' TUMBLEWEED!
HA!
FREDDY!
BLOO-SEF! HO! HO!
MARGEET! FUZZY BLUE MOTHSTER ON OUR DOORSTEP! WANTS TO EAT US!
BLOO! HOW GOOD IT IS TO SEE YOU! COME! COME INSIDE! COFFEE IS ON AND HOT!
SHING!
EXCUSE ME! THIS IS A COUCHETTE CAR!
PLEASE TAKE YOUR NO DOUBT SALACIOUS AFFAIRS OUTSIDE, PLEASE!
SO! WHAT BRINGS ALL NINETY-FIVE POUNDS OF THE BOOSE OUT HERE?! CITY LIVIN' MAKING YOU ITCHY?

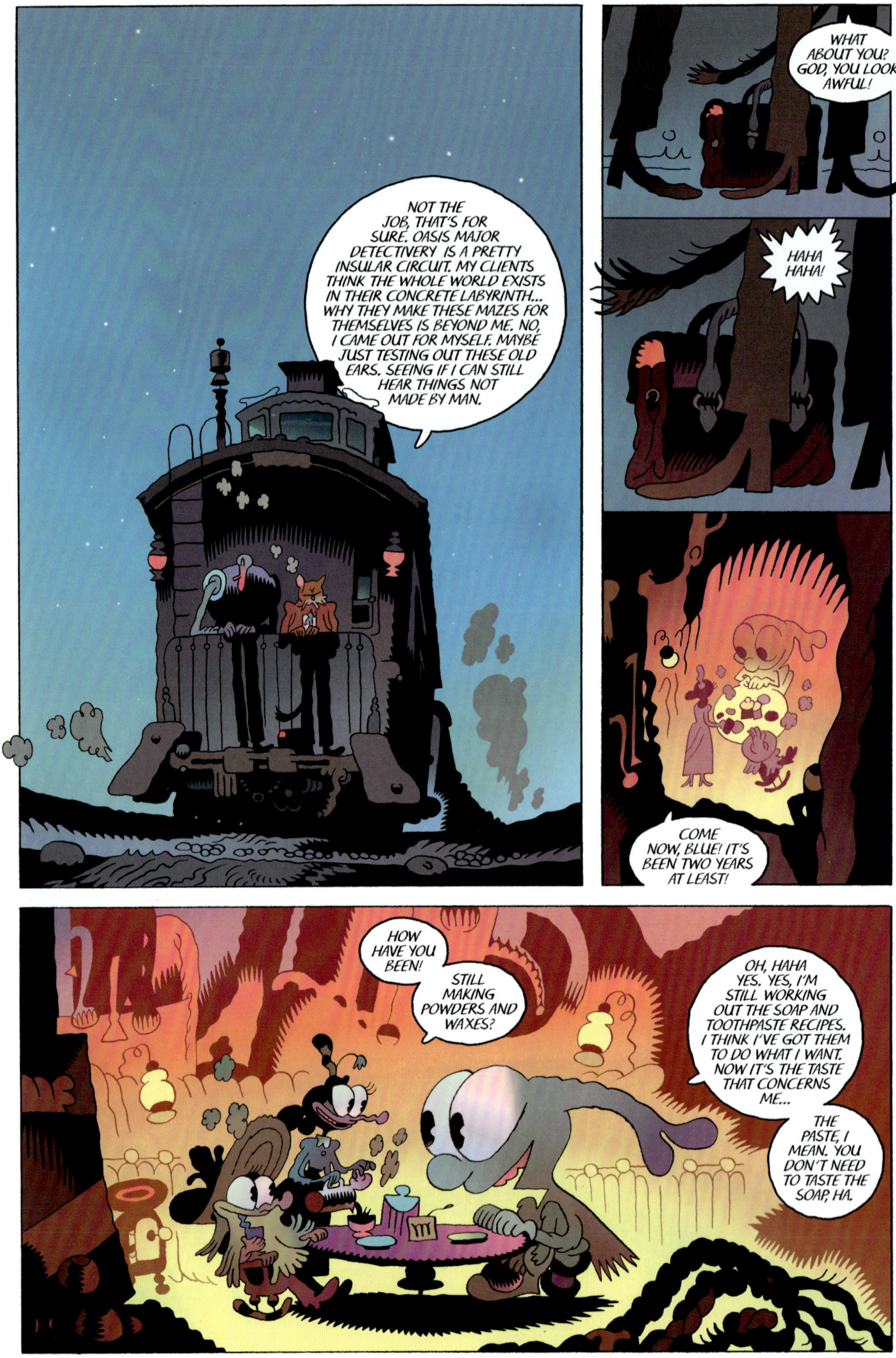
NOT THE JOB, THAT'S FOR SURE. OASIS MAJOR DETECTIVERY IS A PRETTY INSULAR CIRCUIT. MY CLIENTS THINK THE WHOLE WORLD EXISTS IN THEIR CONCRETE LABYRINTH... WHY THEY MAKE THESE MAZES FOR THEMSELVES IS BEYOND ME. NO, I CAME OUT FOR MYSELF. MAYBE JUST TESTING OUT THESE OLD EARS. SEEING IF I CAN STILL HEAR THINGS NOT MADE BY MAN.
WHAT ABOUT YOU? GOD, YOU LOOK AWFUL!
HAHA HAHA!
COME NOW, BLUE! IT'S BEEN TWO YEARS AT LEAST!
HOW HAVE YOU BEEN!
STILL MAKING POWDERS AND WAXES?
OH, HAHA YES. YES, I'M STILL WORKING OUT THE SOAP AND TOOTHPASTE RECIPES. I THINK I'VE GOT THEM TO DO WHAT I WANT. NOW IT'S THE TASTE THAT CONCERNS ME...
THE PASTE, I MEAN. YOU DON'T NEED TO TASTE THE SOAP, HA.

WELL, ONE PROUD CUSTOMER IS MR. FLY HERE! 'IS TEETH HAVE NEVER BEEN BRIGHTER! AND HIS BREATH! BELIEVE ME, A SIGHT FOR SORE EYES, YOU CAN BE SURE!
TRUE, THOUGH I DO NOT LIKE TO ADMIT, HAHA.
BUT IT DOES THE MOST GOOD TO ADMIT IT! GOOD FOR OUR PEOPLE. BUGS AREN'T QUICK TO CHANGE BUT CHANGE IS REQUIRED. THE PROOF IS UNDENIABLE. BUGS WITH PROPER HYGIENE LIVE MUCH LONGER THAN THOSE WITHOUT.
FOR YOU, BLUESIR, I WILL ADMIT THIS. THOUGH I HAVE HAD TO COVER THE SOAPY SMELL ON OCCASION WHEN I GO OUT. THE BOYS WILL TALK, SAY I'VE GONE SOFT. YOU UNDER-STAND?
RIDICULOUS, DARLING! YOU ARE SOFT! 'IS WHY I LOVE YOU!
I'M STILL WALKING. FOLLOWING THE BIRDS, BURYING THE BONES.
MERCY, THERE'S SOME GRIM STUFF GOIN' ROUND...
THESE PEOPLE, YAZZA AND YOOGA, BIG AND SMALL. THEY DO SUCH TERRIBLE THINGS TO EACH OTHER.
YOU THINK THEY ACT ALONE?
WHAT DO YOU MEAN?

A WEDGE IS BEING DRIVEN BETWEEN THEM. THE POWER STRUCTURE OF HATE IS BEING REBUILT. FORKED TONGUE AND CLOVEN HOOF ARE DEALING THE CARDS OUT AGAIN.
DECEIVING AND DIVIDING, DECEIVING AND DIVIDING.
TESTING OLD EARS, MY ASS! WHAT ARE YOU REALLY UP TO?
MOOK-RACKA.
NO! NO WAY. COUNT ME OUT.
YOU'RE NOT INVITED. I WASN'T GOING TO TELL YOU BECAUSE YOU WEREN'T INVITED.
OH YEAH? NOT INVITED BY WHOM?
HA! SO CURIOUS! EH?
ME? NO WAY. CONCERNED, MAYBE.
I'D JUST LIKE TO KNOW WHO'LL BE LEADING YOU OFF A CLIFF THIS TIME.
HA!
IT'S MOOKRAKA JOE, WE WERE ALWAYS DUMB SHEEP.
THE LEAP OF FAITH AND THE CLIFF ARE CONNECTED. YOU CAN'T TOUCH GROUND AND FLY AT THE SAME TIME, MY FRIEND.

BUT MAYBE YOU'RE MAKING THE JUMP EVEN NOW? I SEE LIGHT IN YOUR EYES THOUGH YOU WOULD HIDE IT FROM ME. YOU AREN'T FOLLOWING ANY BIRDS TONIGHT. WHAT ARE YOU HUNTING?
I DON'T KNOW. A SHADOW MAN, SOME SPIRIT OF DARKNESS...NEW CARDS ARE BEING DEALT, AND I HEAR THE CHAINS OF EVIL COILING AGAIN.
NEW CARDS ARE BEING DEALT, AND I HEAR THE CHAINS OF EVIL COILING AGAIN.
BUT PERHAPS ASSEMBLY IS A SOLUTION IN ITS OWN RIGHT? PERHAPS THE ROAD IS BEST TRAVELED TO- -GETHER?
DO YOU REMEMBER THAT TIME WE FELL INTO THE CRACK?
AND THE CORI- OI?
YOU KIDDING?! THEM SPOOKY LITTLE SONS OF BITCHES WERE FAST!
HA! WE GAVE 'EM ONE HELL OF A CHASE. I REMEMBER THAT.
QUICKER FEET HAVE NOT BEEN SEEN ON THESE LEGS BEFORE.
OR SINCE FOR THAT MATTER!

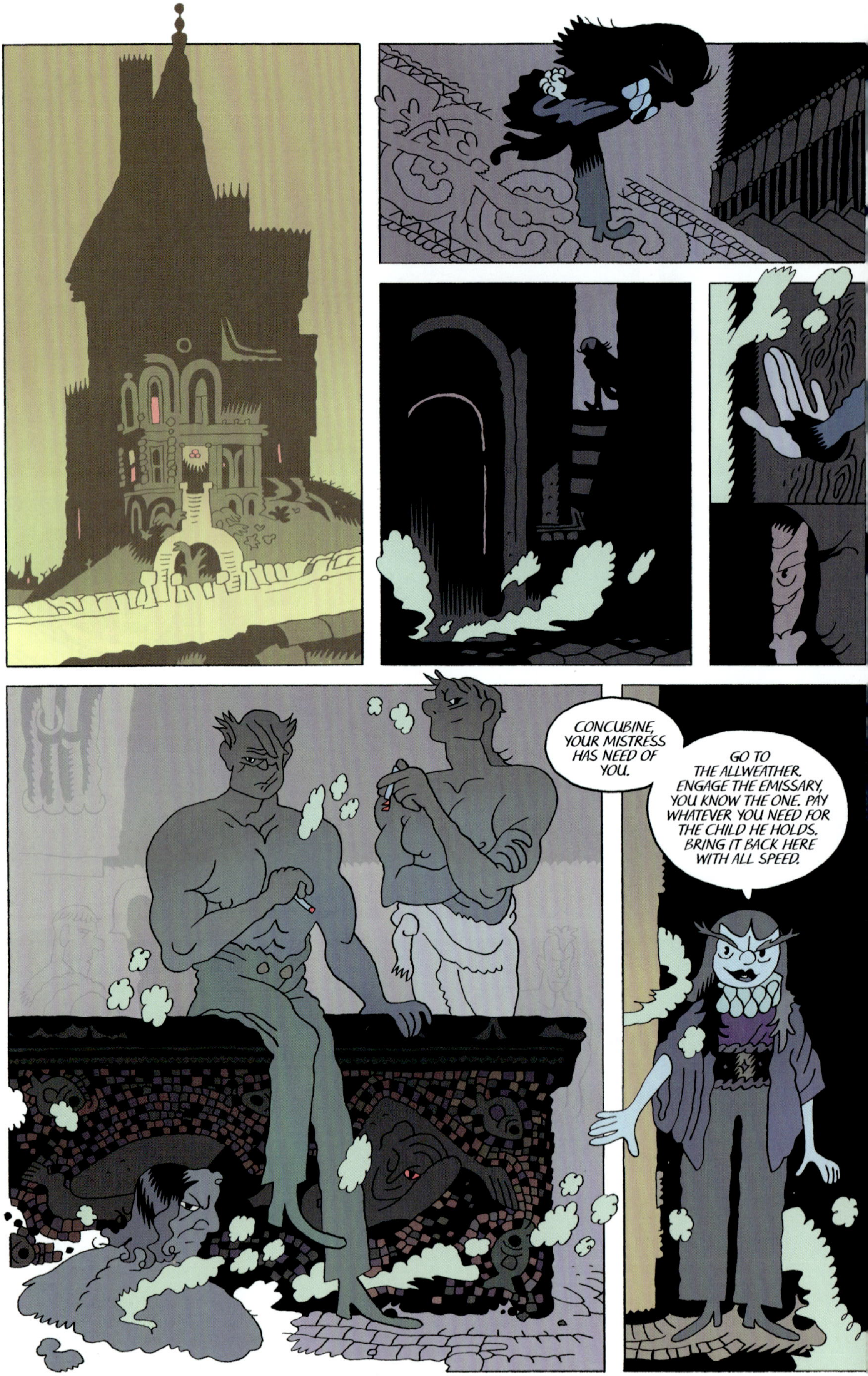
CONCUBINE, YOUR MISTRESS HAS NEED OF YOU.
GO TO THE ALLWEATHER. ENGAGE THE EMISSARY, YOU KNOW THE ONE. PAY WHATEVER YOU NEED FOR THE CHILD HE HOLDS. BRING IT BACK HERE WITH ALL SPEED.

WHAT'S THIS? I BEEN HERE TWO MONTHS AND NOT EVEN SEEN THE LADY!
JUS' YOU. COMIN' AND GOING. TELLIN' US TO DO THIS AND DO THAT.
LITTLE TOADY, THIS AIN'T WHAT I SIGNED UP FOR.
ISN'T IT?
LOOK AROUND YOU, BOY.
THERE SHE IS.
PAINTED WITH COLORS BRIGHT. TILED IN TITILLATING PATTERN.
HAVE HER NOW. HAVE HER LATER. SHE'LL ALWAYS BE THERE FOR YOU. AND SHE'LL NEVER, EVER, GROW OLD.
NOW ISN'T THAT A DREAM?
ISN'T THAT MORE THAN YOU WERE OFFERED, HMM?
AND, DON'T FORGET. THE ALLWEATHER IS A PLACE FOR ADULTS. MAKE SURE TO WEAR SOMETHING NICE.
SLAM

MY, WHAT A FINE JOB YOU'VE DONE WITH THOSE BOYS.
EVEN TAUGHT THEM TO CALL ME "LITTLE TOADY," I SEE?
WELL, I'VE HOPED YOU'VE ENJOYED KICKING "UGLY IRIS" AROUND BECAUSE IT WILL SOON BE OVER.
THE CHILD'S BLOOD WILL BE MINE AND YOU SHALL LOOK UPON IRIS TRANS-FORMED!
A VISION OF TERRIBLE BEAUTY.
POWER BEYOND COMPARE!

I SHALL RIVAL DARK MODEEBA, AND PINK SHAY-ORIA!
I SHALL CALL ALL MEN TO ME AND THEY WILL KILL THEM-SELVES FOR MY BEAUTY.
I WILL WALK IN THE CRIMSON RIVER.
AND IT WILL BE A BALM TO THE FEET THEY ONCE MADE FUN OF.
A NECTAR TO THE FLOWER OF THE WORLD! IRIS! IRIS! IRIS!
AND YOU?
YOU WILL ROT HERE IN THIS SANCTUM. WATCHING YOURSELF AGE WHILE I GROW MORE BEAUTIFUL EVERY DAY!
JUST AS SOON AS THE PIECES FALL INTO PLACE.

ANY PURSUIT WILL PASS. WE'LL HOP BACK ON THE TRAIN TOMORROW.
WHAT'S WRONG WITH 'IM? HE DON'T LOOK SO GOOD, DO 'E?
LOOK GOOD?! LOOK GOOD?!
SHARA-GORE SHALL-A-HOOT! THIS BODY IS DYING... THIS BOY IS FIGHTING ME... DEEP INSIDE HE CONTENDS ...
HE WILL NOT LAST LONG...BUT A BEATING HEART I STILL NEED TO REMAIN IN THE MORTAL VALE...
I NEED A NEW BODY... WHERE DID YOU FIND THIS ONE, MAGGOT? SOME SHY SCRAP WITH A LITTLE HATE IN HIS HEART?
I NEED SOMETHING NEW, SOMEONE BETTER. DO YOU HEAR ME?! OR YOUR HEAD WILL ROLL!

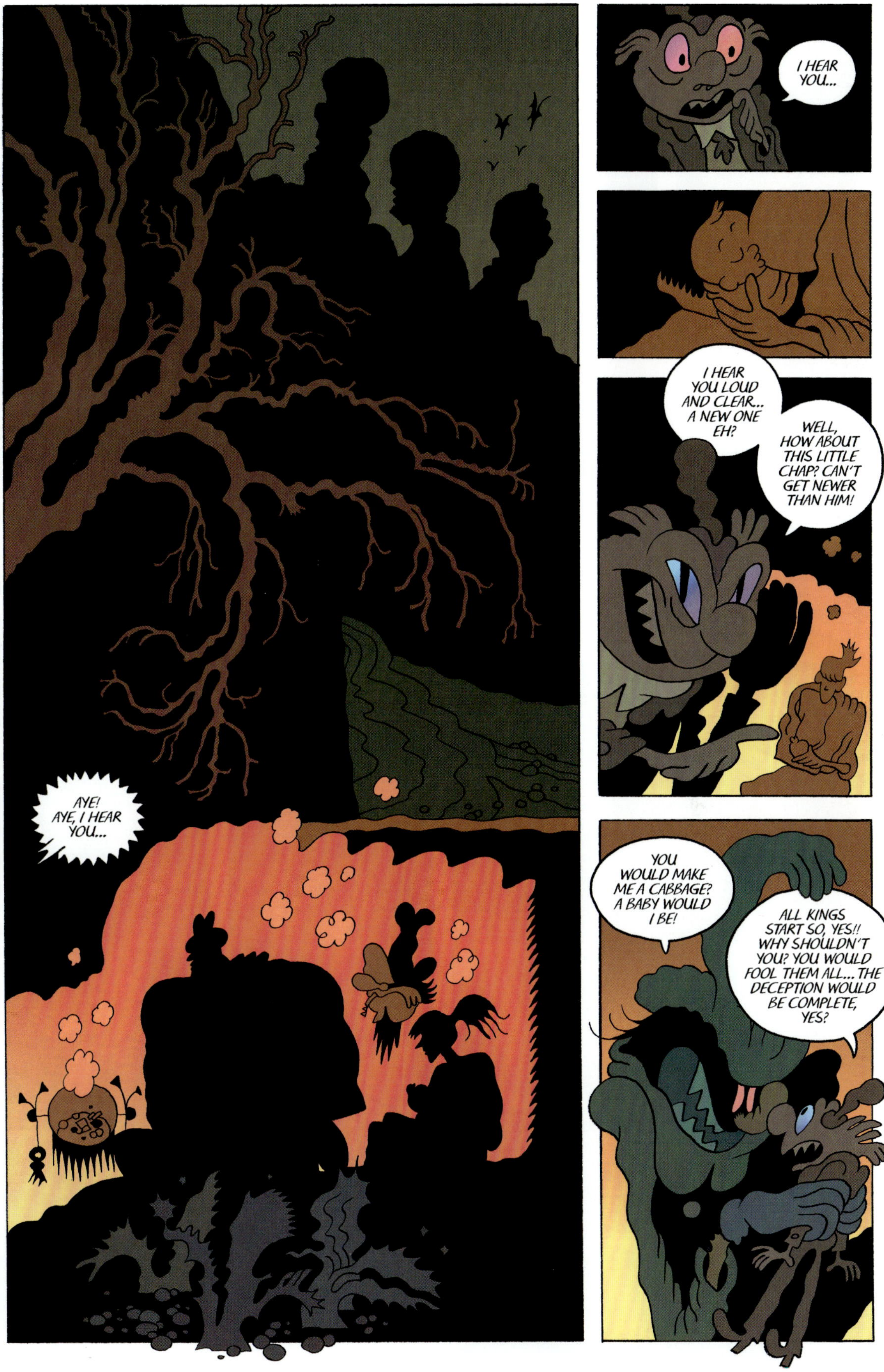
AYE! AYE, I HEAR YOU...
I HEAR YOU...
I HEAR YOU LOUD AND CLEAR... A NEW ONE EH?
WELL, HOW ABOUT THIS LITTLE CHAP? CAN'T GET NEWER THAN HIM!
YOU WOULD MAKE ME A CABBAGE? A BABY WOULD I BE!
ALL KINGS START SO, YES!! WHY SHOULDN'T YOU? YOU WOULD FOOL THEM ALL... THE DECEPTION WOULD BE COMPLETE, YES?

YES...A NEW START. AN EARLIER BEGINNING. IT WOULD BE A LONG GAME.
IT WOULD GIVE ME MORE TIME...
MORE TIME...MORE TIME TO...
TO SIGN THE SOUL...
MAKE THE DEAL!
TO BE THE ONE!

YOU HAVE SOME-THING FOR THE MASTER?!
NO!
WE WILL!
NOT YET WE DON'T. BUT WE WILL!
YOU BETTER HAVE, AND FAST. YOUR SOUL STONE ISN'T LOOKING VERY BRIGHT. NOT VERY BRIGHT AT ALL... THAT MAKES US VERY HUNGRY...
HUNGRY...
BUT CAN IT BE DONE?
CAN A BABY ACCEPT US IN?

THE DOORS MUST BE OPENED TO US ...HATE, JEALOUSY, PRIDE, ANGER, THE MALIGNANT KEYS MUST BE ACCEPTED.
MALE-VOLENCE INGESTED...EVIL REQUESTED.
CAN THE DOOR BE FORCED IN?
FORCED OPEN?
THE FIVE FINGERS WILL HAVE REPRESENTATIVES AT THE ALLWEATHER IN STACY! TWO STOPS UP THE GORECKI LINE.
THEY'RE WITCHES! THEY'LL KNOW!
YES... MORE TIME. IT WILL GIVE US MORE TIME...
MORE TIME.
MORE TIME.
MORE TIME.
MORE TIME.
MORE TIME.
MORE TIME.
MORE TIME.
MORE TIME.
MORE TIME.
MORE TIME.
MORE TIME.

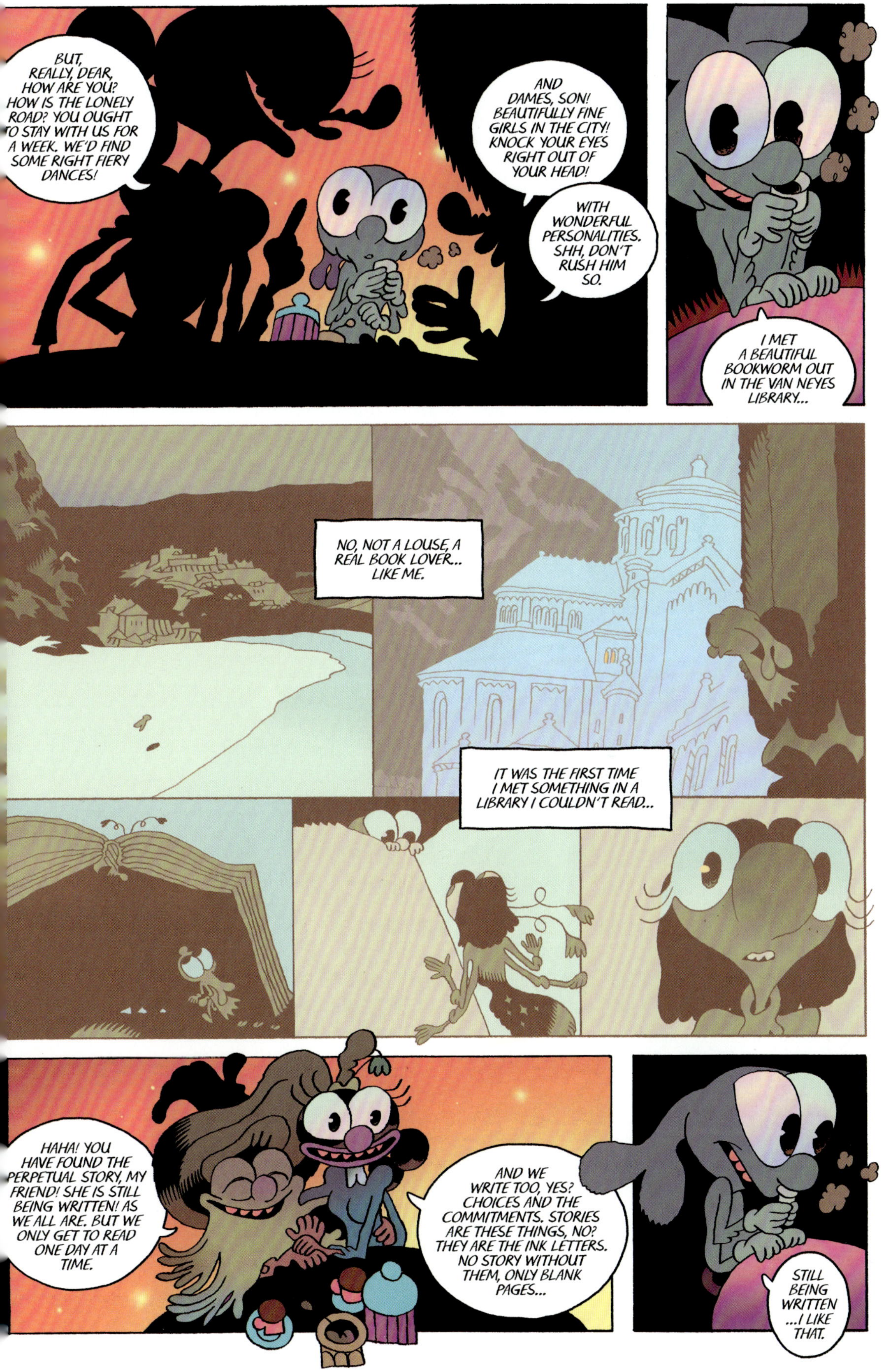
BUT, REALLY, DEAR, HOW ARE YOU? HOW IS THE LONELY ROAD? YOU OUGHT TO STAY WITH US FOR A WEEK. WE'D FIND SOME RIGHT FIERY DANCES!
AND DAMES, SON! BEAUTIFULLY FINE GIRLS IN THE CITY! KNOCK YOUR EYES RIGHT OUT OF YOUR HEAD!
WITH WONDERFUL PERSONALITIES. SHH, DON'T RUSH HIM SO.
I MET A BEAUTIFUL BOOKWORM OUT IN THE VAN NEYES LIBRARY...
NO, NOT A LOUSE, A REAL BOOK LOVER... LIKE ME.
IT WAS THE FIRST TIME I MET SOMETHING IN A LIBRARY I COULDN'T READ...
HAHA! YOU HAVE FOUND THE PERPETUAL STORY, MY FRIEND! SHE IS STILL BEING WRITTEN! AS WE ALL ARE. BUT WE ONLY GET TO READ ONE DAY AT A TIME.
AND WE WRITE TOO, YES? CHOICES AND THE COMMITMENTS. STORIES ARE THESE THINGS, NO? THEY ARE THE INK LETTERS. NO STORY WITHOUT THEM, ONLY BLANK PAGES...
STILL BEING WRITTEN ...I LIKE THAT.

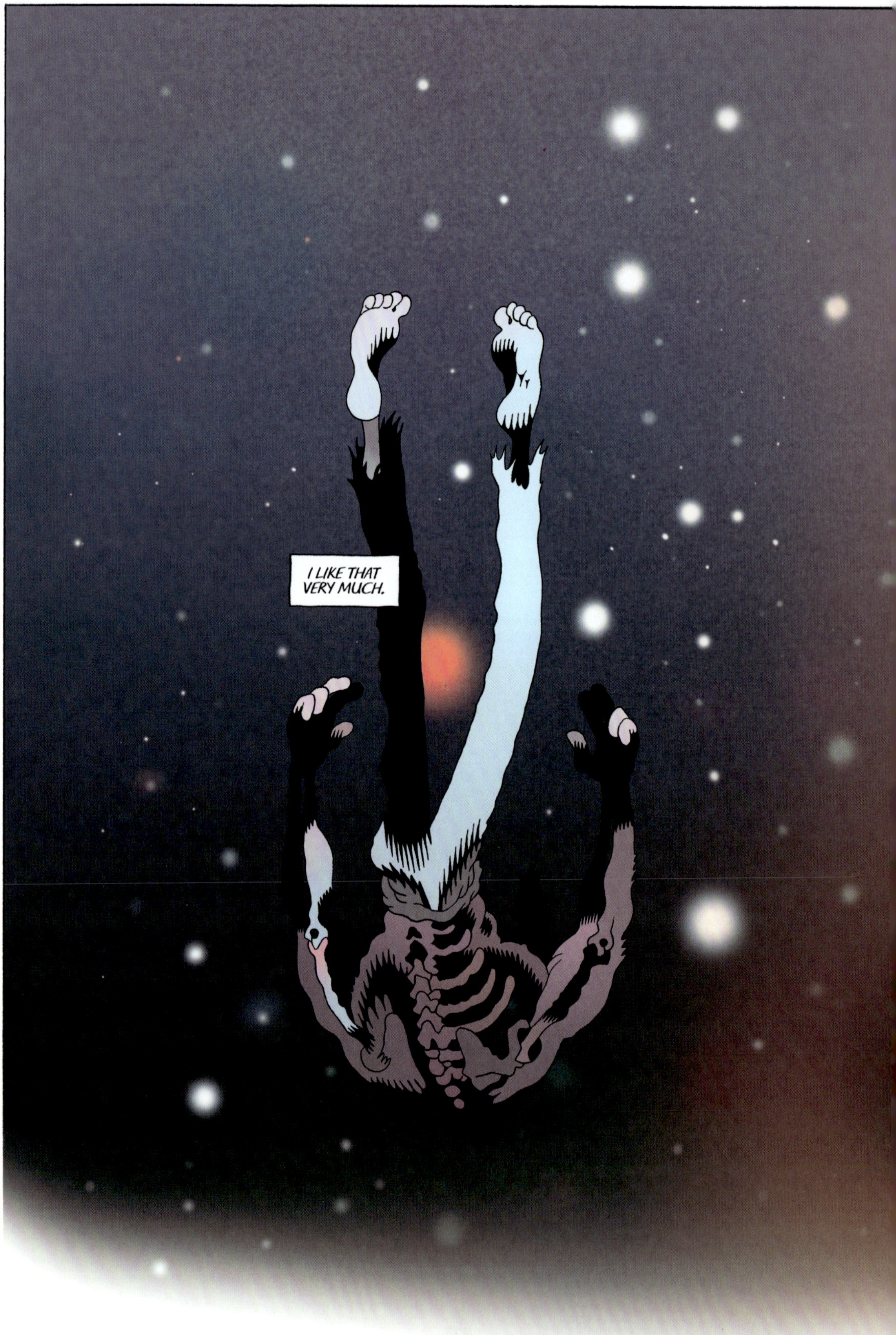
I LIKE THAT VERY MUCH.

IV
MAMBO
JAMBO
IN THE
GREEN
GOLDEN
HOUR

Cotton heads in plenty,
They are precious too.
But cotton heads in safety?
There are precious few.

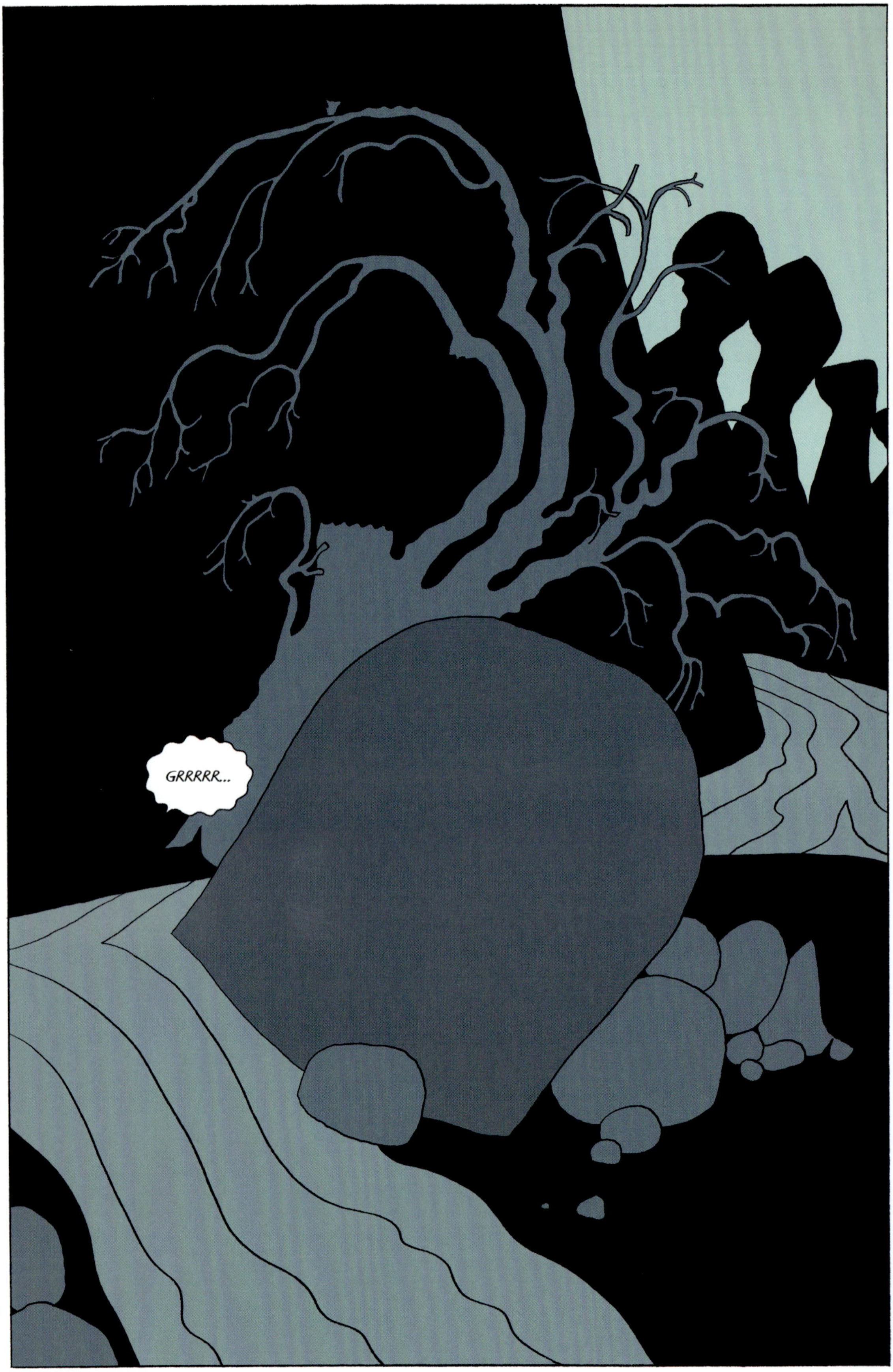
GRRRRR...

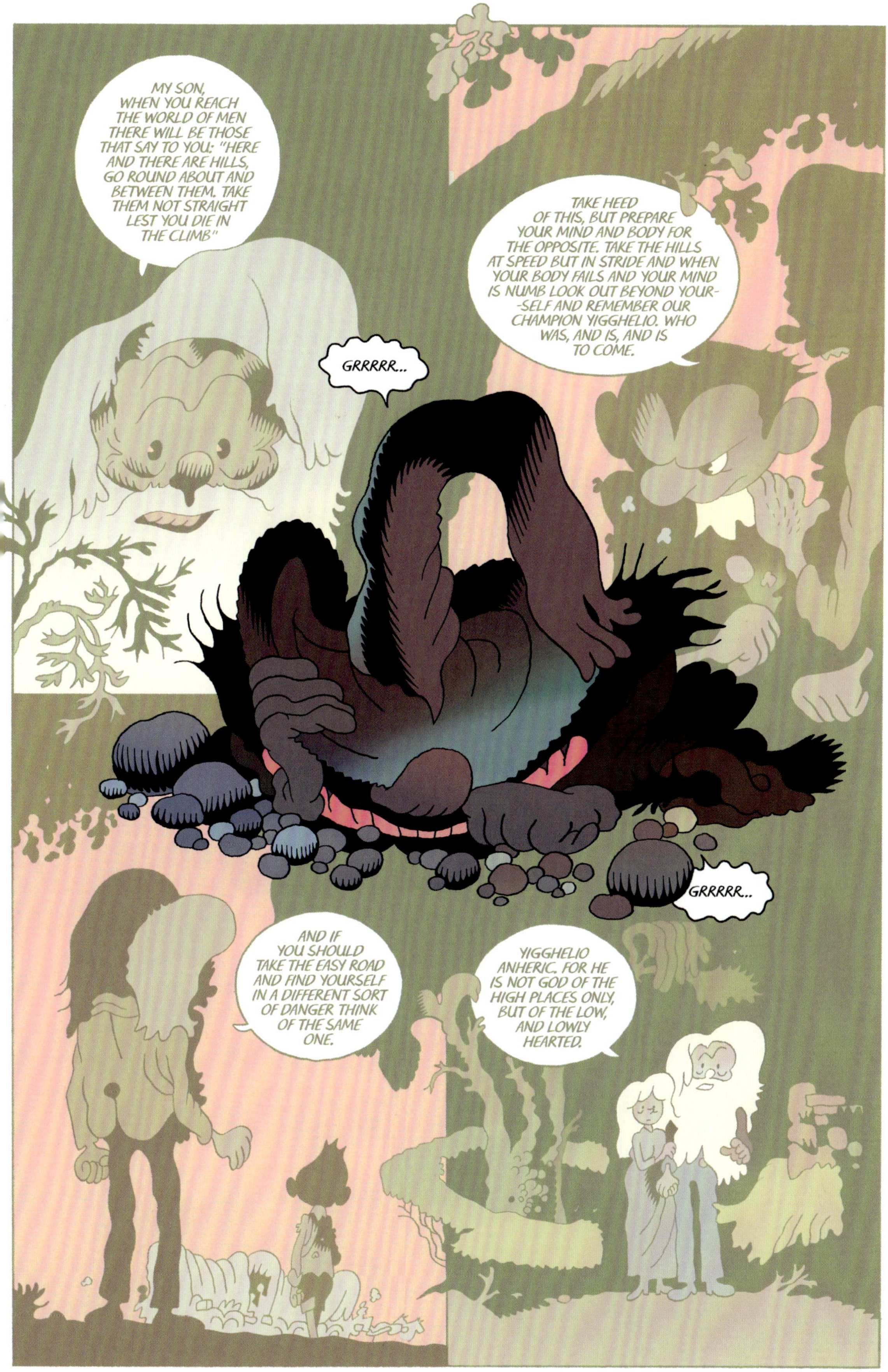
MY SON, WHEN YOU REACH THE WORLD OF MEN THERE WILL BE THOSE THAT SAY TO YOU: "HERE AND THERE ARE HILLS, GO ROUND ABOUT AND BETWEEN THEM. TAKE THEM NOT STRAIGHT LEST YOU DIE IN THE CLIMB"
TAKE HEED OF THIS, BUT PREPARE YOUR MIND AND BODY FOR THE OPPOSITE. TAKE THE HILLS AT SPEED BUT IN STRIDE AND WHEN YOUR BODY FAILS AND YOUR MIND IS NUMB LOOK OUT BEYOND YOUR--SELF AND REMEMBER OUR CHAMPION YIGGHELIO. WHO WAS, AND IS, AND IS TO COME.
GRRRRR...
GRRRRR...
AND IF YOU SHOULD TAKE THE EASY ROAD AND FIND YOURSELF IN A DIFFERENT SORT OF DANGER THINK OF THE SAME ONE.
YIGGHELIO ANHERIC. FOR HE IS NOT GOD OF THE HIGH PLACES ONLY, BUT OF THE LOW, AND LOWLY HEARTED.

SAY BUB-BY TO DADDY?
NAH, HE'S JUST SOME CRAZY CULTIST.
BUB-BY TO THE OL'T ORPHANAGE THEN! AND WELCOME TO THE REAL FAMILY!
GRRRRR...
GRRRRR...

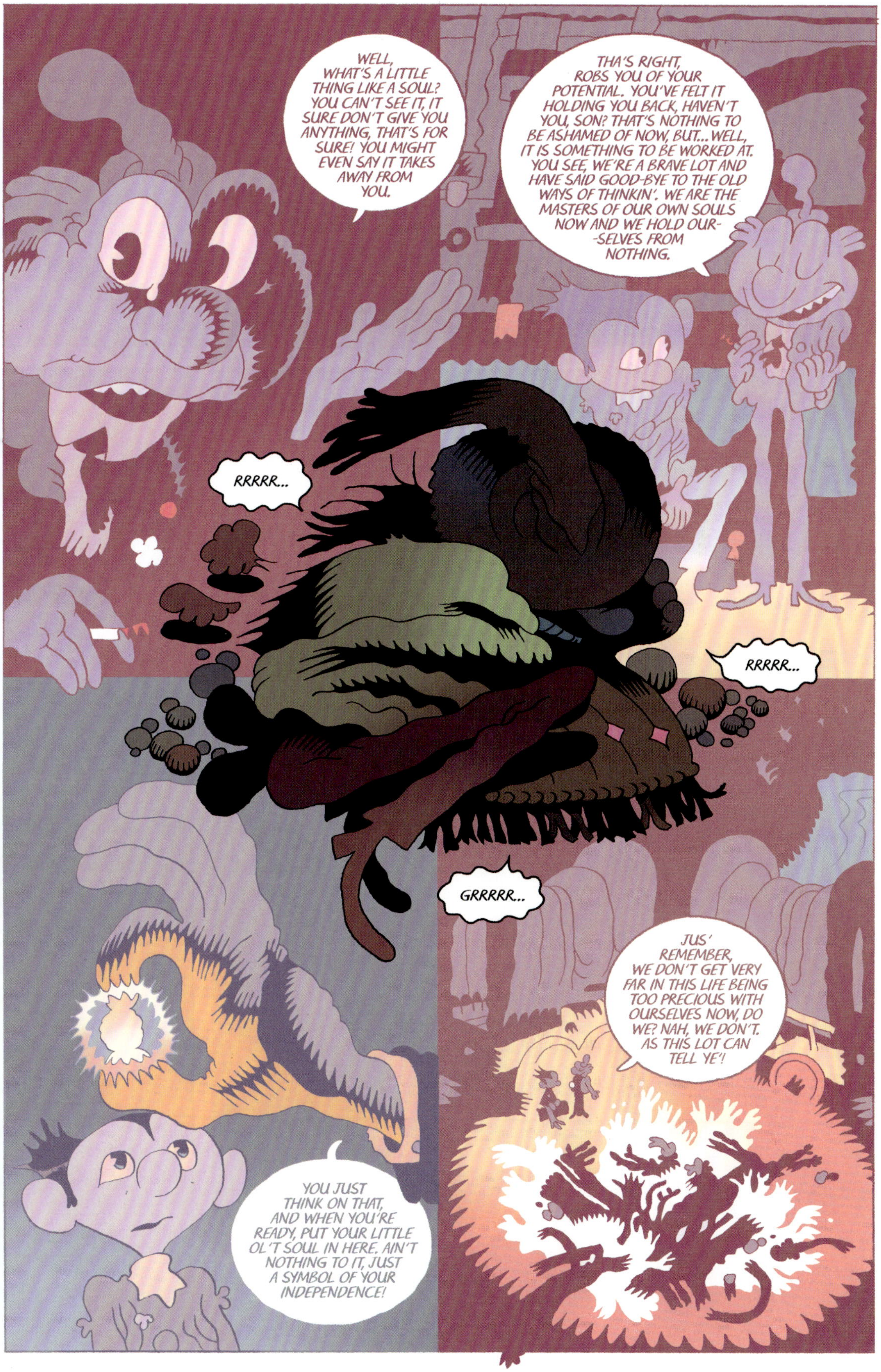
WELL, WHAT'S A LITTLE THING LIKE A SOUL? YOU CAN'T SEE IT, IT SURE DON'T GIVE YOU ANYTHING, THAT'S FOR SURE! YOU MIGHT EVEN SAY IT TAKES AWAY FROM YOU.
THA'S RIGHT, ROBS YOU OF YOUR POTENTIAL. YOU'VE FELT IT HOLDING YOU BACK, HAVEN'T YOU, SON? THAT'S NOTHING TO BE ASHAMED OF NOW, BUT... WELL, IT IS SOMETHING TO BE WORKED AT. YOU SEE, WE'RE A BRAVE LOT AND HAVE SAID GOOD-BYE TO THE OLD WAYS OF THINKIN'. WE ARE THE MASTERS OF OUR OWN SOULS NOW AND WE HOLD OUR--SELVES FROM NOTHING.
RRRRR...
RRRRR...
GRRRRR...
JUS' REMEMBER, WE DON'T GET VERY FAR IN THIS LIFE BEING TOO PRECIOUS WITH OURSELVES NOW, DO WE? NAH, WE DON'T. AS THIS LOT CAN TELL YE'!
YOU JUST THINK ON THAT, AND WHEN YOU'RE READY, PUT YOUR LITTLE OL'T SOUL IN HERE. AIN'T NOTHING TO IT, JUST A SYMBOL OF YOUR INDEPENDENCE!

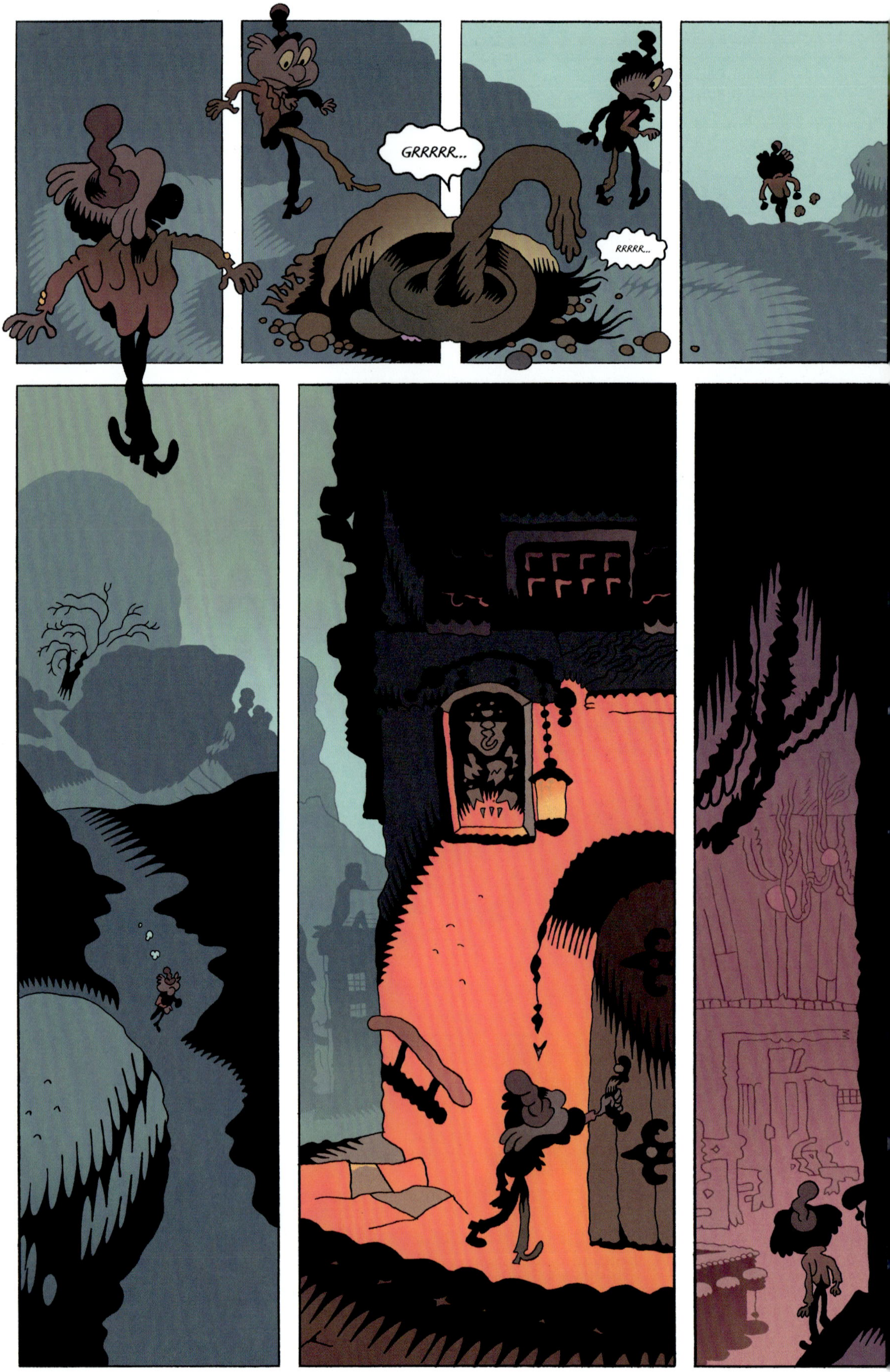
GRRRRR...
RRRRR...

THOUGHT I SAW YOU SLINK INTO THE STATION TODAY. LOOKS LIKE YOU'RE A COUPLE BOYS SHORT OF A CARNY!
THESE HUMANS, THEY WEAR OUT. NOT LIKE US, 'EY? NOT LIKE US. WE BEEN KICKIN' THE CAN DOWN THE ROAD FOR A WHILE NOW.
WELL, IT'S FUNNY YOU SHOULD MENTION THE BOYS, CAUSE AH...I GOT ONE OF 'EM LEFT, SEE, BUT HE, UH, WELL...HE DON'T LISTEN TO ME ANY--MORE. GOT PLANS OF HIS OWN AND ALL.
DOES HE NOW?! HO, HO!
HOW DID THIS HAPPEN?
I SOLD YOUR BATCH UP THE RIVER.
TO WHO?!

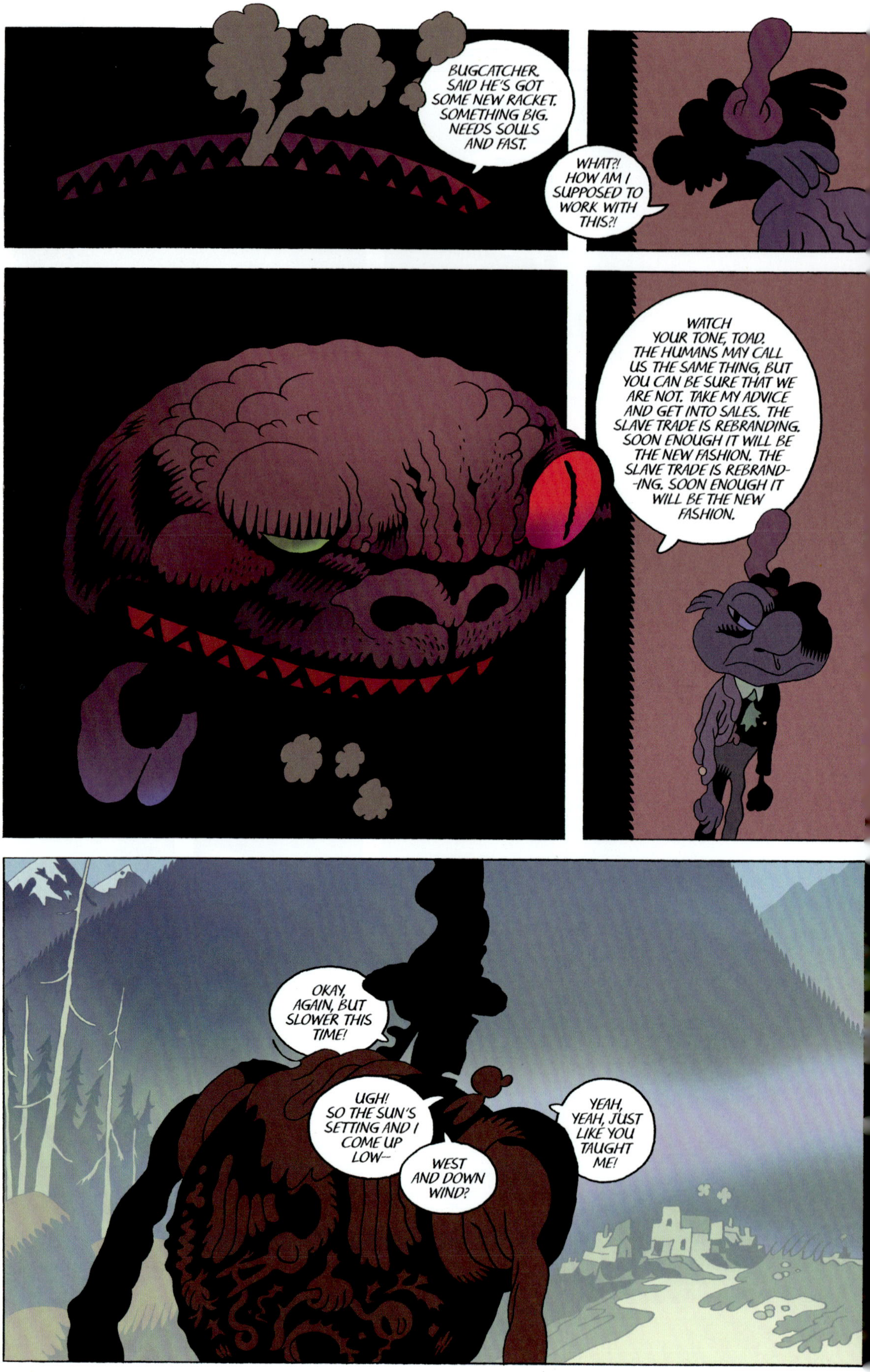
BUGCATCHER SAID HE'S GOT SOME NEW RACKET. SOMETHING BIG. NEEDS SOULS AND FAST.
WHAT?! HOW AM I SUPPOSED TO WORK WITH THIS?!
WATCH YOUR TONE, TOAD. THE HUMANS MAY CALL US THE SAME THING, BUT YOU CAN BE SURE THAT WE ARE NOT. TAKE MY ADVICE AND GET INTO SALES. THE SLAVE TRADE IS REBRANDING. SOON ENOUGH IT WILL BE THE NEW FASHION. THE SLAVE TRADE IS REBRAND--ING. SOON ENOUGH IT WILL BE THE NEW FASHION.
OKAY, AGAIN, BUT SLOWER THIS TIME!
UGH! SO THE SUN'S SETTING AND I COME UP LOW--
WEST AND DOWN WIND?
YEAH, YEAH, JUST LIKE YOU TAUGHT ME!

SO I SEE THESE TWO FIGURES, ONLY TWO AND I THINK, OH NO! THEY DID THE KID ALREADY!
BUT AS I GET CLOSER IT'S CLEAR SOMETHING'S WRONG. NO MOVEMENT, NO HORSES. I COME AROUND AND THESE WITCHES ARE STONE COLD!
DEAD I TELL YOU, EYES LIKE MARBLES. IT WAS KNIFE WORK AND VERY MESSY.
THE GIRL WAS GONE. NOWHERE TO BE FOUND.
HM. WELL, LUCKY BREAK FOR MISS STRANGER.
HEY! I'M SURE I MADE IT BACK IN TIME.
OH, YOU PROBABLY DID, BUT...WELL, I'M JUST GLAD SHE GOT AWAY. EVERY TIME WE ROLL INTO TOWN THE WORLD SEEMS DIMMER. MAYBE A FINE GIRL LIKE THAT WILL BRIGHTEN UP SOME CORNER OUT THERE.

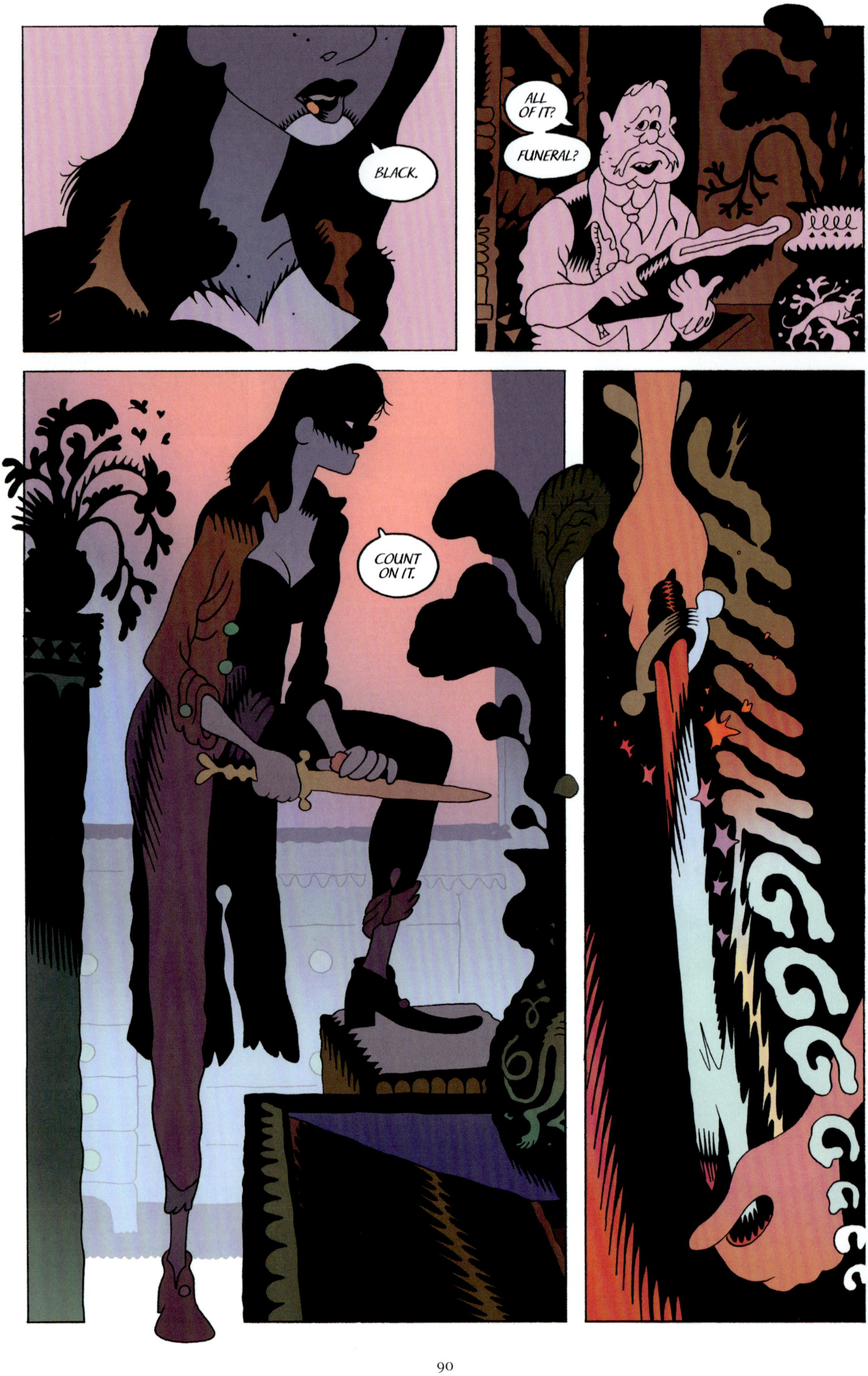
BLACK.
ALL OF IT?
FUNERAL?
COUNT ON IT.

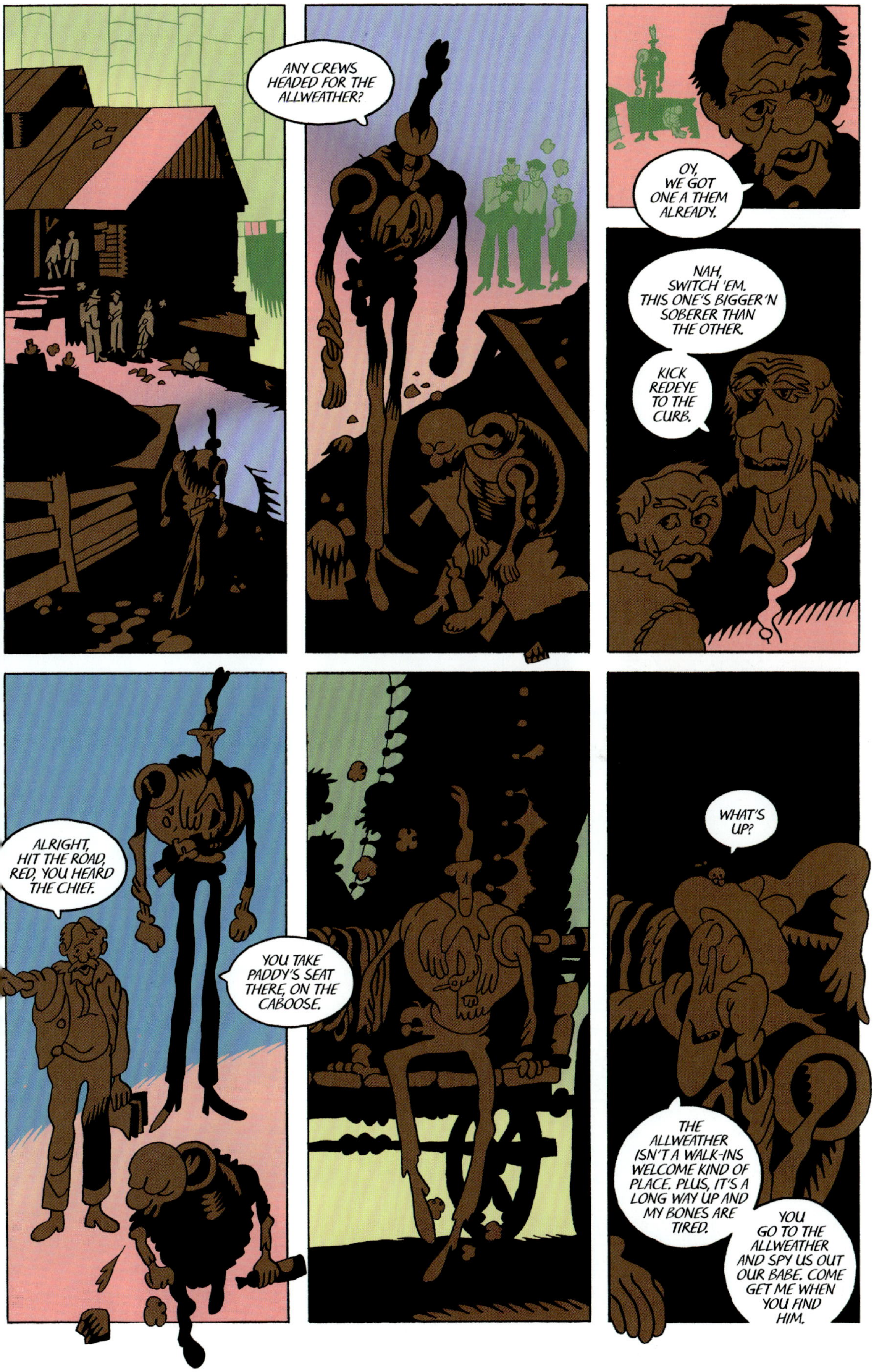
ANY CREWS HEADED FOR THE ALLWEATHER?
OY, WE GOT ONE A THEM ALREADY.
NAH, SWITCH 'EM. THIS ONE'S BIGGER'N SOBERER THAN THE OTHER.
KICK REDEYE TO THE CURB.
ALRIGHT, HIT THE ROAD, RED, YOU HEARD THE CHIEF.
YOU TAKE PADDY'S SEAT THERE, ON THE CABOOSE.
WHAT'S UP?
THE ALLWEATHER ISN'T A WALK-INS WELCOME KIND OF PLACE. PLUS, IT'S A LONG WAY UP AND MY BONES ARE TIRED.
YOU GO TO THE ALLWEATHER AND SPY US OUT OUR BABE. COME GET ME WHEN YOU FIND HIM.

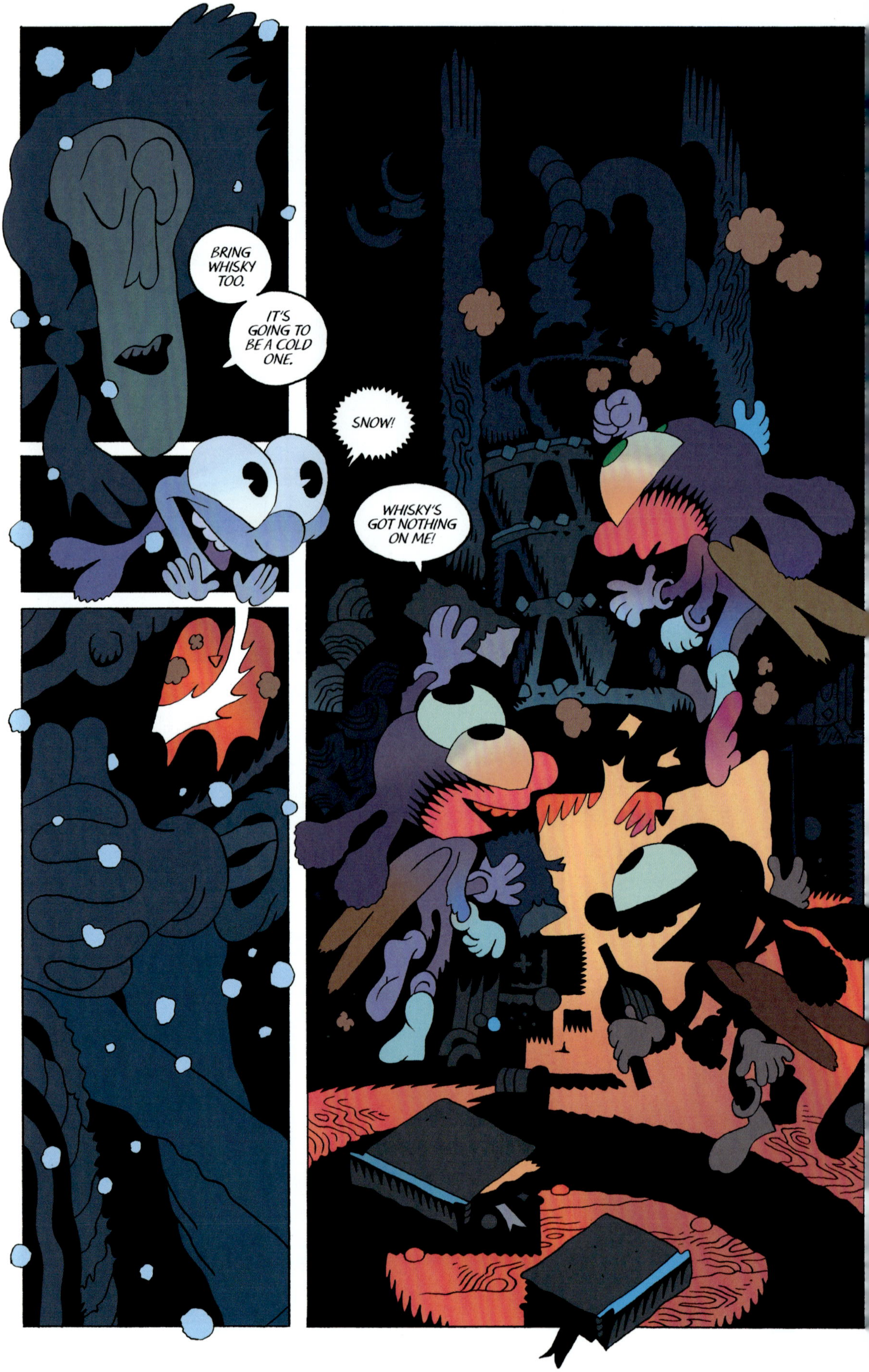
BRING WHISKY TOO.
IT'S GOING TO BE A COLD ONE.
SNOW!
WHISKY'S GOT NOTHING ON ME!

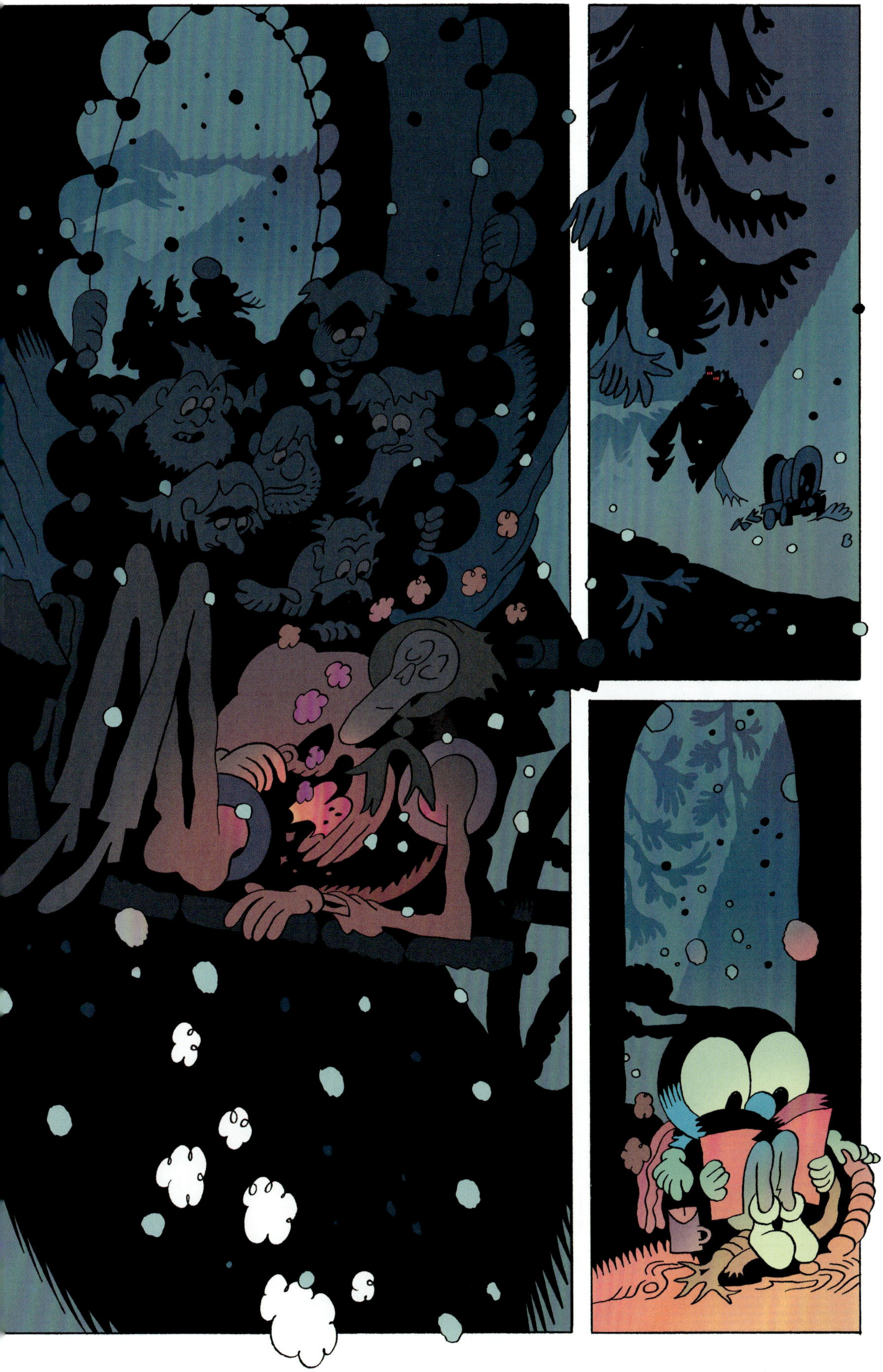

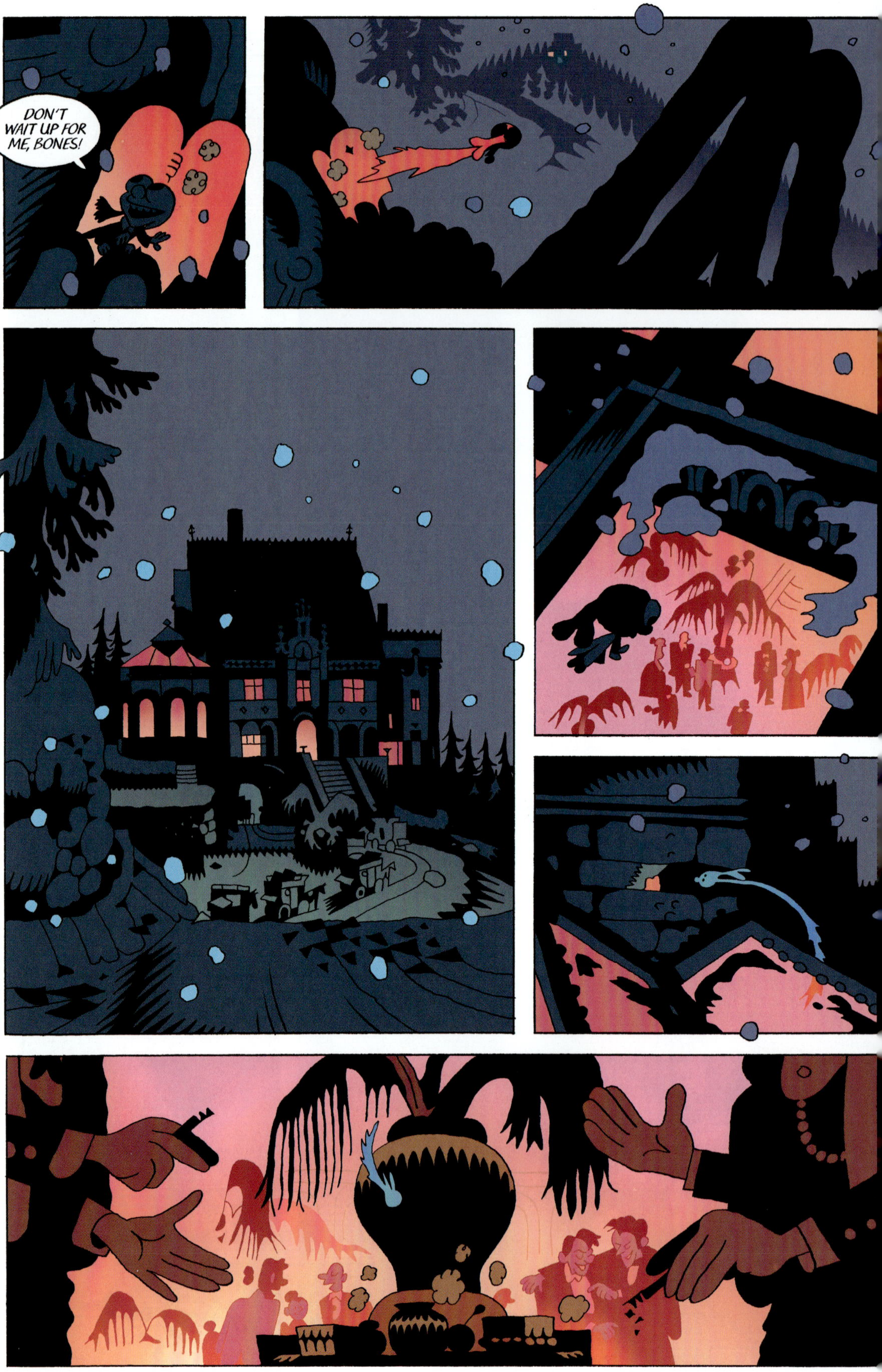
DON'T WAIT UP FOR ME, BONES!

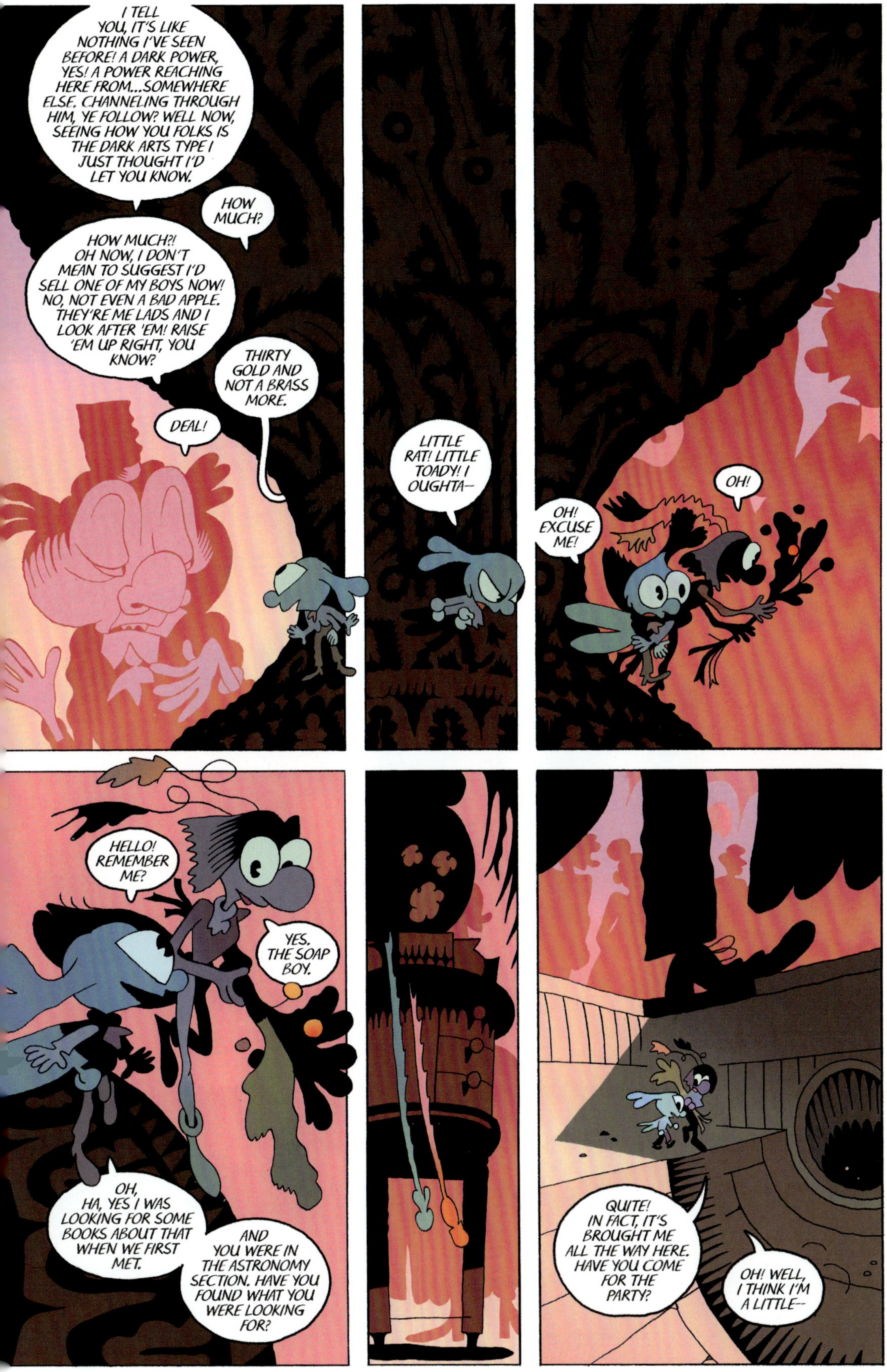
I TELL YOU, IT'S LIKE NOTHING I'VE SEEN BEFORE! A DARK POWER, YES! A POWER REACHING HERE FROM...SOMEWHERE ELSE. CHANNELING THROUGH HIM, YE FOLLOW? WELL NOW, SEEING HOW YOU FOLKS IS THE DARK ARTS TYPE I JUST THOUGHT I'D LET YOU KNOW.
HOW MUCH?
HOW MUCH?! OH NOW, I DON'T MEAN TO SUGGEST I'D SELL ONE OF MY BOYS NOW! NO, NOT EVEN A BAD APPLE. THEY'RE ME LADS AND I LOOK AFTER 'EM! RAISE 'EM UP RIGHT, YOU KNOW?
THIRTY GOLD AND NOT A BRASS MORE.
DEAL!
LITTLE RAT! LITTLE TOADY! I OUGHTA--
OH! EXCUSE ME!
OH!
HELLO! REMEMBER ME?
YES. THE SOAP BOY.
OH, HA, YES I WAS LOOKING FOR SOME BOOKS ABOUT THAT WHEN WE FIRST MET.
AND YOU WERE IN THE ASTRONOMY SECTION. HAVE YOU FOUND WHAT YOU WERE LOOKING FOR?
QUITE! IN FACT, IT'S BROUGHT ME ALL THE WAY HERE. HAVE YOU COME FOR THE PARTY?
OH! WELL, I THINK I'M A LITTLE--

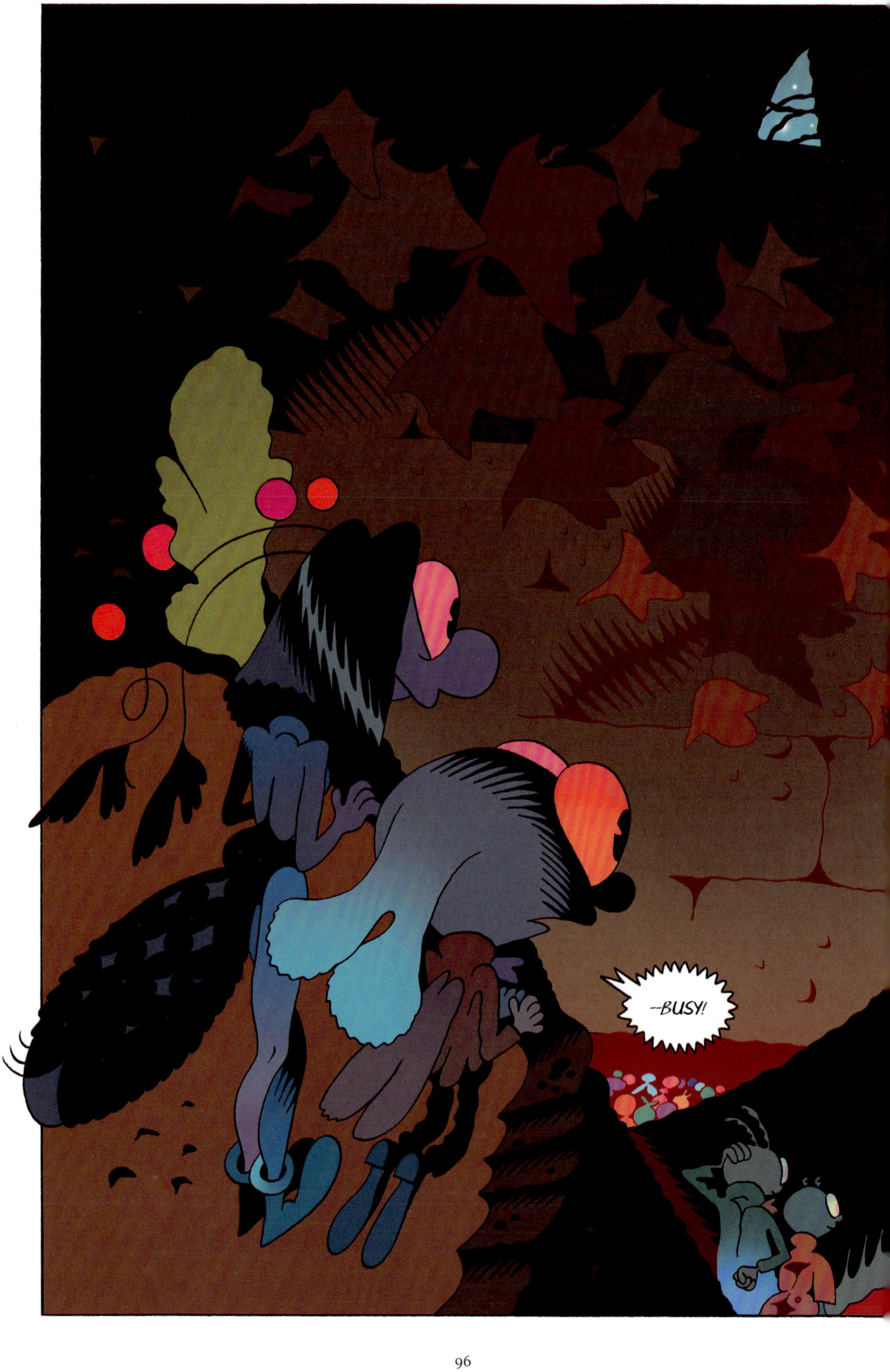
--BUSY!

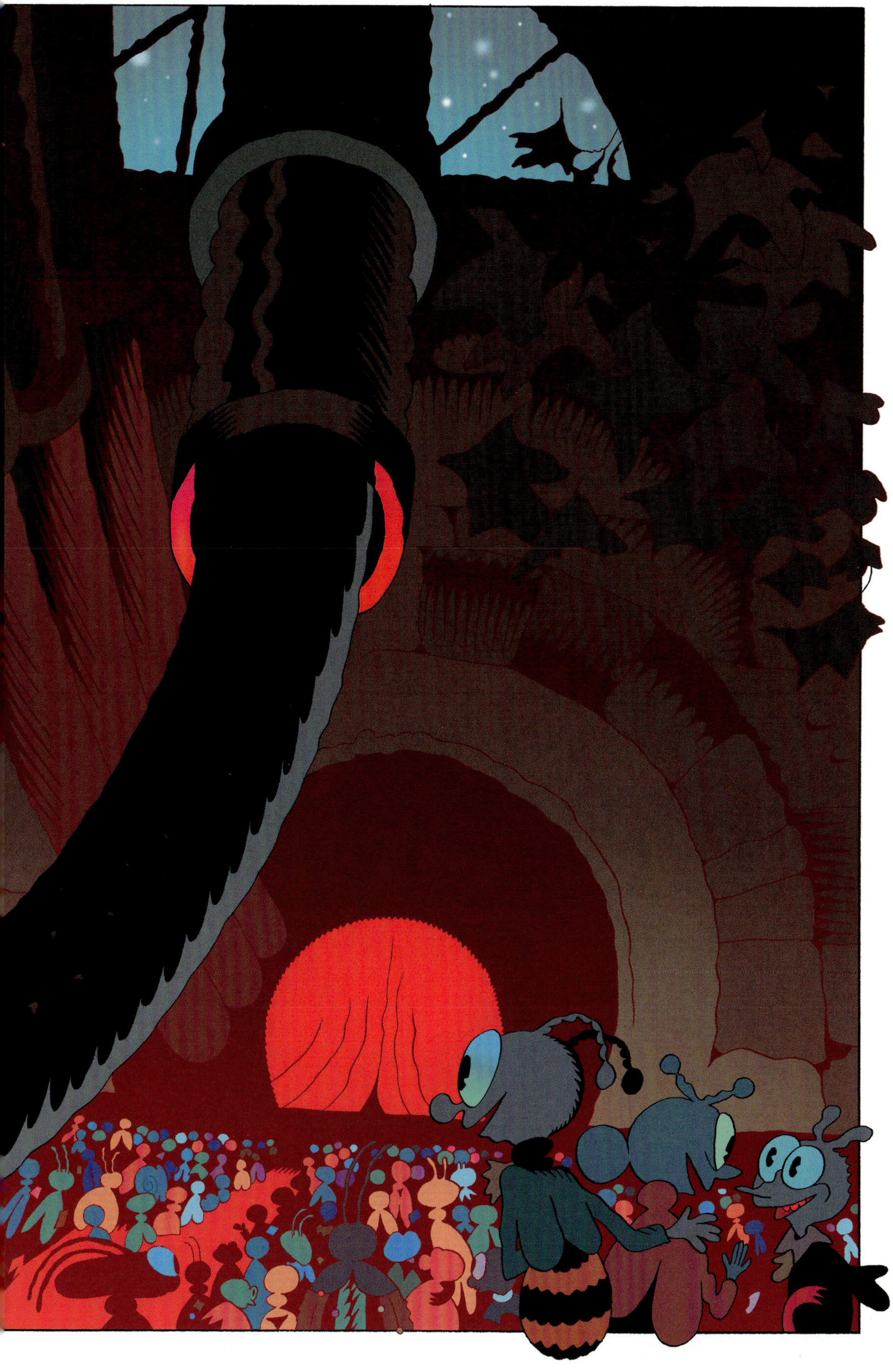

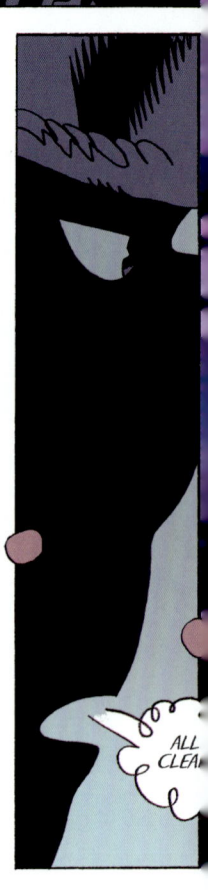

"ALRIGHT, PADDY, LET'S GET ON WITH IT."

"WHAT?"

"THE MAMBO JAMBO, THE YAKKETY YAK YOU SPOOKS DO. PRAY TO THE EARTH GOD FOR GOOD FORTUNE. MAKES THE LADS FEEL BETTER CHOPPIN' DOWN THE OL' TIMBERS."

"WHY'D YOU THINK WE SWAPPED YOU OUT FOR THE OTHER PADDY? ONLY NEED ONE OF YA!"

"KILL THEM, KILL THEM ALL! YOU KNOW WE COULD DO IT! BY YOUR HAND I COULD DO IT!"

"ALL CLEA"

YEAH?! WELL! THAT WASN'T SO HARD NOW, WAS IT?
RIGHT, LADS. MORE SAWING, LESS JAWING.

IT'S NOT SO HARD. NOT SO HARD BEING KICKED TO THE SIDE. OVER-LOOKED AND UNDER-FED.
NOT SO BAD TO BE TAKEN FROM ONE WORLD AND BROUGHT TO ANOTHER. NOT SO BAD TO BE DOME-STICATED, DECLAWED, DETHRONED, DEFORMED!
WILD ONE! RETURN TO US!
TURN OVER THE CHILD'S CRADLE AND DEVOUR HIM! DRINK UP HIS BLOOD BEFORE HIS HEEL IS SHOD WITH IRON.
BEFORE HE PRESS US OUT LIKE THE GRAPE, AND CONSUME US LIKE WINE.

YOU FEAR THE CHASM BECAUSE YOU FORGET THE BRIDGE.
YOU PARROT HIS WORDS BECAUSE YOU CAN. NOT BECAUSE YOU BELIEVE THEM. GO. PLAY YOUR TRICKS TO PLEASE YOUR GOD. DANCE FOR THE CLAPPING OF HANDS.
YOU WILL REMEMBER OUR WORDS WHEN THE SONS AND DAUGHTERS OF MAN CHOKE THIS WORLD.

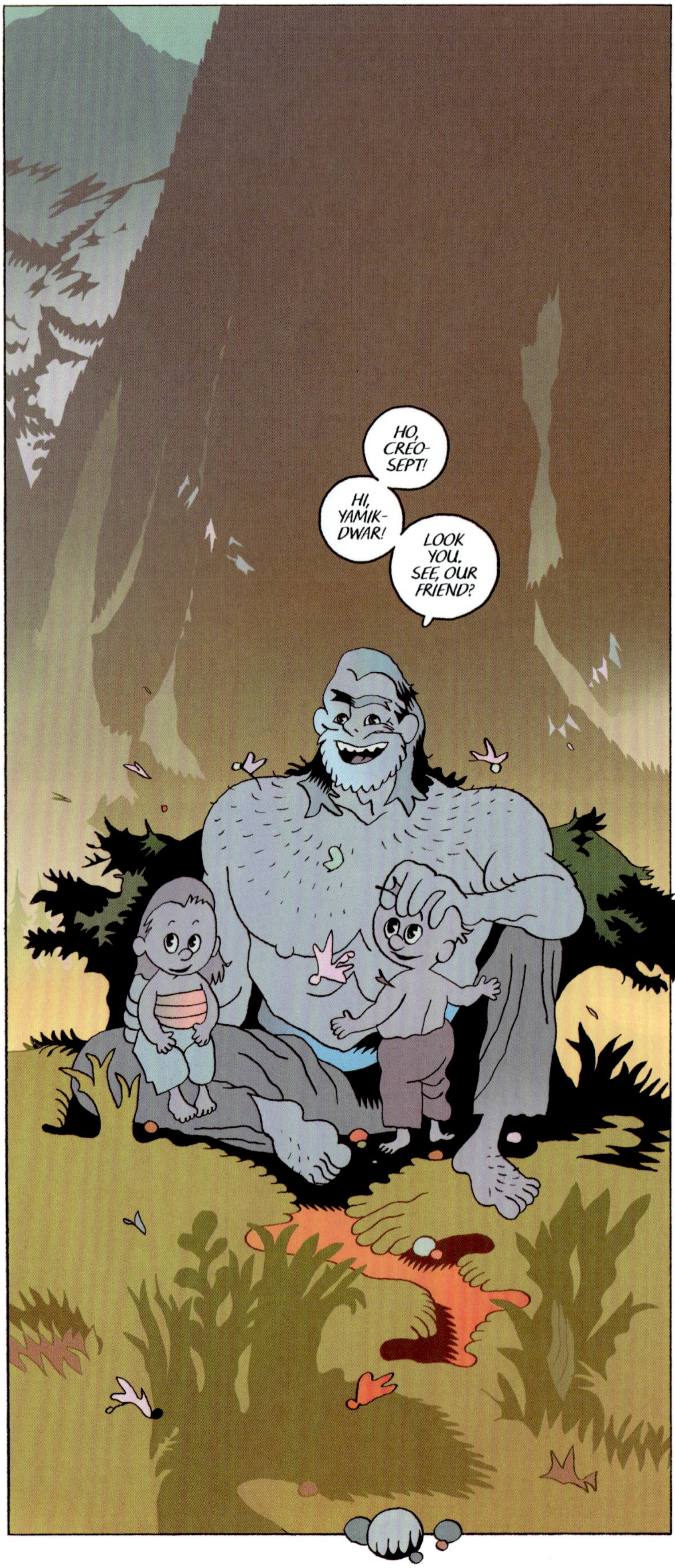
HO, CREO-SEPT!
HI, YAMIK-DWAR!
LOOK YOU. SEE, OUR FRIEND?

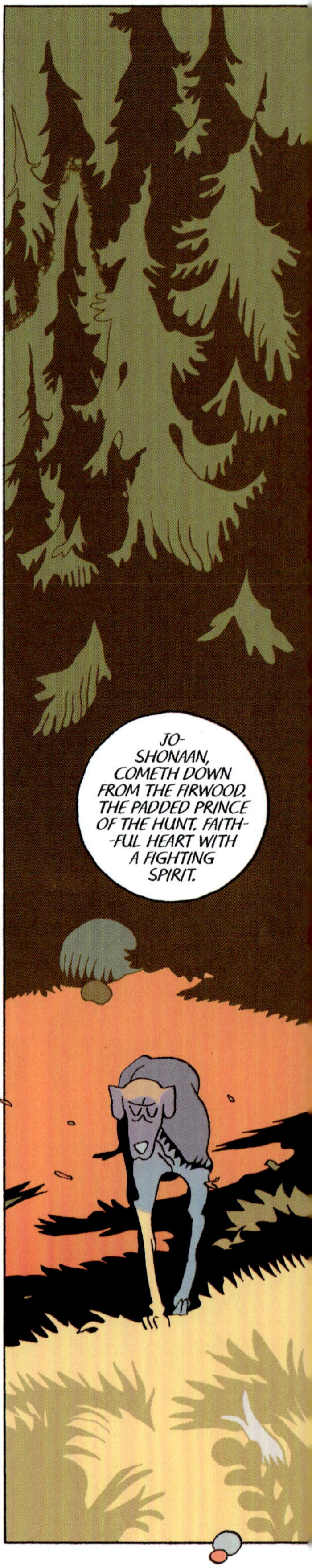
JO-SHONAAN, COMETH DOWN FROM THE FIRWOOD. THE PADDED PRINCE OF THE HUNT. FAITH--FUL HEART WITH A FIGHTING SPIRIT.

HE IS ONE TO TRUST AND TO BE GOOD UNTO.
MEET HIM NOW. BE NOT AFRAID.
BE NOT AFRAID.

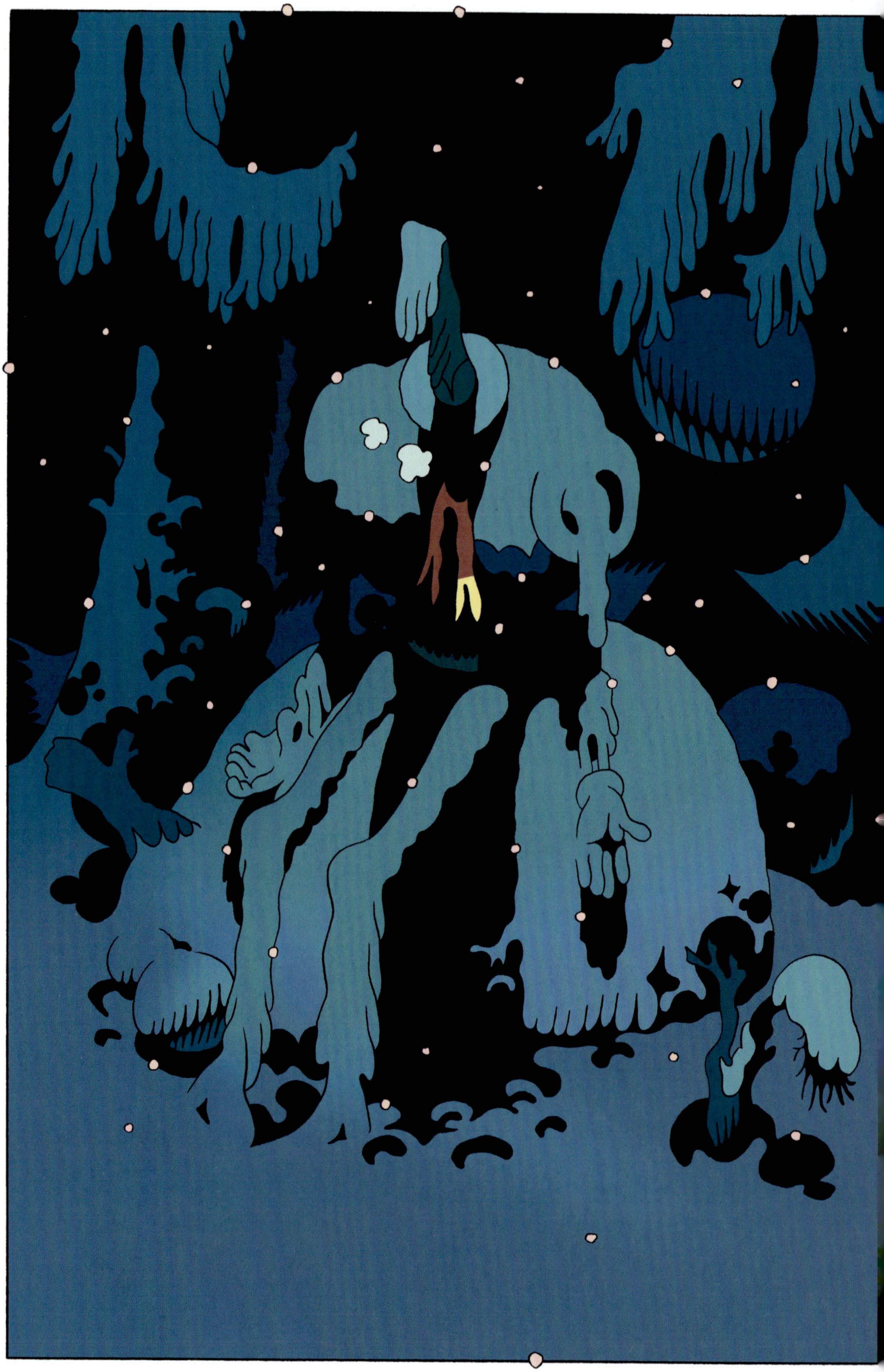

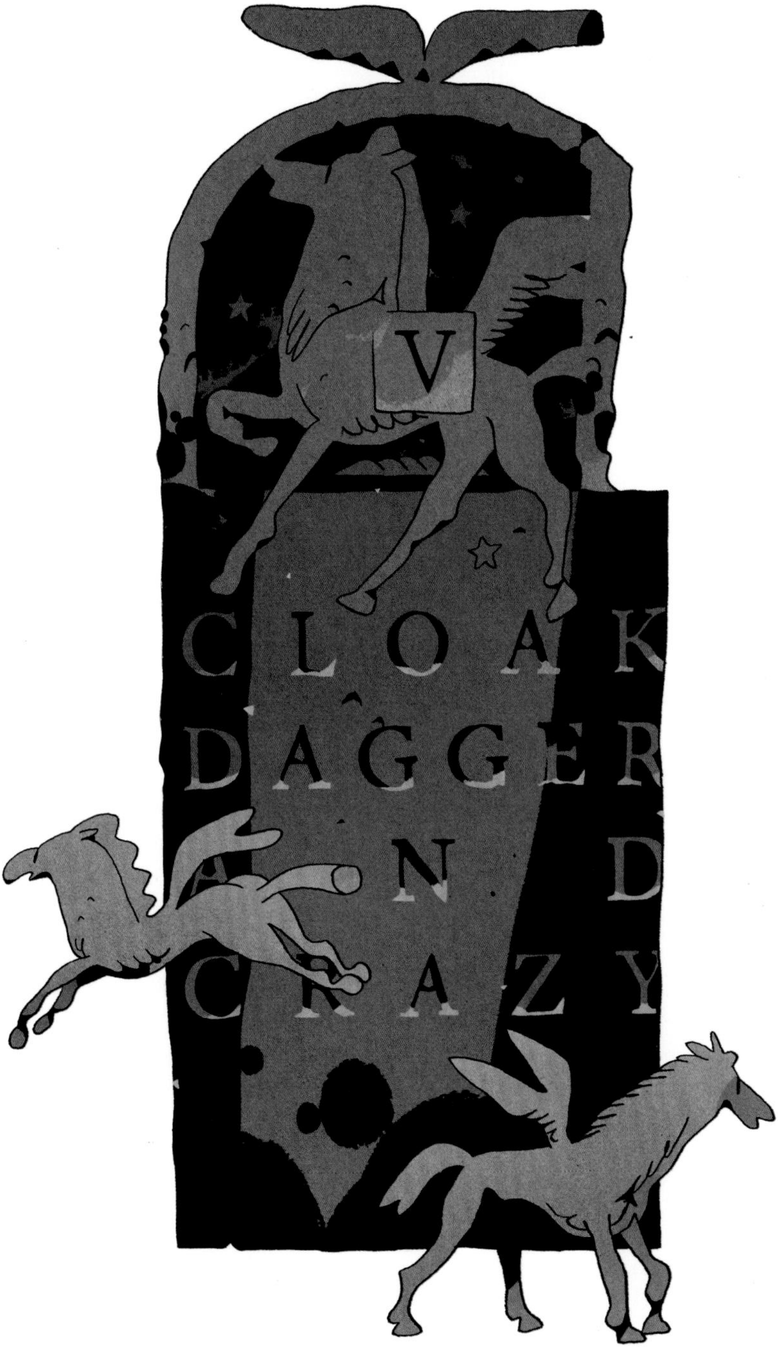
V
CLOAK
DAGGER
AND
CRAZY

Wooded rings of promise,
Wrapped round the emerald crown.
Petals pledged forever,
In foever lay me down.

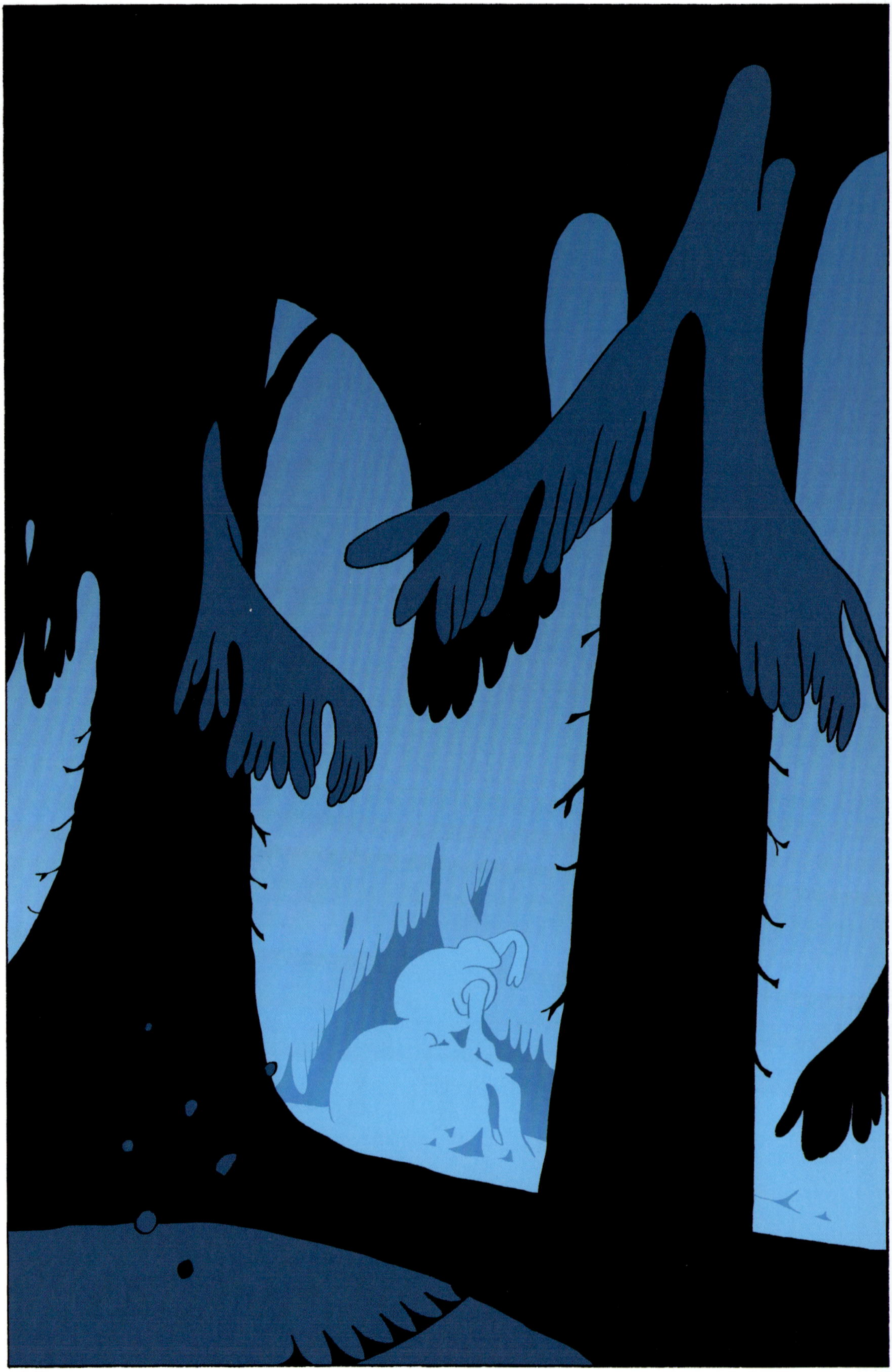

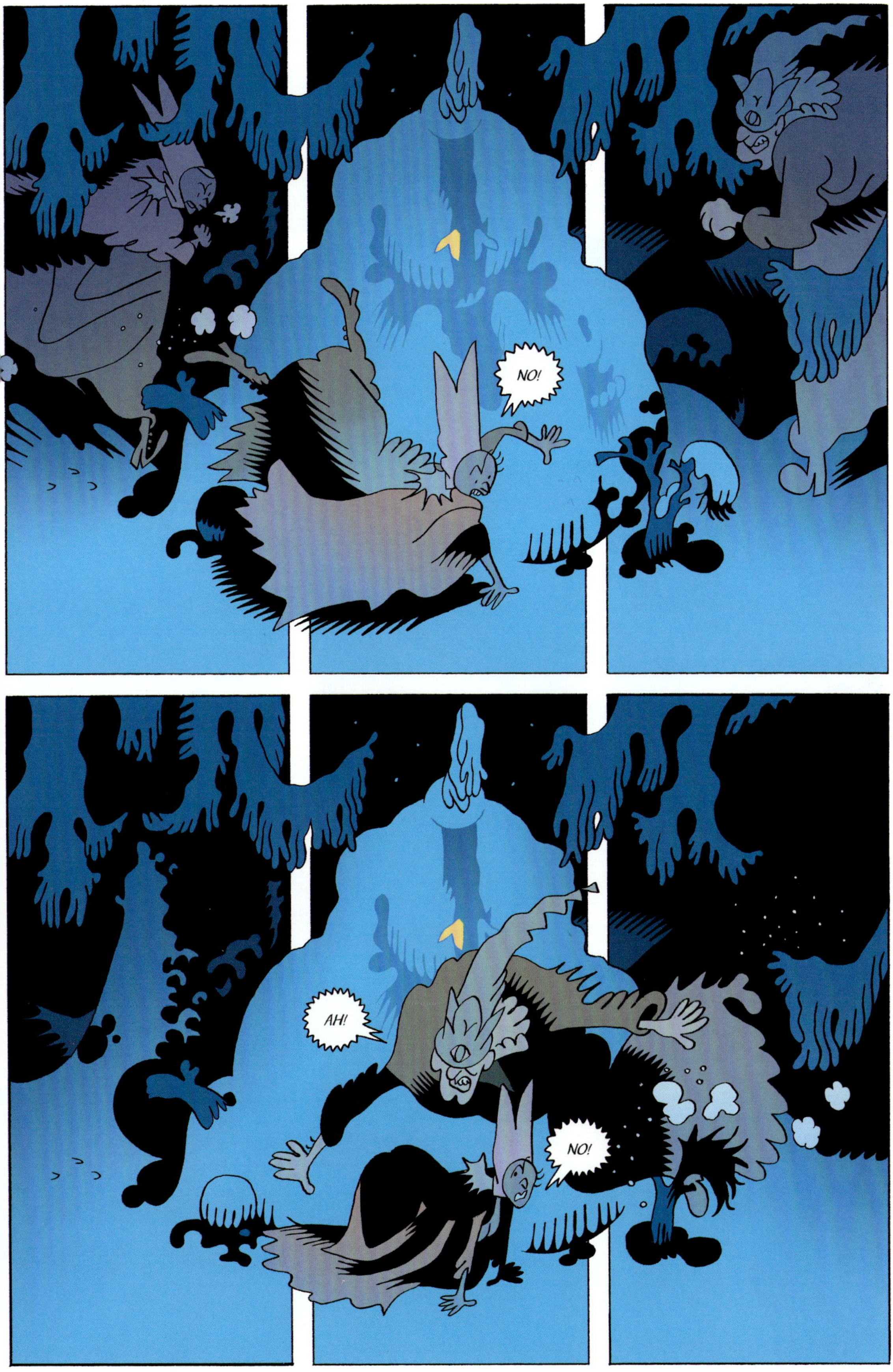
NO!
AH!
NO!

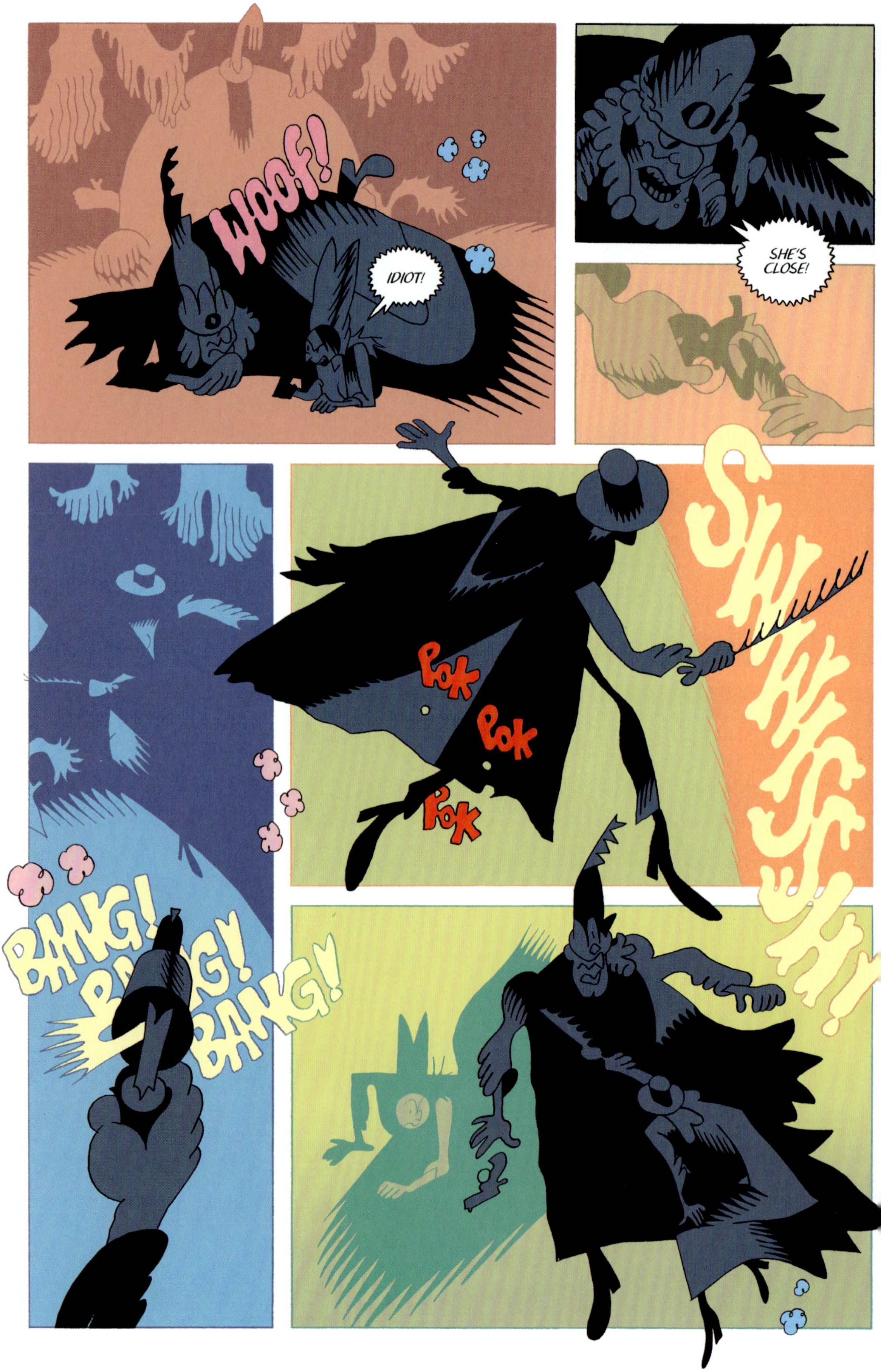
WOOF!
IDIOT!
SHE'S CLOSE!
BANG! BANG! BANG!
POK POK POK
SHHHHHH!

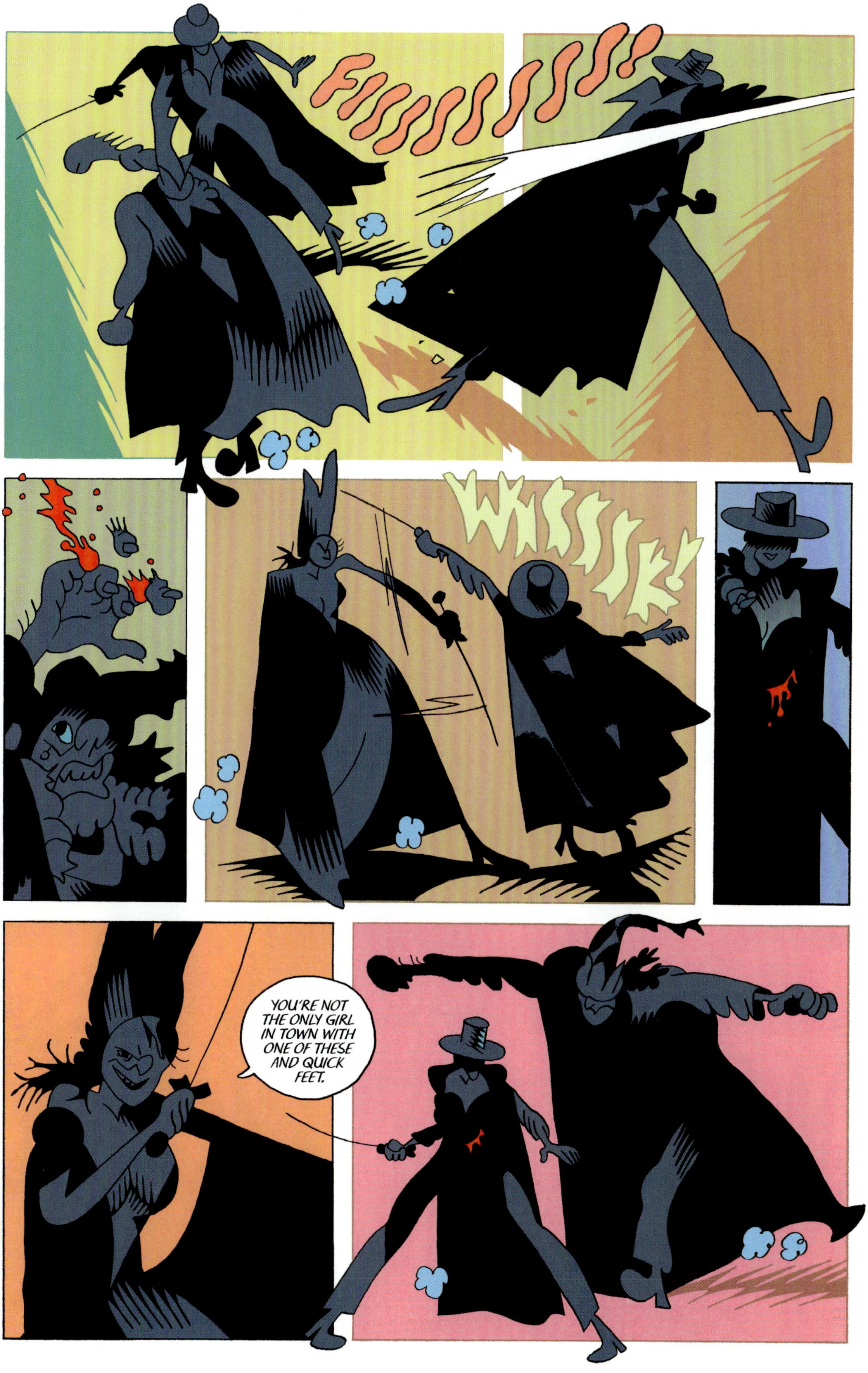
FISSSSSS!!
WHSSSK!
YOU'RE NOT THE ONLY GIRL IN TOWN WITH ONE OF THESE AND QUICK FEET.

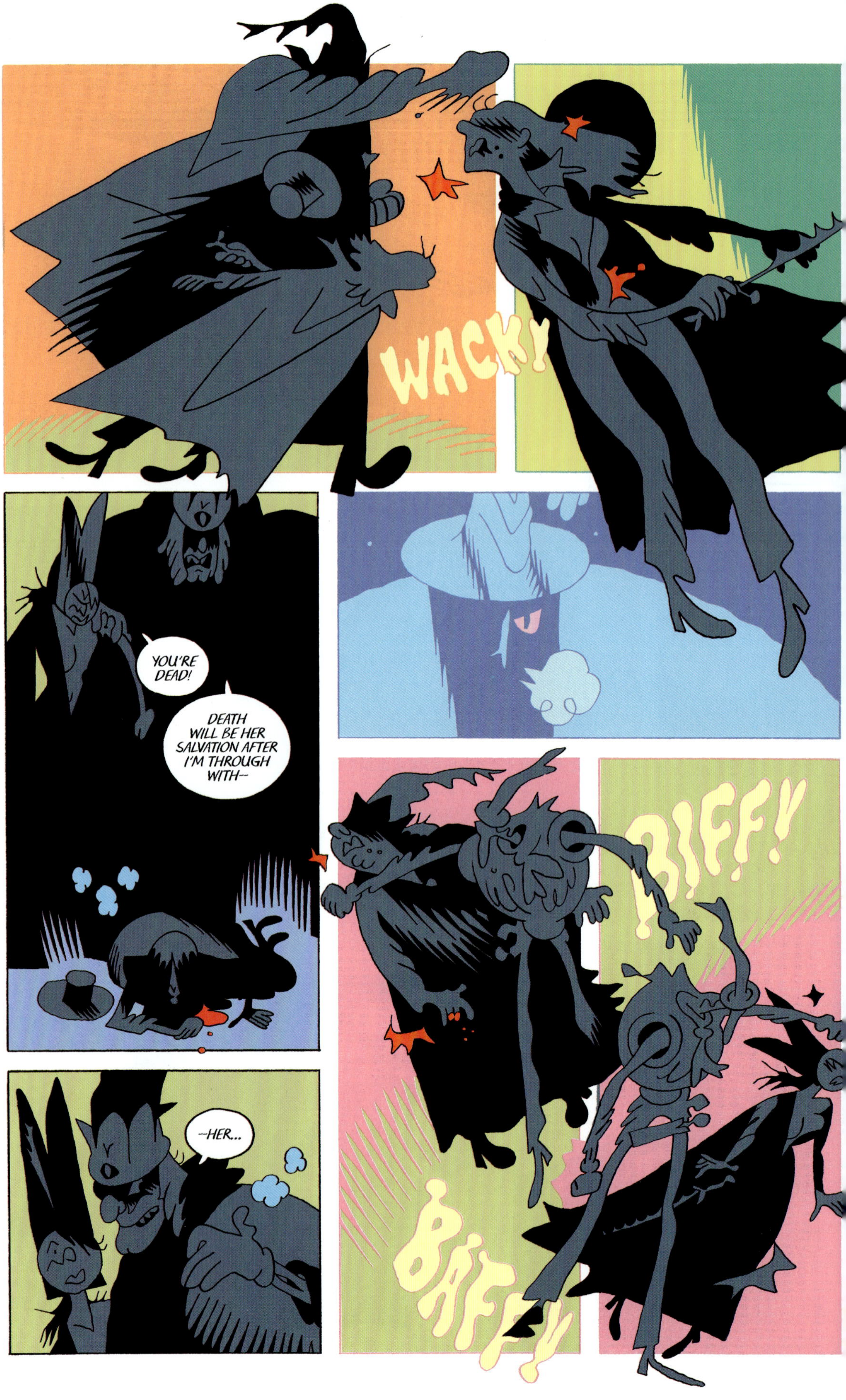
WACK!
YOU'RE DEAD!
DEATH WILL BE HER SALVATION AFTER I'M THROUGH WITH--
--HER...
BIFF!
BAFF!

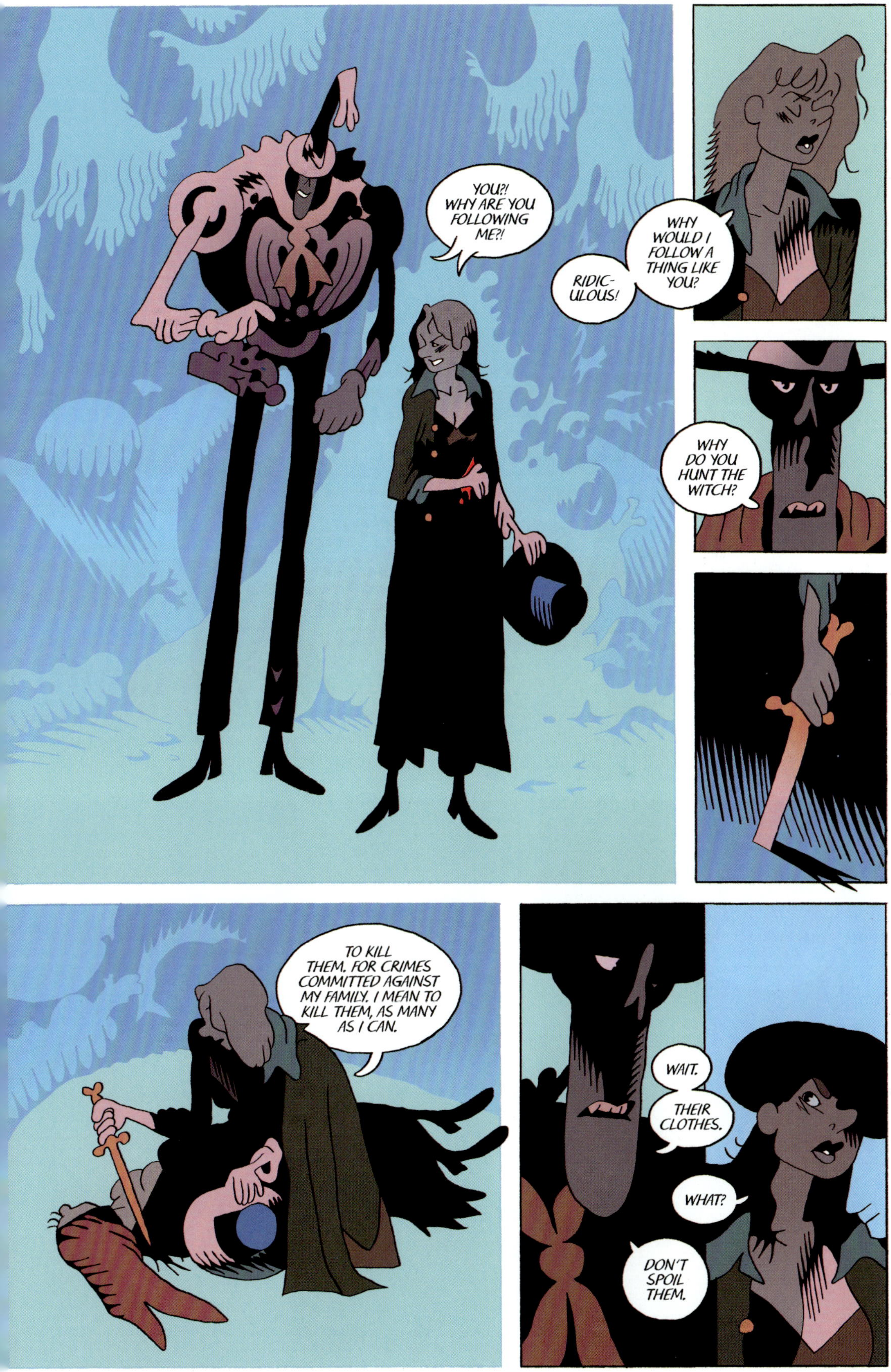
YOU?! WHY ARE YOU FOLLOWING ME?!
WHY WOULD I FOLLOW A THING LIKE YOU?
RIDIC-ULOUS!
WHY DO YOU HUNT THE WITCH?
TO KILL THEM. FOR CRIMES COMMITTED AGAINST MY FAMILY. I MEAN TO KILL THEM, AS MANY AS I CAN.
WAIT.
THEIR CLOTHES.
WHAT?
DON'T SPOIL THEM.

YOU WANT TO FIND WITCHES? THIS IS A GOOD WAY TO DO IT.
RIDICULOUS!
I SAID I WANT TO KILL WITCHES, NOT LOOK LIKE THEM WHILE DOING IT!
THIS IS COWARD--ICE.
IS BRAVERY AT STAKE OR VANITY? THE TWO ARE NOT THE SAME.
AND AS FOR REVENGE... ARE YOU RIGHTEOUS TO WIELD IT? SOMEONE HURT YOU SO YOU CAN HURT THEM?
THE HUNTER AND THE HUNTED SOUND VERY SIMILIAR.

QUICK! TO THE FRONT!
THIS IS MARVELOUS! I HAD NO IDEA I WAS AMONG SO MANY SEEKERS AND STAR-GAZERS! TO THINK, WE ALL COME TO HONOR OUR BELOVED MOTHER!
MM...
HERE, I SAY! BLACKTHORN AND SLOE, OF WHO I AM NAMED AFTER! TAKE IT UPON THY ALTAR AS I HONOR THE EARTH THAT BORE ME ALSO!
HUH?
A FINE BABBLER FROM THE COUNTRY. BE GONE, GIRL, THE RIMHORN HAS NO USE OF THIS MESS.
WHAT? WHO? ISN'T IT THE APPOINTED HOUR OF TRANS-FORMATION?
DOES THE PRIEST HERE NOT KNOW THE RITE? I'M GIVING MYSELF TO THE EARTH TONIGHT, NOT THESE THINGS, THEY ARE ONLY SYMBOLS...
WELL! THAT IS A DIFFERENT STORY! A DIFFERENT STORY ENTIRELY! YES, I THINK WE COULD TAKE A CLOSER LOOK AT YOU!
OH YES! I THINK I HAVE JUST THE JOB FOR YOU...

OOO-
-KAY...WELL, I THINK I'LL JUST TAKE MY SISTER HERE TO HER SEAT BEFORE THE, UHM, CEREMONY BEGINS.
WHAT?! LET GO! THEY WERE ABOUT TO ACCEPT ME IN!
I'M SURE THEY WERE! BUT I DOUBT YOU WOULD'VE LIKED IT!
I KNOW WHAT I'M ABOUT, YOU-- --YOU--! YOU'RE JUST A LITTLE MAN... OBSESSED WITH SAFETY. I'VE SEEN YOUR KIND BEFORE, I WISH TO SEE THEM NO MORE.
WAIT-- NO!
IT'S ABOUT TO START!
SIT DOWN YOUNG MAN!
HUSH!
HE'S HERE!
MY FINE FRIENDS, ENLIGHTENED COMPANY, GOOD PEOPLE. I'VE JUST COME IN FROM THE COUNTRY, AND THE DUST OF DISEASE, ILL TEMPER, AND SUPERSTITION CLING TO ME...
EVEN AFTER ALL THIS FINE WINE!
HA!
THE POOR DEAR!
HA!
THAT'S OUR RIM-HORN!
HAHA!
HAHA!
YES!
YES!
THE GOLD!
FOR GOOD!
FOR BETTER!
I DON'T HAVE TO BEAT AROUND THE BUSH WITH ANY OF YOU! NOBODY HERE NEEDS REMINDING OF OUR DARK DAYS BEFORE THE GOLDEN COIN ILLUMINATED OUR LIVES.
YES!
YES!

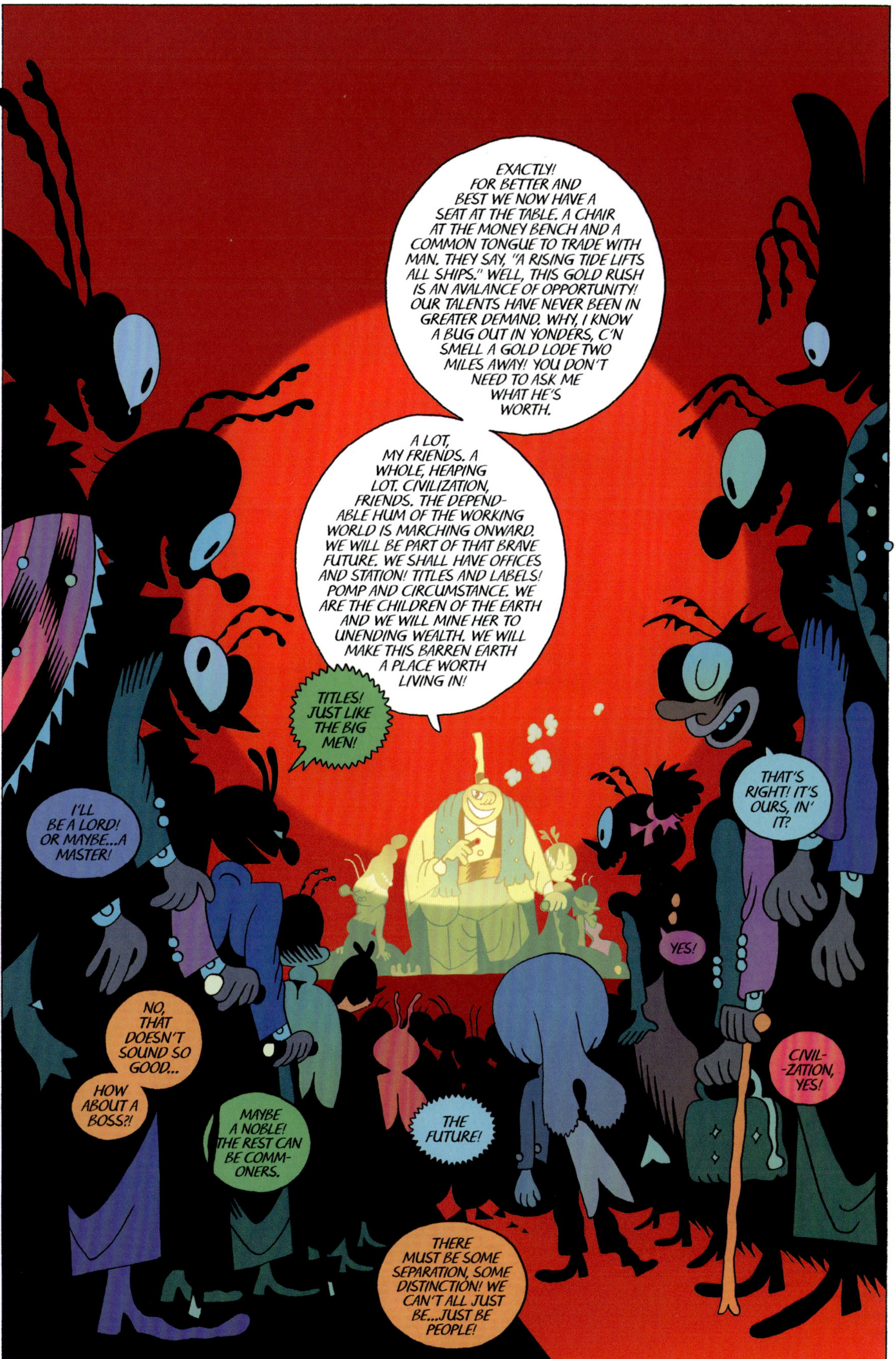
EXACTLY! FOR BETTER AND BEST WE NOW HAVE A SEAT AT THE TABLE. A CHAIR AT THE MONEY BENCH AND A COMMON TONGUE TO TRADE WITH MAN. THEY SAY, "A RISING TIDE LIFTS ALL SHIPS." WELL, THIS GOLD RUSH IS AN AVALANCE OF OPPORTUNITY! OUR TALENTS HAVE NEVER BEEN IN GREATER DEMAND. WHY, I KNOW A BUG OUT IN YONDERS, C'N SMELL A GOLD LODE TWO MILES AWAY! YOU DON'T NEED TO ASK ME WHAT HE'S WORTH.
A LOT, MY FRIENDS. A WHOLE, HEAPING LOT. CIVILIZATION, FRIENDS. THE DEPEND-ABLE HUM OF THE WORKING WORLD IS MARCHING ONWARD. WE WILL BE PART OF THAT BRAVE FUTURE. WE SHALL HAVE OFFICES AND STATION! TITLES AND LABELS! POMP AND CIRCUMSTANCE. WE ARE THE CHILDREN OF THE EARTH AND WE WILL MINE HER TO UNENDING WEALTH. WE WILL MAKE THIS BARREN EARTH A PLACE WORTH LIVING IN!
TITLES! JUST LIKE THE BIG MEN!
THAT'S RIGHT! IT'S OURS, IN' IT?
I'LL BE A LORD! OR MAYBE...A MASTER!
YES!
NO, THAT DOESN'T SOUND SO GOOD...
HOW ABOUT A BOSS?!
CIVIL-ZATION, YES!
MAYBE A NOBLE! THE REST CAN BE COMM-ONERS.
THE FUTURE!
THERE MUST BE SOME SEPARATION, SOME DISTINCTION! WE CAN'T ALL JUST BE...JUST BE PEOPLE!

MM! YES SIR!
I'LL HAVE ME SOME O' THAT!
NOW, I KNOW THERE MUST BE AT LEAST A FEW SKEPTICS OUT THERE. SOME HIVE LEADERS UNSURE OF THIS NEW WORLD... I DON'T BLAME YOU... AND I'M ALSO NOT ANXIOUS FOR YOU TO CUT IN ON OUR PROFIT MARGINS! HA! STAY OUTSIDE FOR ALL I CARE! HAHA!
MY HIVE IS FULL TILT FOR GOLD!
SO'S MINE!
SHOO-WEE!
IF THE WEAVERS ARE IN THEN SO ARE WE!
YOU SEE THOSE GIRLS?!
THE RACE IS ON!
YOU SMELL THAT MONEY?!
GOTTA KEEP UP!
JUST GOTTA!
THE TRAP!
NO!
FOOLS!
THE TRICK!
NO!
OH NO!
THE CHAIN!
THE LADDER!
RUN!

SISTER SORCERERS, BROTHER WITCHES. YOU WITHOUT BORDER AND EDGE. IT'S GOOD TO BE AMONG YOU TONIGHT. TRULY WE ARE ONE AND PART OF EACH OTHER, CELEBRATING ON THE INFINITE PLAIN. GONE ARE THE MOUNTAINS AND GONE ARE THE VALLEYS. NO GODS ABOVE AND NO DEVILS BELOW, BUT SPIRITS COMMUNING AS ONE. I KNOW WHY IT WAS YOU CAME OUT HERE TONIGHT. FORSAKING THE WARMTH OF WEALTH FOR THE COLD OF THE WILD. IT IS STIFLING, YES? THAT STINK OF MONEY, THAT CANKER OF GOLD! THE MATERIAL WEIGHT, AND THE BODY SUFFOCATING THE SOUL?
BUT THERE IS HOPE HERE IN THE NIGHT! HOPE FOR POWER AND FREE--DOM.
I HAVE WITH ME HERE ONE WHO HAS DONE IT! ONE WHO HAS GIVEN HIMSELF COMPLETELY OVER TO THE INFINITE! HE SWIMS IN THE COSMIC FLOW, THE PARADISE OF ENDLESS BEING, LIMITLESS AND UNTETHERED FROM THIS BODY OF DECAY! NOW ONE WITH THAT GREAT AND INFINITE STRENGTH!
ACCESSOR OF POWER BEYOND THE REACH OF THIS MORTAL VALE. THINK YOU NOW HOW YOU WOULD USE THAT POWER? WHAT COULD YOU ACCOMPLISH WITH SUCH A UNION? HM? THAT OPPORTUNITY IS NOW. OUR FRIEND HERE IS GRADUATING TO THE NEXT STAGE. PASSING BEYOND AND GIVING UP THIS GIFT TO ONE OF YOU. SIEZE NOW THE SPIRIT OF FREEDOM AND THROW AWAY THAT GOLD THAT WEIGHS YOU SO LOW!
TEN PIECES! HERE!
THIRTEEN! OVER HERE! HERE!
TWENTY!
TWENTY-FIVE!
THIRTY!

HE SWIMS IN THE COSMIC FLOW... THE PARADISE OF ENDLESS BEING, LIMITLESS AND UNTETHERED FROM THIS BODY OF DECAY!
PARADISE? WHERE?
FREE?
HOW?
SHSSS, SHUSSSH, DEAR. YOU ARE IN IT. YOU ARE FREE HERE.
DON'T FEEL SO WELL. DON'T FEEL SO FREE... SWIMMING? SHOULD BE... RUN-NNNING...?
SHSS, OH, SHSS, SWEET CHILD. DON'T SAY SUCH THINGS. SIT. SIT BACK DOWN! HAVEN'T WE GIVEN YOU EVERYTHING YOU EVER WANTED? HAVEN'T WE CROWNED YOU KING OF YOUR OWN COUNTRY? YOU OWN SOUL?

YOU'LL HURT US SO IF YOU TAKE ANOTHER STEP! DON'T DO IT!
NO!
NO!
THE HILLS! I WILL MAKE FOR THEM! I MUST...
NO!
BUT OH! HILLS?! I ONLY SEE MOUNTAINS TO THE HEAVENS! AND ALL SO FAR AWAY...AND ON THE ROAD ...

ON THE ROAD I SEE DEATH! DEATH LIKE A MONOLITH!
AND THE NAKED SWORD IN HIS HAND! A LIVING FIRE!
THAT PULLS A VEIL ACROSS THE SKY!
THE HEAVENS ARE DIMMED.

DIMMED...
YES! HE STANDS READY TO DEVOUR US, CHILD. QUICKLY, TURN BACK!
OUR MASTER WILL TAKE YOU IN AGAIN! HE ALWAYS TAKES THE ONES THAT COME BACK TO HIM.
YES! THEY ARE TREATED EVEN BETTER THAN BEFORE, YES!

NO.
I DON'T BELIEVE YOU ANY- -MORE.
THAT LIFE WAS HORROR. I WOULD GO BACK IF I WANTED MORE OF IT.
I DO NOT.
DO YOU?
AND WOULDN'T DEATH BE BETTER?

NOT IF THEY CATCH US.

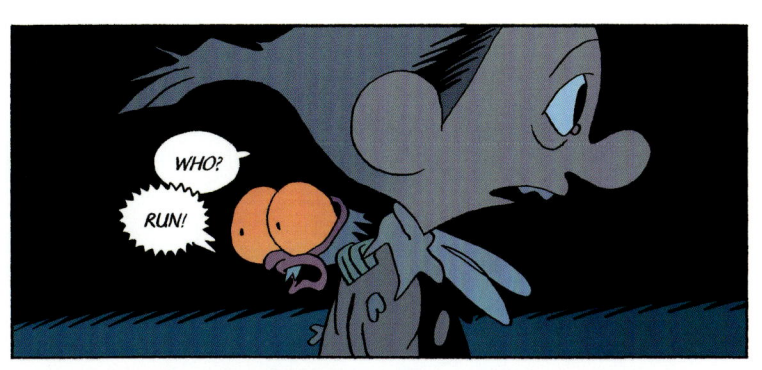

WHO?
RUN!

BACK! STAY BACK OR I WILL BREAK HIM! I'LL SQUEEZE HIS GUTS OUT!
I HAVE WHAT I CAME FOR, AND IT WAS NOT FOR HIM. BUT I AM NO FRIEND OF YOURS... WHO IS HE?
MIIII-IIIIIIIIIIII-NEEE.
NO...
NO...
YIGG-HELIO...AN-HERIC...

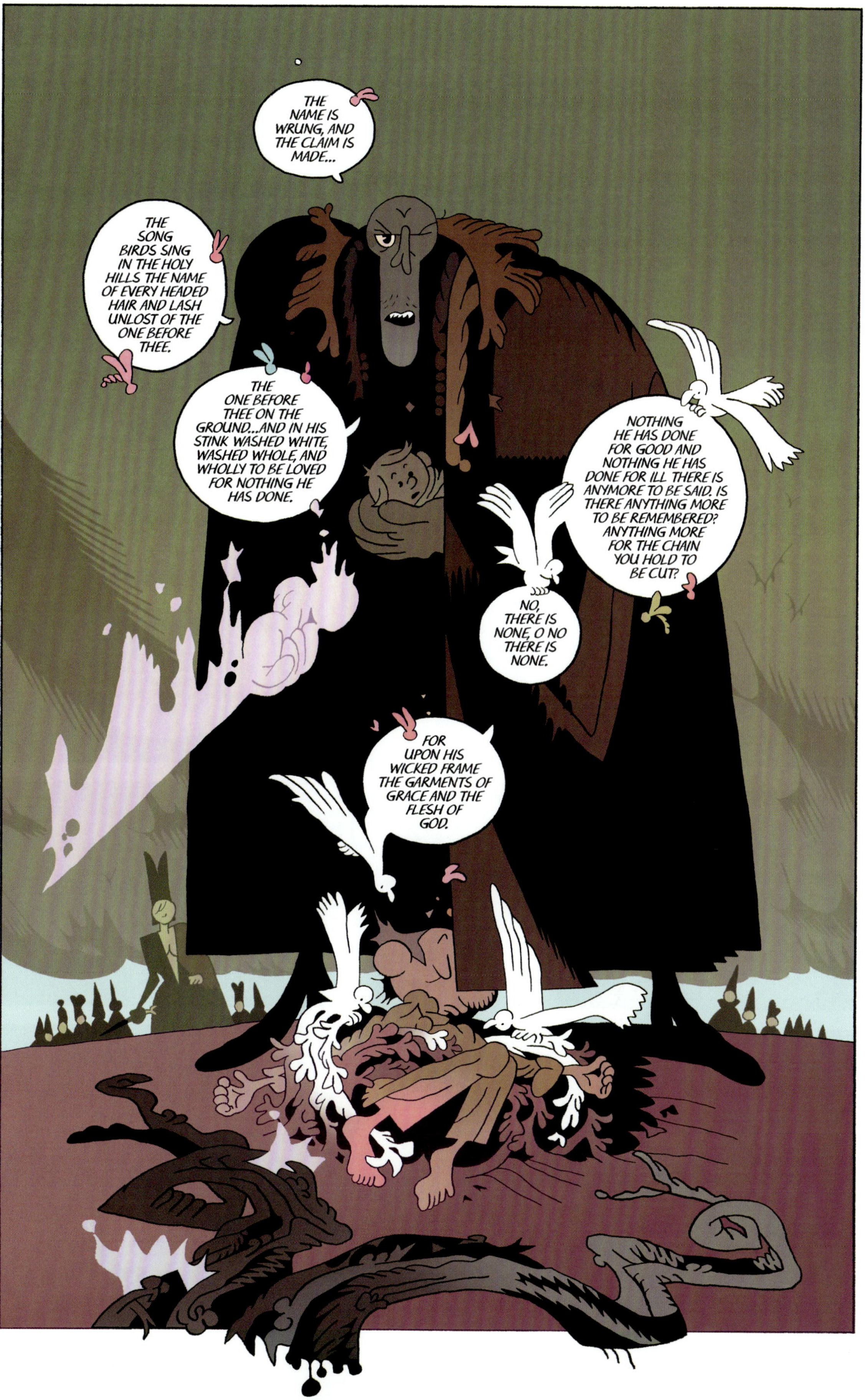
THE NAME IS WRUNG, AND THE CLAIM IS MADE...
THE SONG BIRDS SING IN THE HOLY HILLS THE NAME OF EVERY HEADED HAIR AND LASH UNLOST OF THE ONE BEFORE THEE.
THE ONE BEFORE THEE ON THE GROUND...AND IN HIS STINK WASHED WHITE, WASHED WHOLE, AND WHOLLY TO BE LOVED FOR NOTHING HE HAS DONE.
NOTHING HE HAS DONE FOR GOOD AND NOTHING HE HAS DONE FOR ILL THERE IS ANYMORE TO BE SAID. IS THERE ANYTHING MORE TO BE REMEMBERED? ANYTHING MORE FOR THE CHAIN YOU HOLD TO BE CUT?
NO, THERE IS NONE, O NO THERE IS NONE.
FOR UPON HIS WICKED FRAME THE GARMENTS OF GRACE AND THE FLESH OF GOD.

YOU! HA! I REMEMBER YOU... FOREVER FONDLING FORGIVENESS. YOU WANT IT TO BE TRUE...IT ISN'T.
HE'S NOT TAKING YOU BACK. IT DOESN'T MATTER WHAT YOU DO. HE'S CHOSEN THEM OVER YOU. PATHETIC, TRY STANDING ON YOUR OWN TWO FEET FOR ONCE. COME AND JOIN US IN THE NEW WORLD.
THERE'S A PLACE FOR YOU...
A HIGH SEAT AND HIGHLY COVETED...RETIREMENT PLANS, FOUR-OH-ONE-KAY'S, HEALTH INSURANCE, SECURITY, ALL SURROUNDING AND IMPENETRABLE FINANCIAL SECURITY...
BE GONE, SNAKE.
DENTAL COVERAGE ...

TO ME, SPIRIT!
TO ME FOR THE PERSECUTION OF THE WITCH AND THE WIZARD! THAT SWINE HERD WHO THOUGHT YOUR POWER COULD BE BOUGHT FOR GOLD!
TO ME AND ENTER!
NO!
FOOL!
HA HA!
KEEP THE SCRAPS, OLD BOY! I'LL TAKE THE FULL DISH!

CONCU-
-BINE'S IN THE
HALL. WHAT
ROOM?
FINGER?
WHICH OF
THE FIVE?
THEY'RE UNMARKED, BUT
SMELL LIKE RING TO ME.
BUNCH O' DANDY'S.
ROOM FIVE-
TWO, THEN.
STEP-
PING
OUT?
AFTER
RIDING FOR
DAYS? WHAT
FOR?
HAVEN'T
WE A JOB TO
DO? AND WON'T
THERE BE WOMEN IN
THIS PLACE? REAL
WOMEN?

REAL WOMEN? WHO NEEDS THEM?!
HA!
YOU FIND ME REAL WOMEN LIKE THESE AND I'LL FIGHT YOU FOR 'EM. BUT I'LL BET ANYTHING YOU CAN'T!
SONNY, YOU JUST AIN'T KNOCKED AROUND ENOUGH TO KNOW THERE'S MORE PAIN THAN PLEASURE ON THAT ROAD!
GO DANCE THEIR GAMES AND PLAY THEIR TRICKS AND END UP WITH NOTHING TONIGHT.
FACE IT, KID, THE MOST BEAUTIFUL THINGS IN LIFE ARE FANTASY.

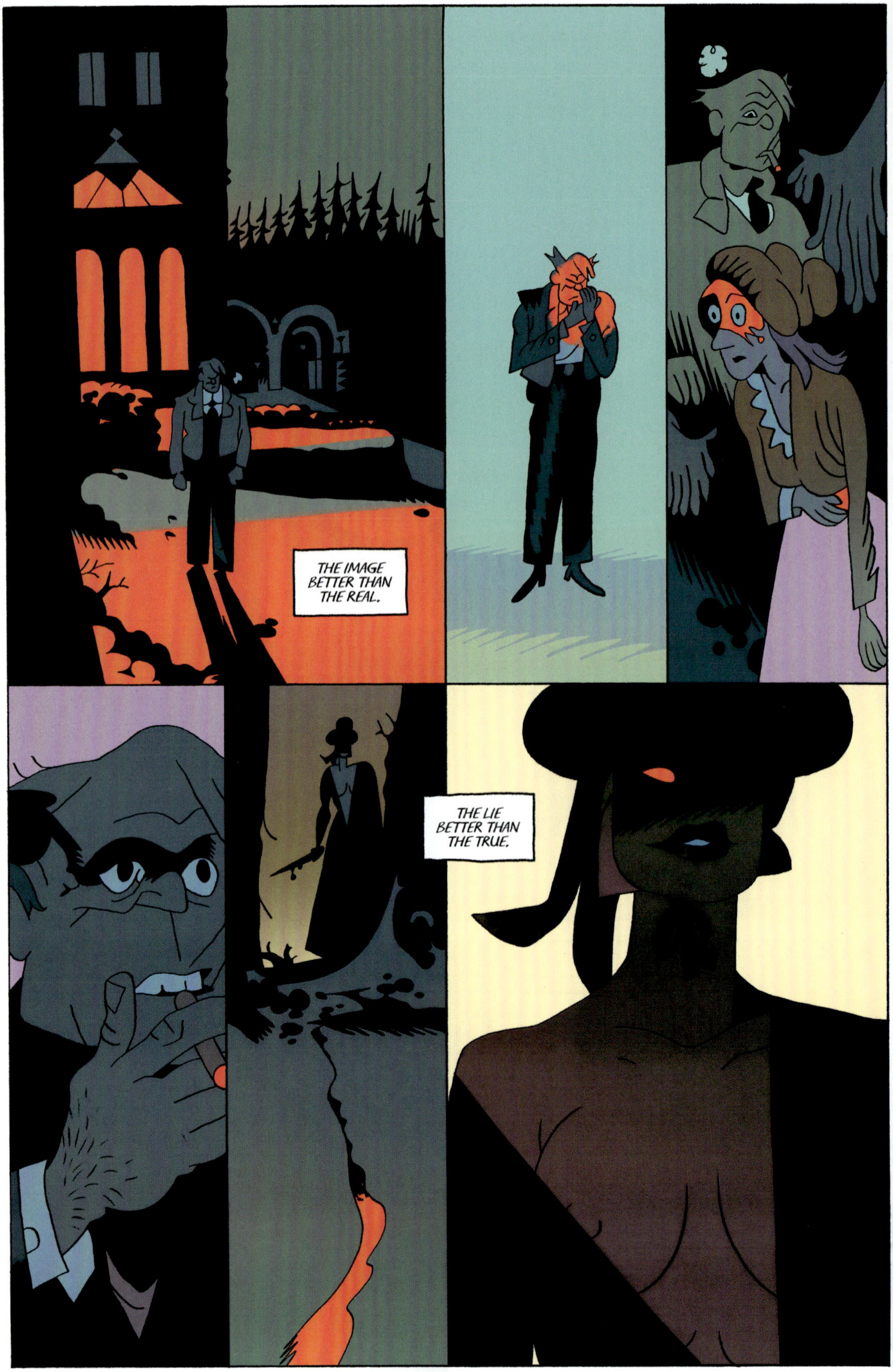
THE IMAGE BETTER THAN THE REAL.
THE LIE BETTER THAN THE TRUE.

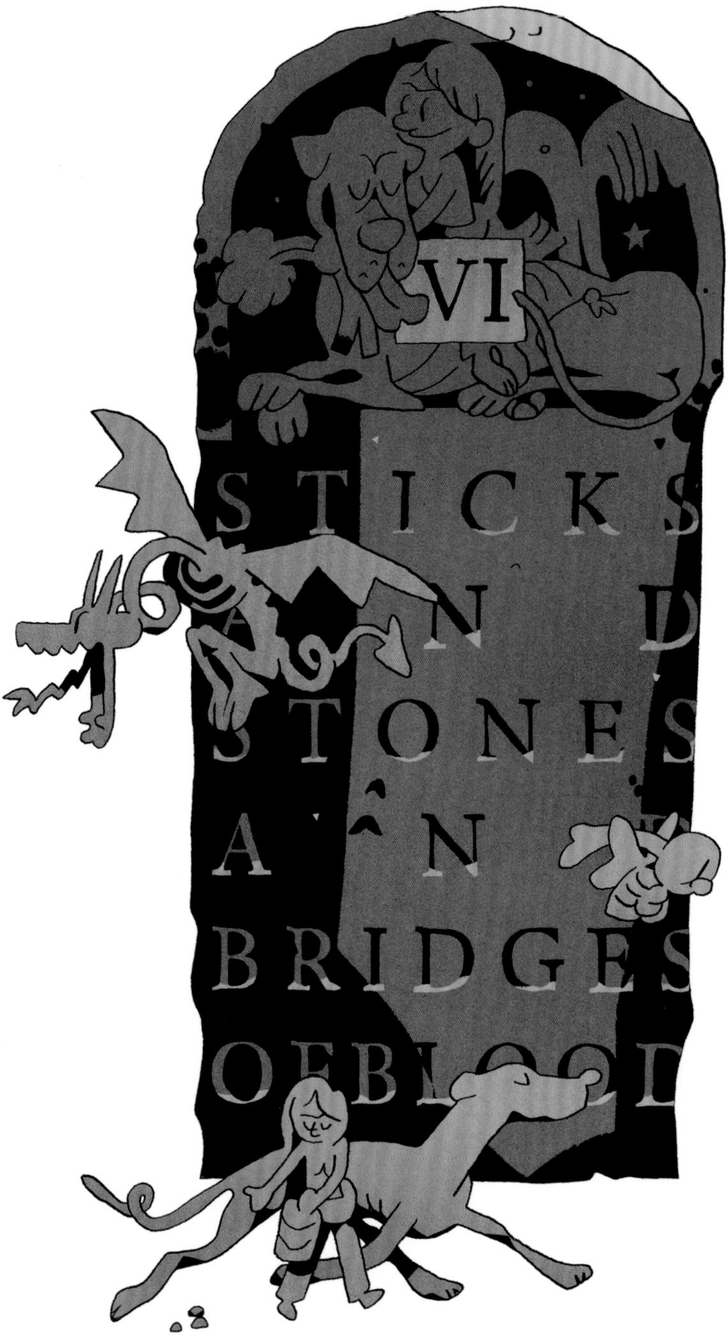
VI
STICKS
AND
STONES
AND
BRIDGES
OF BLOOD

A piece of something bigger,
A splinter off the shoulder.
All the stops are poppin'
And the chips of glory nearer.

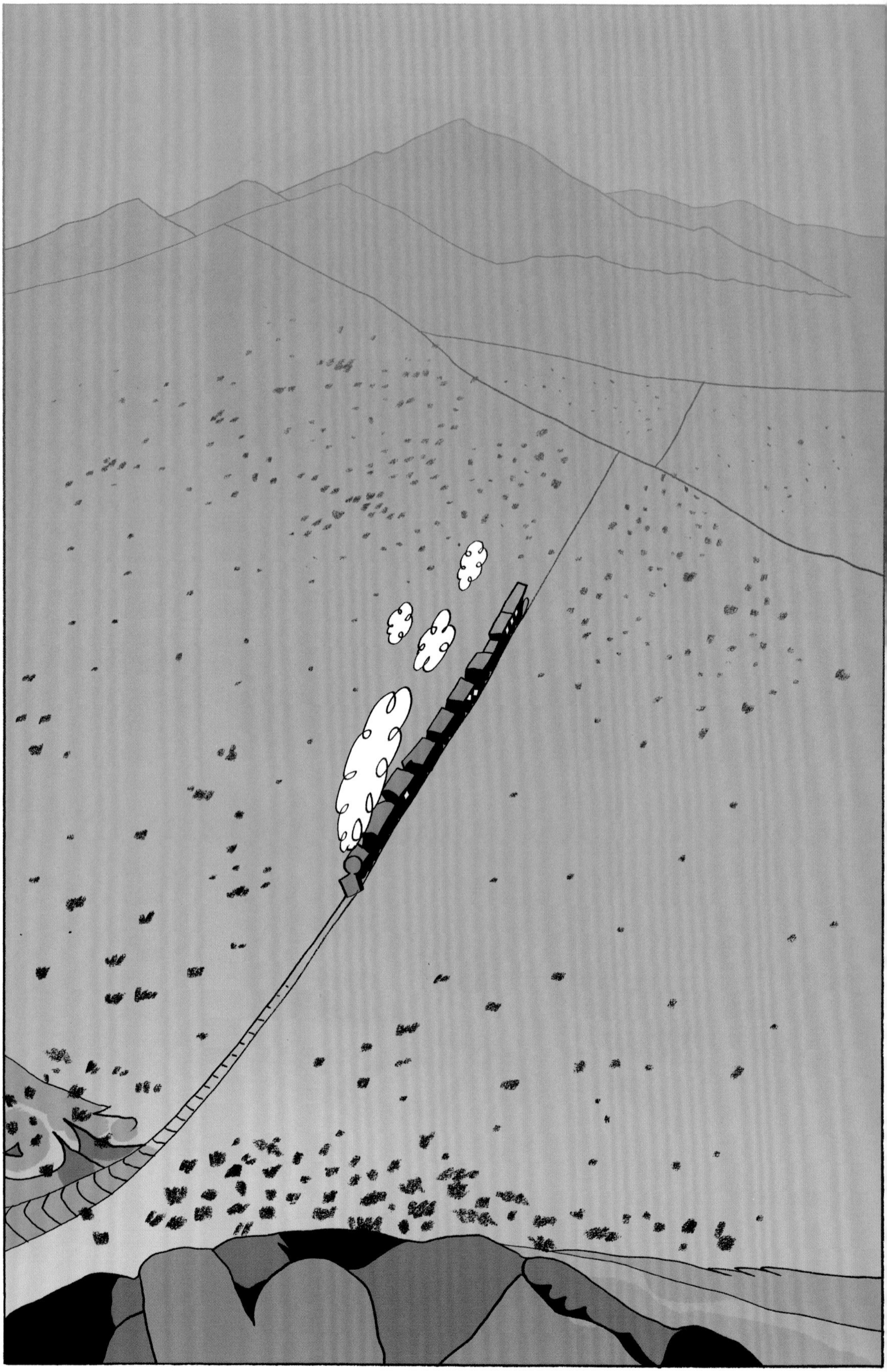

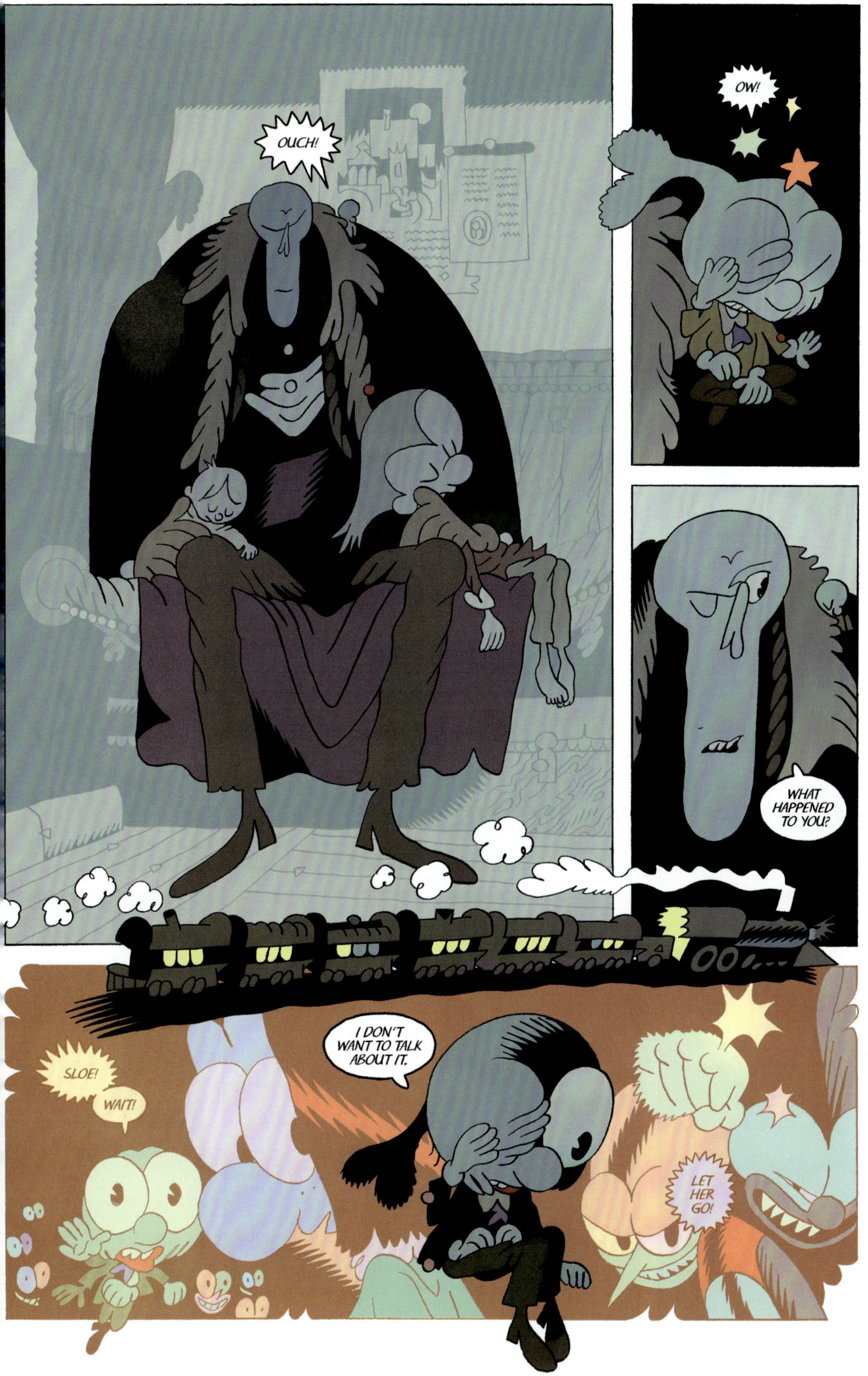
OUCH!
OW!
WHAT HAPPENED TO YOU?
I DON'T WANT TO TALK ABOUT IT.
SLOE!
WAIT!
LET HER GO!

WHO'S HE?
JUST A BOY.
AND THE BABY?
HIM TOO.
AT LEAST OUR LUCK WITH THE LADIES IS CON- SISTENT. AND WHAT ARE YOU WEARING? YOU'RE NOT GOING ALL ARTY ON ME, I HOPE.
IT WAS COLD, AND YOU NEVER BROUGHT ME WHISKY. BESIDES, MAYBE I LIKE IT.
GOOD GRIEF! I BETTER STICK CLOSER TO YOU... THEY'LL HAVE YOU IN THE CIRCUS NEXT TIME. HAVE YOU PULLING FRIGGIN' RABBITS OUT OF HATS ...
SO, BACK TO SAUHER- DOUGH?
YAW.
WE DID IT, THEN.
WE DID SOME- -THING...DO YOU KNOW WHAT?
SAVED SOMEBODY, I GUESS?
FROM WHAT?
DEATH, OR A FATE WORSE THAN?

FOR HOW LONG? TERROR WILL FIND THEM. TIME WILL BURY THEM.
WHAT'S THE POINT?
RIGHT AND WRONG ARE PRESENT CONCERNS. THE FUTURE, HOWEVER GRIM, HASN'T POWER TO CHANGE THE IMMEDIATE RESPONSIBILITY OF LIVING. BRIDGES CAN BE CROSSED ONLY AFTER THE ROAD IS CHOSEN.
AND PERHAPS BRIDGES WILL BE BURNED ALSO?
I EXPECT SO. NO ONE CAN BE FRIENDS WITH EVERYONE, AND ALL SIDES AREN'T EQUAL. CHOOSE NOW HOW YOU SHOULD LIVE.
MAYBE I BETTER START PAYING ATTENTION THEN. SOMETHING AT THE END OF THIS ISN'T SQUARING UP IN MY NOGGIN'.

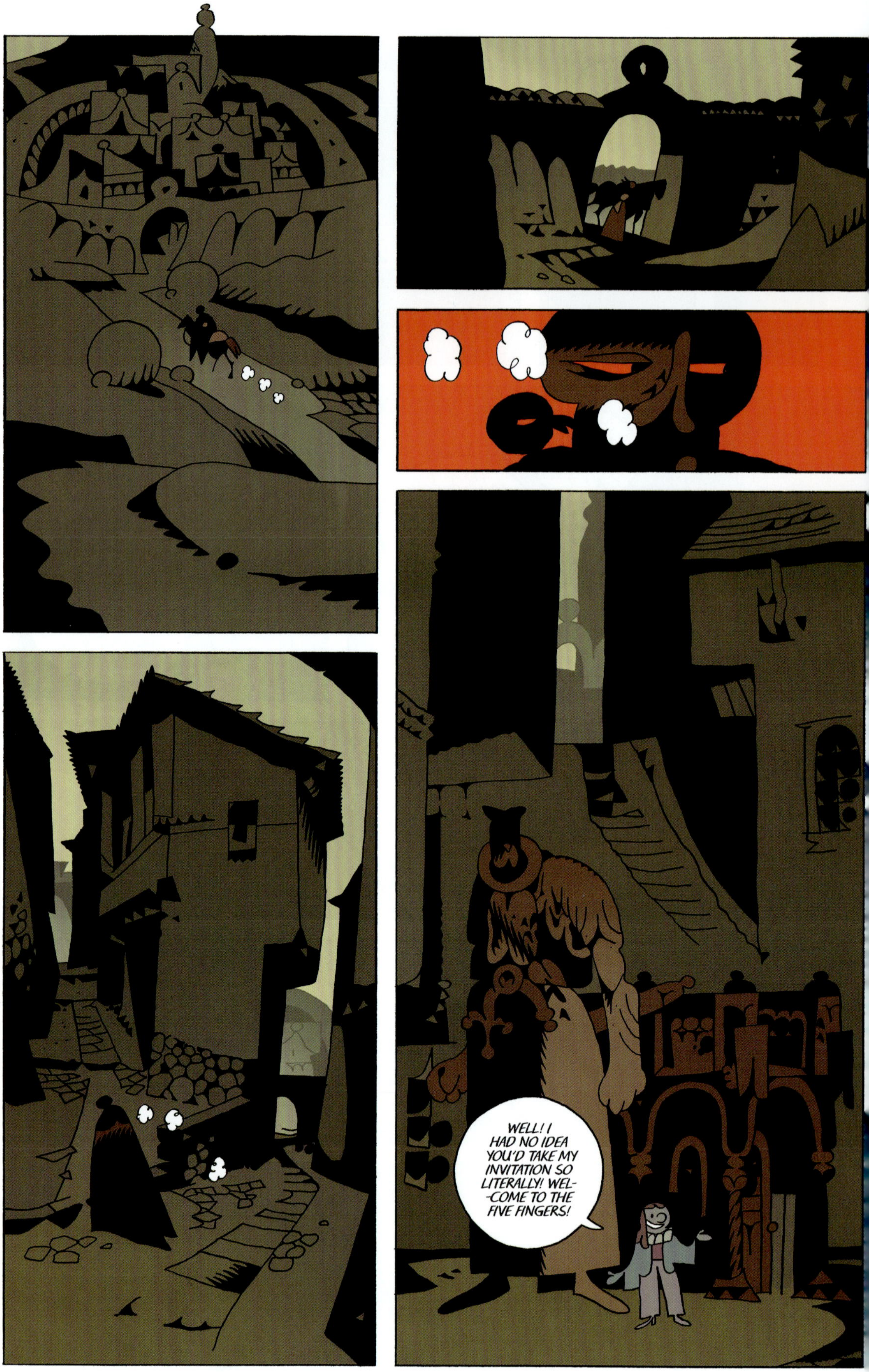
WELL! I HAD NO IDEA YOU'D TAKE MY INVITATION SO LITERALLY! WEL--COME TO THE FIVE FINGERS!

THE PARADISE GARDEN?
WHAS SSAT?
WHERE IS IT? THE GARDEN YOU PROMISED UPON OUR RETURN.
YES!
YES OF COURSE. I SIMPLY REQUIRE THE CHILD TO PERFORM THE MAGIC.
NO. SACRIFICE SOMETHING OF YOUR OWN. GIVE OF YOUR OWN BLOOD.
WHAT DO I NEED FROM A GARDEN? I HAVE MY CASTLE! REMEMBER, THIS IS FOR YOU, MY FRIEND.
IS IT? THE MIRROR SEEMED TO SHOW OTHER--WISE...IS IT FOR YOU?
FOR HIM?
WHY NOT FOR ALL THREE OF US? HM?
FOUR.
THERE ARE FOUR OF US HERE, THE CHILD IS ONE AMONG US.
I DON'T THINK YOU SEE HOW THIS WORKS, MY FRIEND. A SACRIFICE OF BLOOD MUST BE MADE, A TRANSFER OF LIFE FROM ONE TO ANOTHER. YOU ARE BONE, HE IS STONE, AND I AM THE ONE TO PERFORM THE MAGIC.
YOU BOTH NEED WHAT I OFFER AND I NEED THE BLOOD TO PERFORM IT. THE NONESSENTIALITY OF THE BABY SHOULD BE OBVIOUS AT THIS POINT.

IT SHOULD BE... SHOULDN'T IT? BUT IT WON'T ACCOUNT FOR A FEELING. NO, NOT THIS ONE.
THAT IT WOULD BE WRONG FOR WE THREE DEVILS, RUNNING FROM OUR OWN TWIST AND PAIN TO INFLICT IT ON SOME--ONE ELSE. YEA, AND THE LEAST ONE AMONG US.
YOU COULD BE AT THE CENTER, YOU KNOW? YOU COULD RULE YOUR LIFE AS YOU SEE FIT. NOT LEASHED TO A MASTER THAT HAS FORSAKEN YOU.
YOU'RE STILL ON THAT OTHER SIDE OF THE COIN, I SEE...STILL FEELING WHEN YOU SHOULD BE THINKING. STILL BELIEVING IN THE CHAINS OF SOMEONE ELSE'S RIGHT AND WRONG. STILL INCAPABLE OF DOING WHAT NEEDS TO BE DONE IN ORDER TO MOVE FORWARD...
THAT JUST WON'T PULL...NO, IT WONT.
AND I DOUBT THIS WILL, EITHER. THOUGH THE VAMPIRE SUCK FOR A THOUSAND YEARS YOU WON'T GET ANY BLOOD FROM THIS GUY...
STICKS AND STONES. STICKS AND STONES...AT THE END OF THE DAY IT WILL ALWAYS COME DOWN TO STICKS AND STONES.
YOUR TURN, MY FRIEND.

I'LL BE STICK AND YOU CAN BE STONE.
IDIOT, WHY HOLD ON TO A PAST THAT HAS PASSED US BY? IT'S MOVED ON TO THEM, HIS OWN CHILDREN, AND IT'S ONLY WAR BETWEEN US NOW. IT TOOK ME SO LONG TO SEE IT, BUT IT'S RIGHT IN FRONT OF US. THEY INCREASE AND WE DECREASE.
HAVE THE PINES AND LITTLE FORESTS BEEN RAPED ENOUGH? HAVE THE RIVERS AND FISH PONDS BEEN POLLUTED FOR NOTHING? HE ISN'T EVEN HERE ANYMORE...LONG LEFT FOR GREENER PASTURES.
WHY HOLD ON TO THE IMAGE OF THE FATHER? WE ARE WILD OATS. DESTROY THE LIE.
I CAN- -NOT. IT IS GRAVEN ON MY HEART.
THEN I MUST DESTROY IT FOR YOU.
YOU ARE FREE TO TRY.
YOOOOOOW

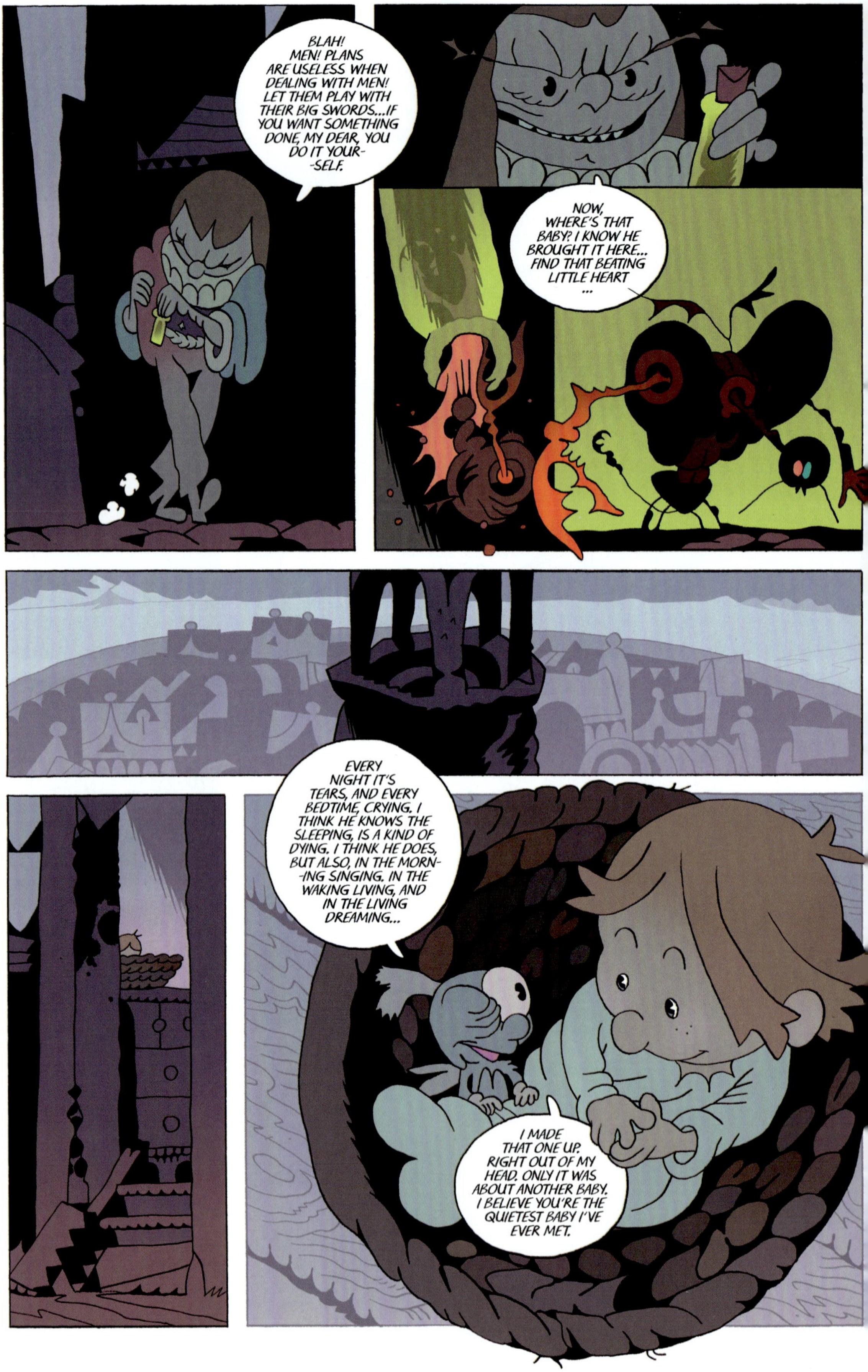
BLAH! MEN! PLANS ARE USELESS WHEN DEALING WITH MEN! LET THEM PLAY WITH THEIR BIG SWORDS...IF YOU WANT SOMETHING DONE, MY DEAR, YOU DO IT YOUR--SELF.
NOW, WHERE'S THAT BABY? I KNOW HE BROUGHT IT HERE... FIND THAT BEATING LITTLE HEART ...
EVERY NIGHT IT'S TEARS, AND EVERY BEDTIME, CRYING. I THINK HE KNOWS THE SLEEPING, IS A KIND OF DYING. I THINK HE DOES, BUT ALSO, IN THE MORN--ING SINGING. IN THE WAKING LIVING, AND IN THE LIVING DREAMING...
I MADE THAT ONE UP. RIGHT OUT OF MY HEAD. ONLY IT WAS ABOUT ANOTHER BABY. I BELIEVE YOU'RE THE QUIETEST BABY I'VE EVER MET.

SCORPION!

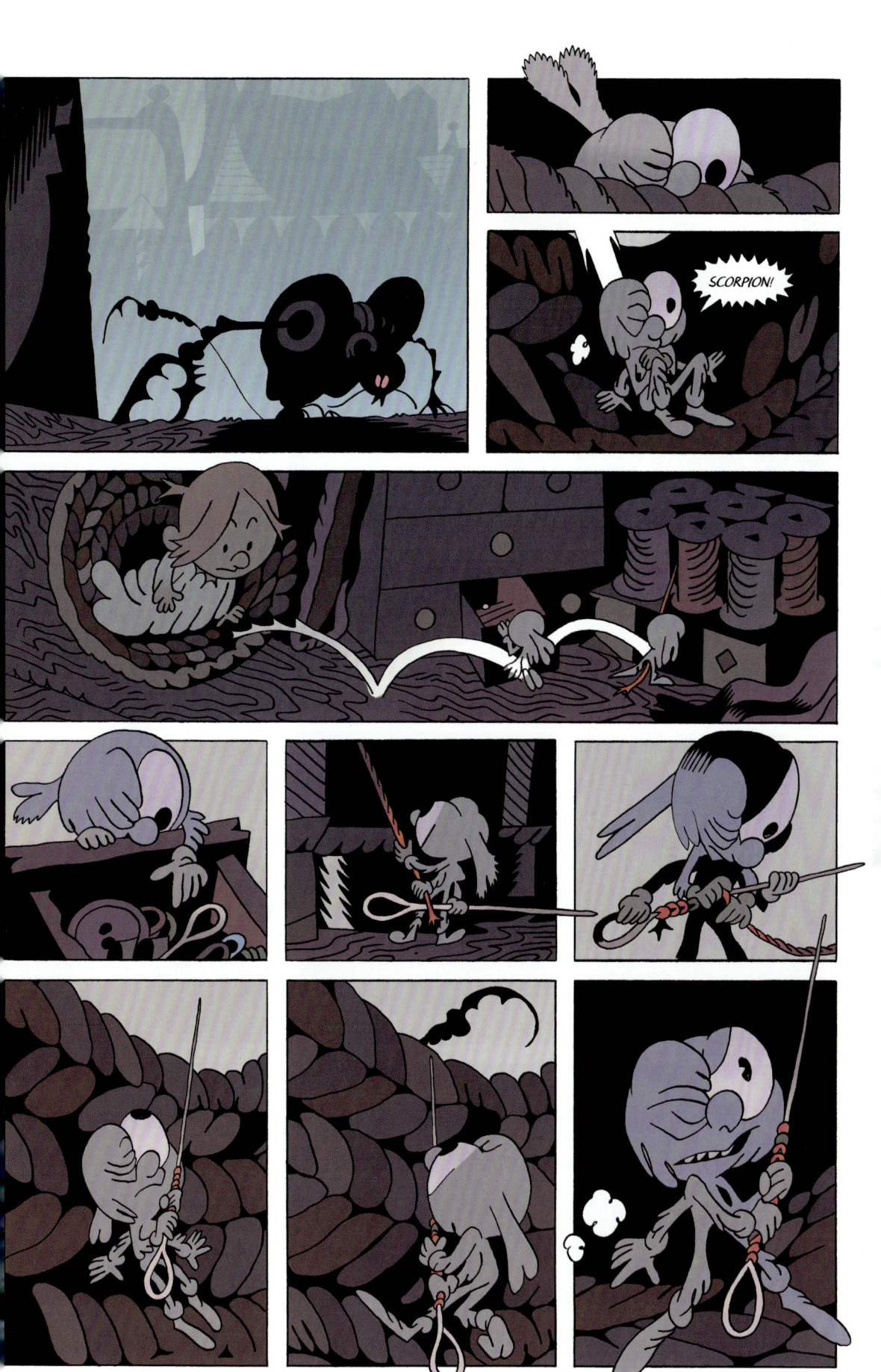

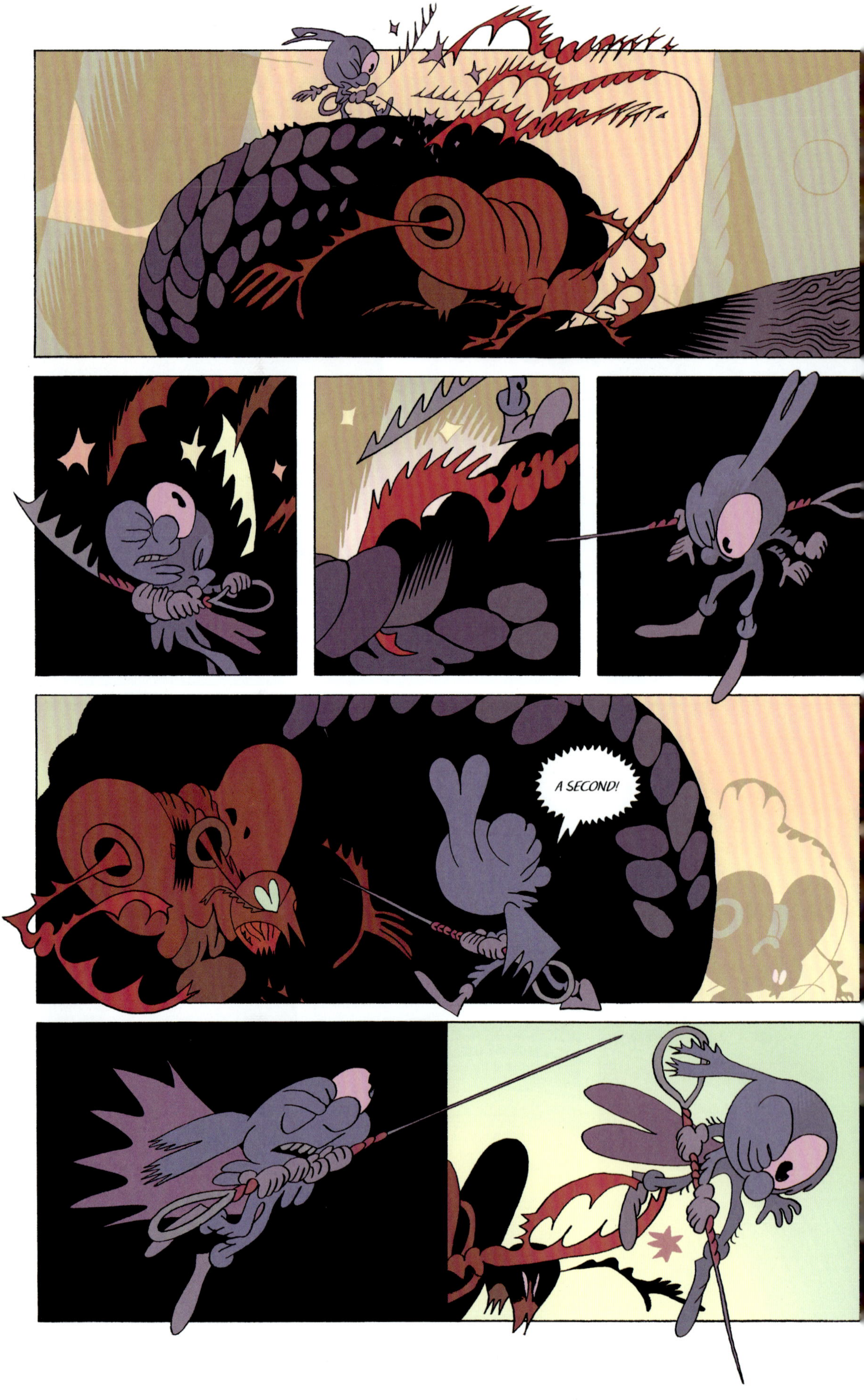
A SECOND!

NO!

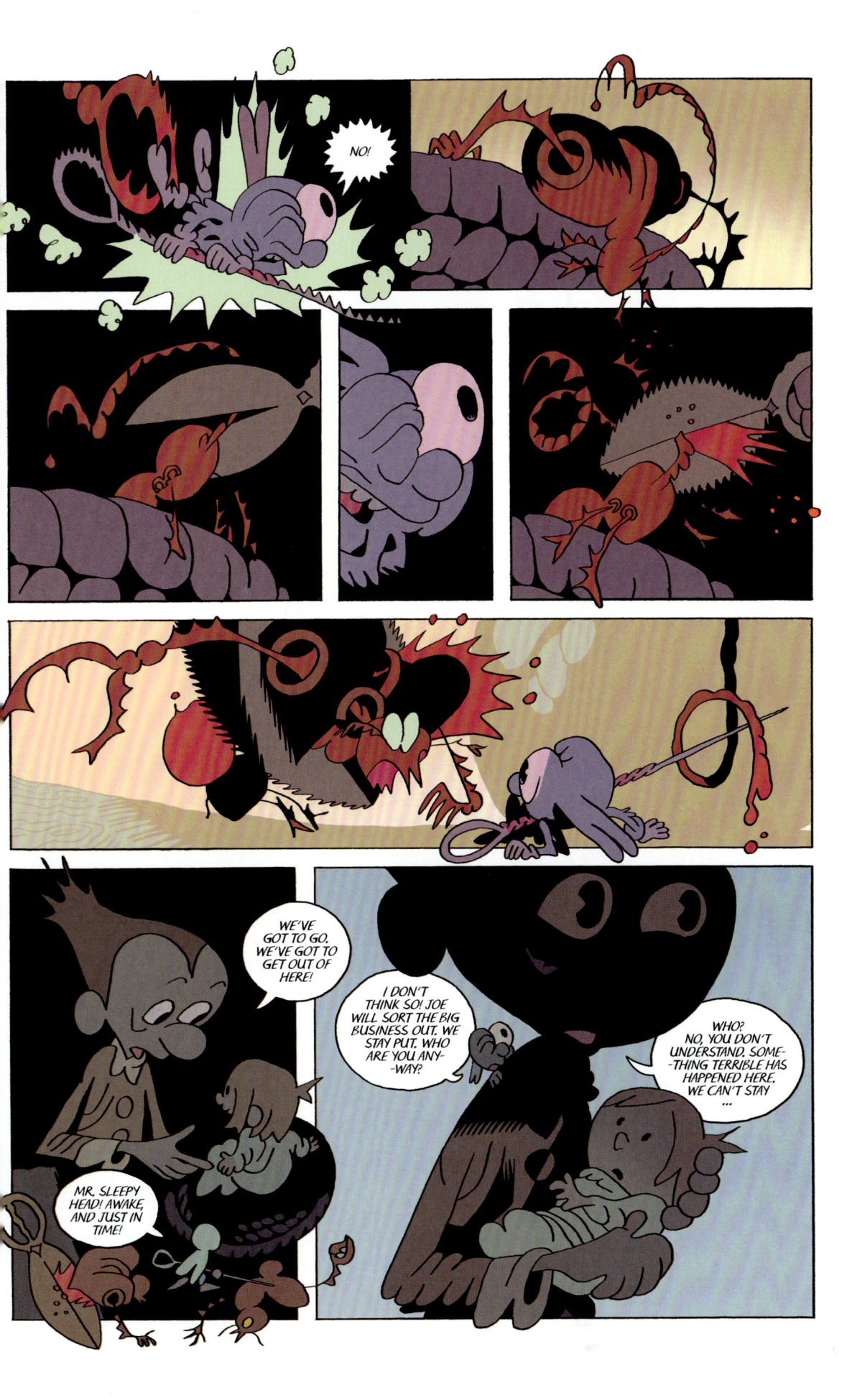

WE'VE GOT TO GO. WE'VE GOT TO GET OUT OF HERE!

I DON'T THINK SO! JOE WILL SORT THE BIG BUSINESS OUT. WE STAY PUT. WHO ARE YOU ANYWAY?

MR. SLEEPY HEAD! AWAKE, AND JUST IN TIME!

WHO? NO, YOU DON'T UNDERSTAND, SOMETHING TERRIBLE HAS HAPPENED HERE. WE CAN'T STAY...

KID, I SAID, WHO ARE YOU?
A PIECE OF SHIT...A GODDAMN FUCKING PIECE OF SHIT.
LOOK, THIS BOY DOESN'T CARE ABOUT YOUR PAST, HE NEEDS YOU HERE. HE NEEDS YOU NOW.
PROTECT HIM. THE HORSE IS TIED IN BACK IF YOU NEED TO RUN.
I'LL FIND JOE!

IT'S TRUE. YOU KNOW IT IS.
NO!
STAY AWAY! STAY BACK!
LEAVE THE BABY WITH ME. YOU CAN'T TRUST YOURSELF ANYMORE, GERICHO ...
THAT'S RIGHT...IT'S THE ONLY WAY TO STOP THAT PAIN INSIDE ...

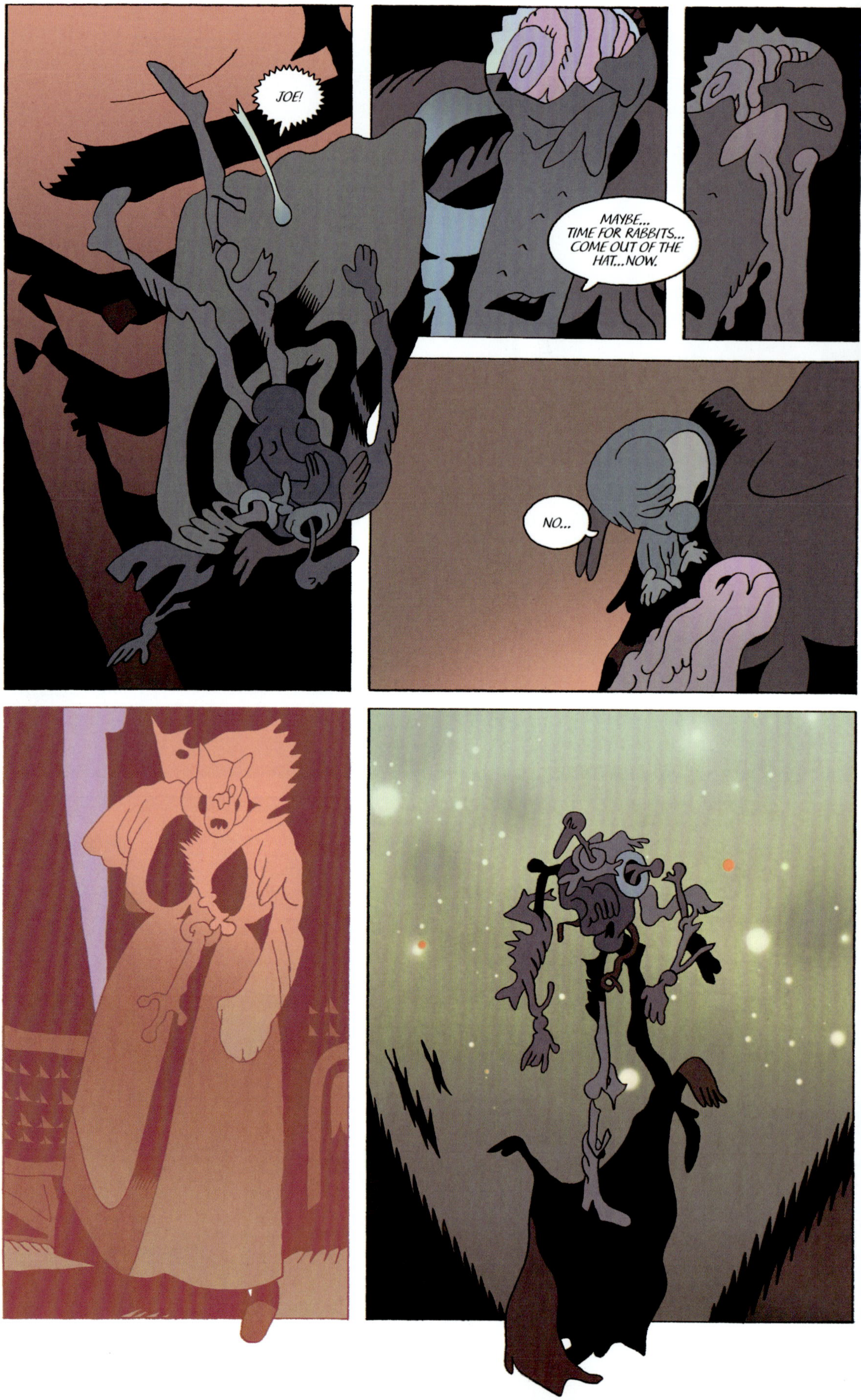
JOE!
MAYBE...
TIME FOR RABBITS...
COME OUT OF THE
HAT...NOW.
NO...

IS IT HE? HE WHO LICKED YOUR BROW AND DRANK YOUR SALT? WHO RAN FROM YOU IN THE DAY OF TROUBLE AND HID HIS TAIL BETWEEN HIS LEGS LIKE A CUR?!
AYE. HIM THAT LICKED MY BROW AND DRANK MY SWEAT. HIM THAT I LET DO SO THOUGH HIS BREATH SMELT LIKE GARBAGE AND HIS FUR LIKE URINE. HIM THAT DEFECATED IN MY FLOWER BEDS AND WET HIS OWN BED AS A CHILD. HIM THAT TURNED AWAY FROM THE DRAGON IN THE DARK--EST HOUR.
HE IS YOURS TO DO WITH AS YOU WILL. BUT DO IT NOW OR I SHALL SMITE HIM TO DEATH AND THE GRAVE FOR A FAITHLESS COMPANION TO MY SON.
HE IS MINE AND I WOULD NOT BE PARTED FROM HIM ANY-MORE...
OH, LOOK WHAT YOU'VE DONE WITH PRECIOUS INFIRMITY ... WASTED IT AS SPEARS AGAINST ME. BUILT WITH IT A GUILTY CAGE TO KEEP ME OUT... THEY WERE CORDS TO DRAW US CLOSER. THEY WERE SINEW FOR YOU TO FLEX.
FOOLISH FRIEND, YOU CANNOT BREATHE WITHOUT ME, BUT I CANNOT FORCE YOU TO. IF YOU WILL RUN FROM ME, I WILL RUN AFTER.
BUT WHEN I STAND AT THE DOOR AND KNOCK, IT MUST BE YOU... YOU MUST ANSWER.

BOOM
BOOM
BOOM

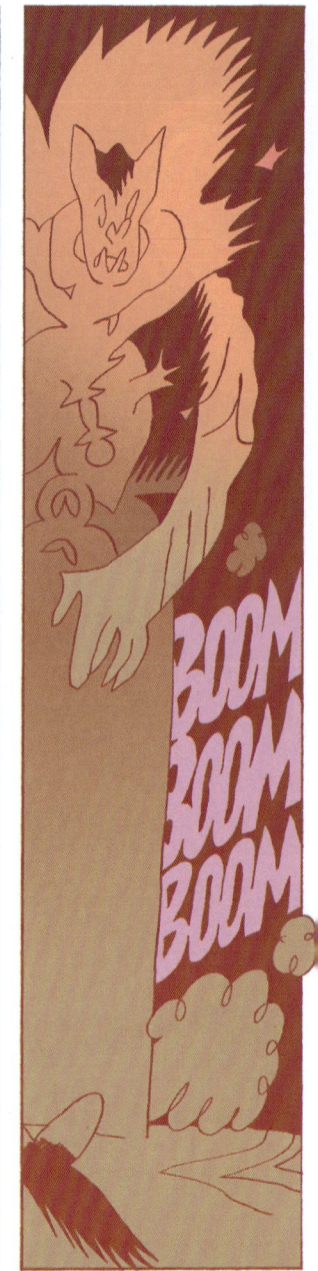

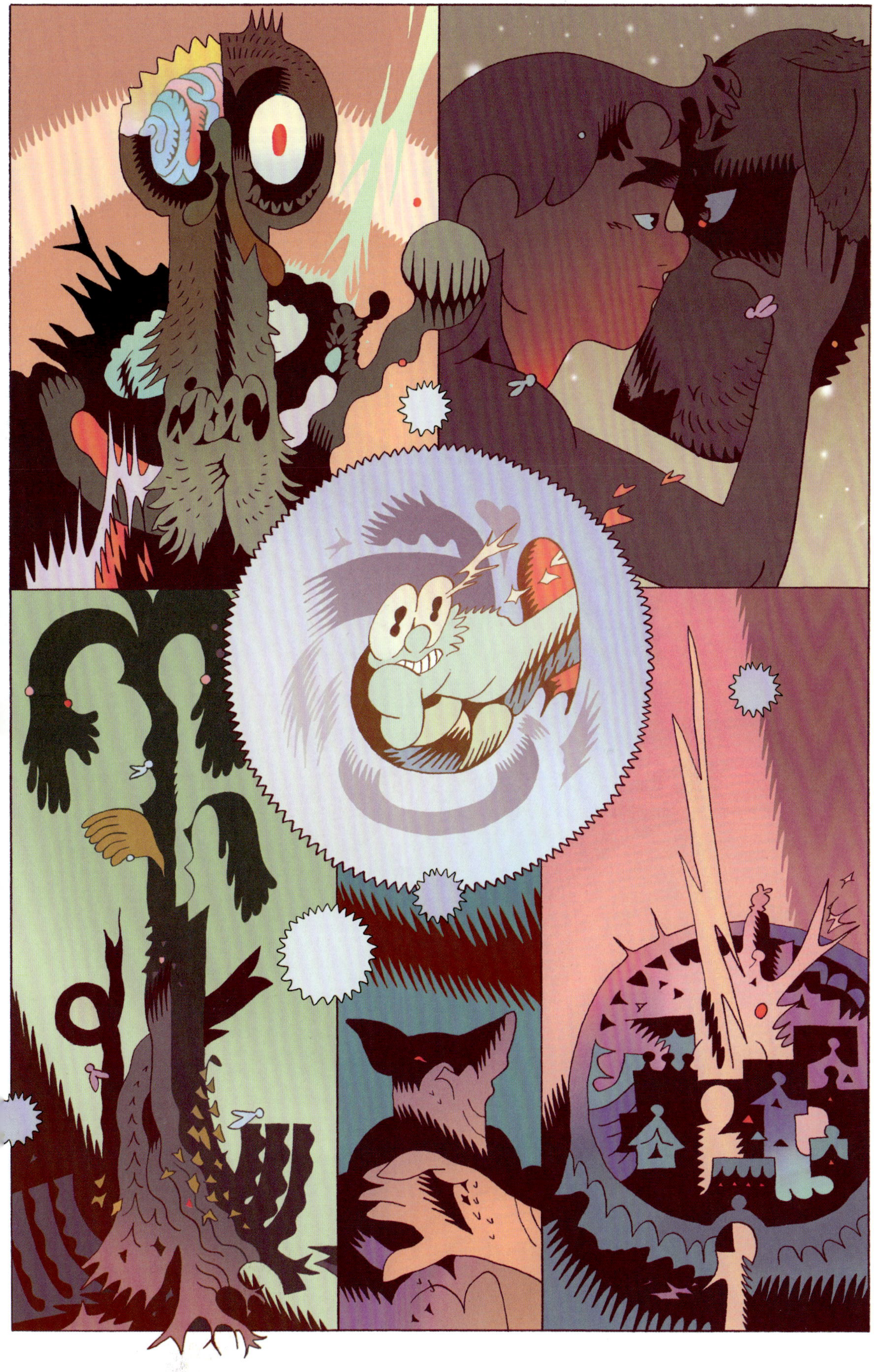

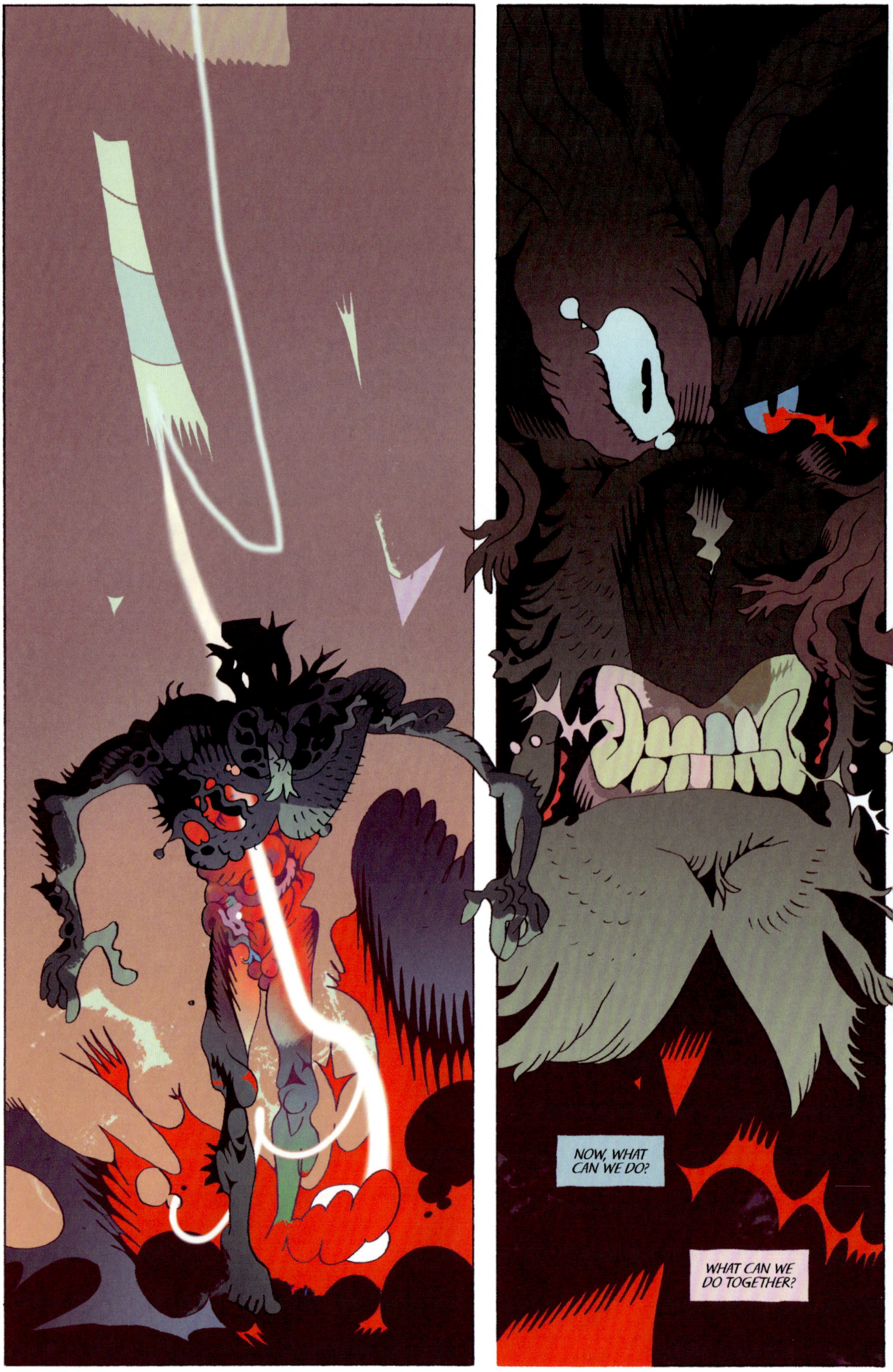
NOW, WHAT CAN WE DO?
WHAT CAN WE DO TOGETHER?

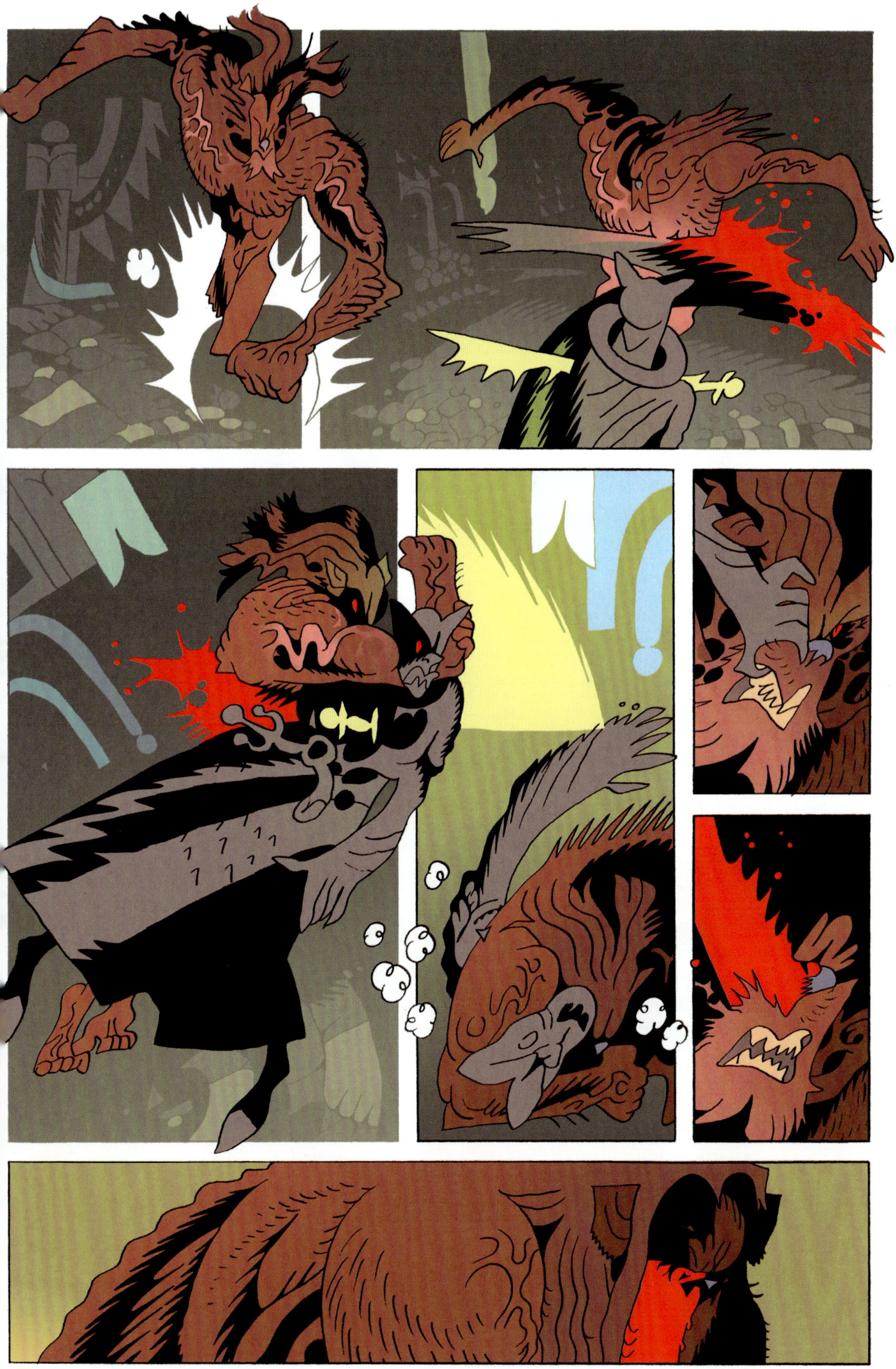

IT COMES BACK NOW. WITH THE BLOOD IT COMES BACK. WITH THE POUND--ING BLOOD IN MY TEMPLES, THE WORD...HE COMES BACK AND IT IS REMEMBERED THAT HE MADE US TO BE PARTICIPANT IN THE RHYTHM OF THE SPHERES, AND IN THE MUSIC OF THE STARS, BOUND UP TOGETHER IN THE RIBBONS OF TIME. THEY ARE STILL TURNING, THEY ARE STILL BURNING, AND ALL OF IT STILL UNFOLDING.
A STORY TO BE LIVED AND A LIFE TO BE WON.
AND TO THINK, THAT OUR PAIN SHOULD BE HIS ALSO. THAT OUR FATES SHOULD TOUCH AND EMBRACE AND BEAR JOY AS HEAVY FRUIT. THAT WE SHOULD GAIN LIFE BY LOSING IT. MYSTERY UPON MYSTERY UPON MYSTERY. AND I COME THROUGH WEIRD AND WEARY WAYS TO BELIEVE THAT IT WAS I.
IT WAS I WHO LEFT THE RELATIONSHIP. IT WAS I WHO FLED THE HALL, TURNED OVER THE TABLE, AND TREAD ON THE FELLOWSHIP BREAD. MIGHTN'T IT HAVE BEEN YOU ALSO, MY BROTHER?

MIGHTN'T IT HAVE BEEN EVERYONE BUT HE?
HE WHO STILL WALKS IN THE COOL GARDEN AND SITS AT THE SUPPER TABLE WITH WINE AND CHEESE AND MILK AND HONEY AND BREAD AND OIL AND FELLOWSHIP DRIPPING FROM THE BOUGHS OF TREES LONG GONE AND RENEWED AND RENEWED AND RENEWED? MIGHTN'T IT STILL BE LIKE THAT IN SOME QUIET CORNER OF OUR MINDS, OF OUR HEARTS, OF OUR BODIES?
AND MIGHTN'T IT BE SO GOOD AS TO OVERFLOW THE DESERT TO BLOSSOM? WITH BIRDS AND BEES AND BUGS AND TREES AND MOONLIGHT AND STAR-LIGHT AND SUNLIGHT AND FIRELIGHT FOREVER AND ON TO THE MUSIC HUM AND THE SWAYING OF WIND AND THE RUSH-ING OF GRASS AND THE LAUGHTER OF GOD.
MIGHTN'T IT BE SO THEN, AND NOW, AND AFTER?

MAD-
-NESS. THIS IS
MADNESS.
GO,
TELL IT ON THE
MOUNTAIN.
BANG
BANG
BANG

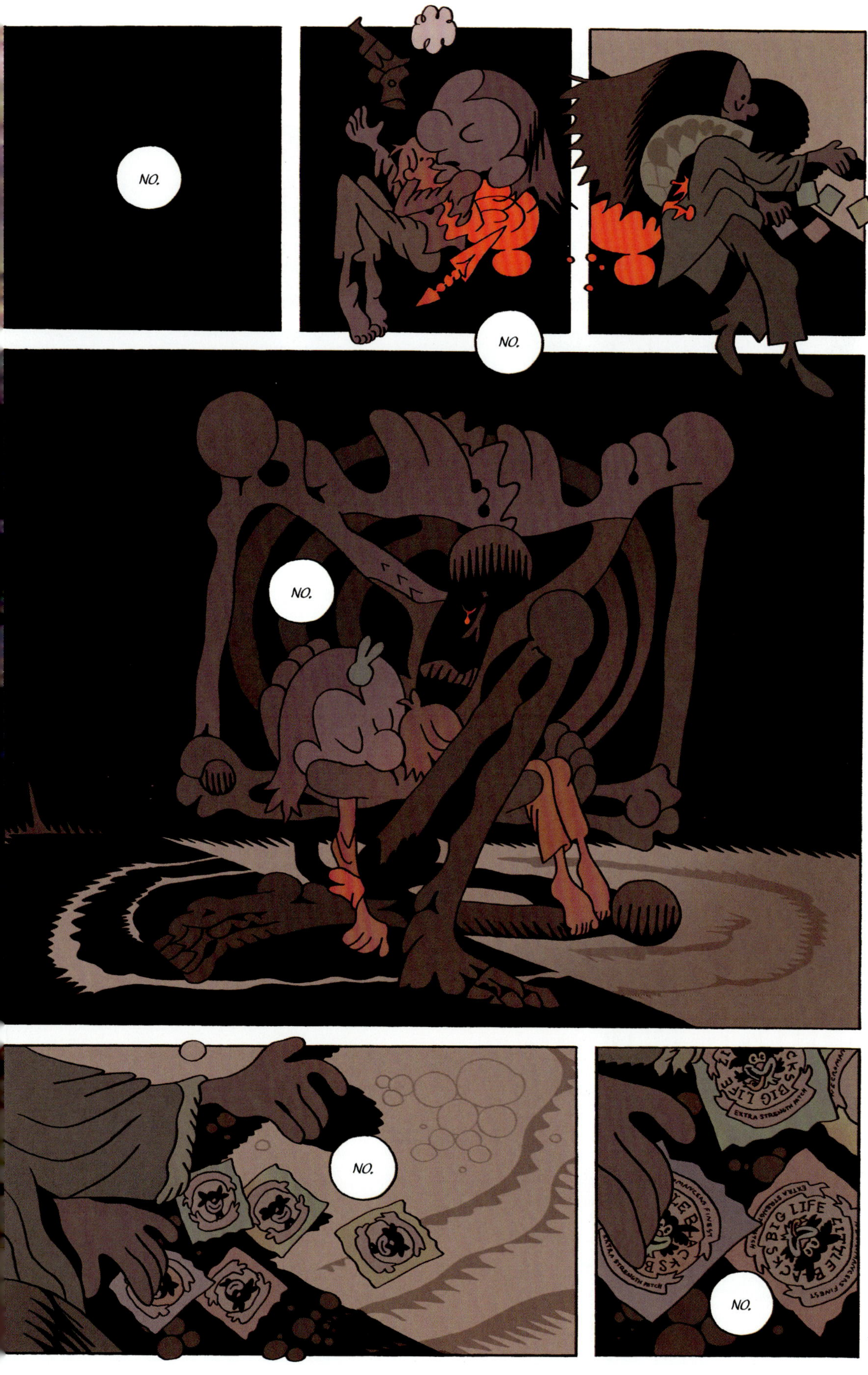
NO.
NO.
NO.
NO.
EXTRA STRENGTH PATCH
BIG LIFE
NO.

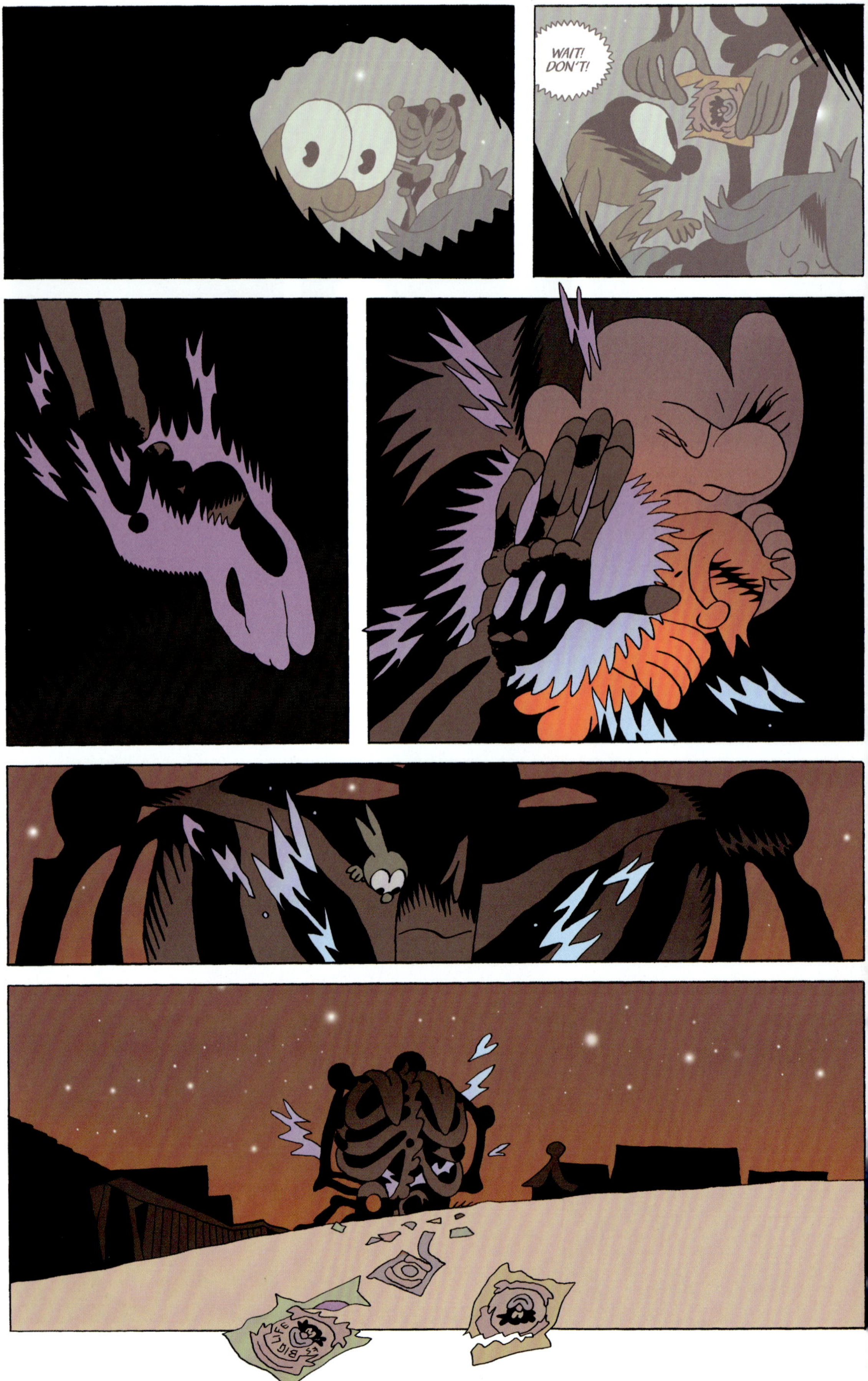
WAIT! DON'T!
BIG LIFE

Benjamin Schipper
Greenville, South Carolina
United States of America
March 10, 2022

Dear Reader,

Thank you for purchasing this book. The money you paid for it supports my family and my further work in comics. If you were wondering, Joe's story isn't done, you could say it's only beginning. This book is the first of many in a series I hope, but that's not something I can do alone.

I need your help.

It's the year twenty-twenty-two and the odds against non-franchise narratives do not look good. The big-box story factories are pumping out content in surprising quantities. Their qualities…bleached out, bled dry, shrink wrapped for the convenience of the global market, do not satisfy me. Give me the works of individual vision, the salty brine of anxious minds, the gifts of those laboring long in quiet studios beneath the earth, exorcizing those demons trapped inside them, drawing them out and baptising them into beauties which pierce like swords and burn like cold iron. I hope that I've provided something new for you in this book to enjoy and I ask only that you share it with others if you have. It takes great effort to make anything anyone can call good, it will take an even greater effort to keep them around after the first printing.

Look me up at benjaminschipper.com. I look forward to hearing from you.

GO ON AN ADVENTURE!

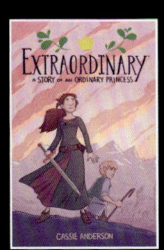

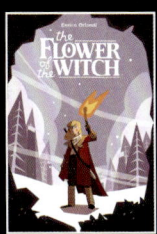

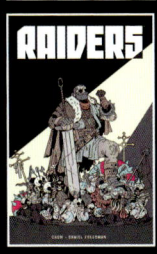

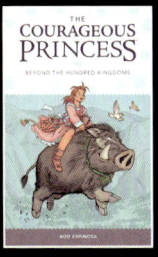

EXTRAORDINARY: A STORY OF AN ORDINARY PRINCESS
Cassie Anderson
After escaping an unconventional kidnapping, Princess Basil finds herself far from her castle and must take fate into her own hands. She tracks down the fairy godmother who "blessed" her, and finds the solution to her ordinariness might be as simple as finding a magic ring. With an unlikely ally in tow, she takes on gnomes, a badger, and a couple of snarky foxes in her quest for a less ordinary life.

ISBN: 978-1-50671-027-3 | $12.99

FLOWER OF THE WITCH
Enrico Orlandi
Tami has traveled long and far from his home in the south, forbidden to return until he has become a man, in this coming-of-age story. Defeating monsters and saving princesses has not been enough, and now he must find the fabled flower of the witch.

ISBN: 978-1-50671-642-8 | $14.99

RAIDERS
Cristian "Crom" Ortiz and Daniel Freedman
Marken and Maron, inseparable brothers, are dungeon raiders in a land ruled by corrupt royals and filled with fantastic dangers around every turn. But just as Marken decides that it's time to give up the raiding life, both brothers find themselves at the wrong end of the powers that be and stumble upon a secret that may unravel the entire political system.

ISBN: 978-1-50671-625-1 | $19.99

THE COURAGEOUS PRINCESS
VOLUME 1: BEYOND THE HUNDRED KINGDOMS
(THIRD EDITION)
Rod Espinosa
Once upon a time, a greedy dragon kidnapped a beloved princess . . . But if you think she just waited around for some charming prince to rescue her, then you're in for a surprise! Princess Mabelrose has enough brains and bravery to fend for herself!

ISBN: 978-1-61655-722-5 | $19.99

GIANTS
Carlos and Miguel Valderrama
A cataclysm of unknown origins unleashed a race of gigantic monsters whose presence has driven humanity underground. There, two orphans discover that the most dangerous monster is ambition, which unchecked, will grow until it devours you!

ISBN: 978-1-50670-624-5 | $19.99

APOCALYPTIGIRL: AN ARIA FOR THE END TIMES
(SECOND EDITION)
Andrew MacLean
Alone at the end of the world, Aria is a woman with a mission! As she traipses through an overgrown city with a cat named Jelly Beans, Aria is on a fruitless search for an ancient relic with immeasurable power. But when a creepy savage sets her on a path to complete her quest, she'll face death in the hopes of claiming her prize.

ISBN: 978-1-50671-464-6 | $19.99

AVAILABLE AT YOUR LOCAL COMICS SHOP OR BOOKSTORE
To find a comics shop near you, visit comicshoplocator.com • For more information or to order direct, visit DarkHorse.com

Extraordinary: A Story of an Ordinary Princess™ © Cassie Anderson. The Flower of The Witch™ © Enrico Orlandi. Raiders™ © Daniel Freedman and Cristian Ortiz. The Courageous Princess™ © Rod Espinosa. Giants™ © Miguel and Carlos Valderrama. Apocalyptigirl™ © Andrew Maclean. Dark Horse Books® and the Dark Horse logo are trademarks of Dark Horse Comics LLC. All rights reserved.

GABRIEL BÁ AND FÁBIO MOON!

"Twin Brazilian artists Fábio Moon and Gabriel Bá have made a huge mark on comics." –*Publishers Weekly*

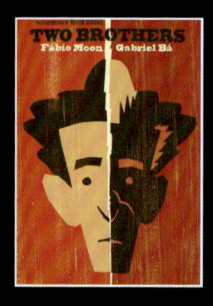

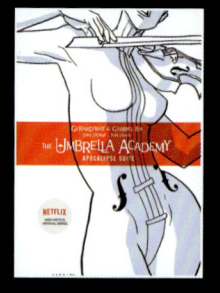

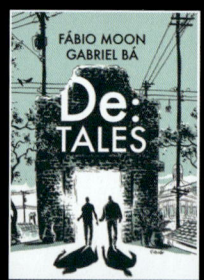

THE UMBRELLA ACADEMY: APOCALYPSE SUITE
Story by Gerard Way
Art by Gabriel Bá
TPB ISBN: 978-1-59307-978-9 | $17.99
Library Edition HC ISBN:
987-1-50671-547-6 | $39.99

THE UMBRELLA ACADEMY: DALLAS
Story by Gerard Way
Art by Gabriel Bá
TPB ISBN: 978-1-59582-345-8 | $17.99
Library Edition HC ISBN:
987-1-50671-548-3 | $39.99

THE UMBRELLA ACADEMY: HOTEL OBLIVION
Story by Gerard Way
Art by Gabriel Bá
TPB ISBN: 978-1-50671-142-3 | $19.99
Library Edition HC ISBN:
978-1-50671-646-6 | $39.99

PIXU: THE MARK OF EVIL
Story and art by Gabriel Bá, Becky Cloonan, Vasilis Lolos, and Fábio Moon
ISBN: 978-1-61655-813-0 | $14.99

B.P.R.D.: VAMPIRE
Story by Mike Mignola, Fábio Moon, and Gabriel Bá
Art by Fábio Moon and Gabriel Bá
ISBN: 978-1-61655-196-4 | $19.99

B.P.R.D.: 1946–1948
Story by Mike Mignola, Joshua Dysart, and John Arcudi
Art by Fábio Moon, Gabriel Bá, Paul Azaceta, and Max Fiumara
ISBN: 978-1-61655-646-4 | $34.99

NEIL GAIMAN'S HOW TO TALK TO GIRLS AT PARTIES
Story by Neil Gaiman
Art by Fábio Moon and Gabriel Bá
ISBN: 978-1-61655-955-7 | $17.99

TWO BROTHERS
Story and art by Gabriel Bá and Fábio Moon
ISBN: 978-1-61655-856-7 | $24.99

DE:TALES
Story and art by Gabriel Bá and Fábio Moon
ISBN: 978-1-59582-557-5 | $19.99

AVAILABLE AT YOUR LOCAL COMICS SHOP OR BOOKSTORE!
To find a comics shop in your area, visit comicshoplocator.com. For more information or to order direct, visit DarkHorse.com

Two Brothers™ © Fábio Moon and Gabriel Bá. De:Tales™ © Fábio Moon and Gabriel Bá. The Umbrella Academy™ © Gerard Way. Pixu™ © Becky Cloonan, Fábio Moon, Gabriel Bá, and Vasilis Lolos. B.P.R.D.™ © Mike Mignola. How to Talk to Girls at Parties™ © Neil Gaiman. Artwork © Fábio Moon and Gabriel Bá. Dark Horse Books® and the Dark Horse logo are registered trademarks of Dark Horse Comics LLC. All rights reserved. (BL 5086)

MORE TITLES FROM THE NEIL GAIMAN LIBRARY

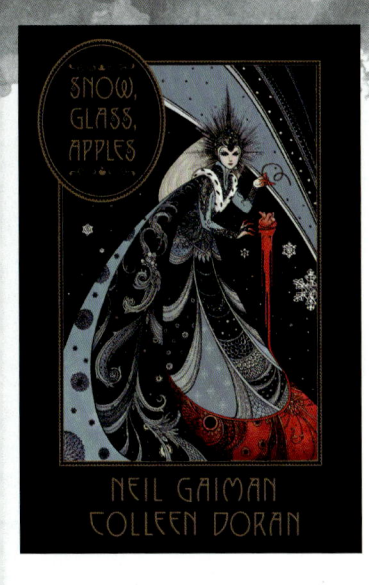

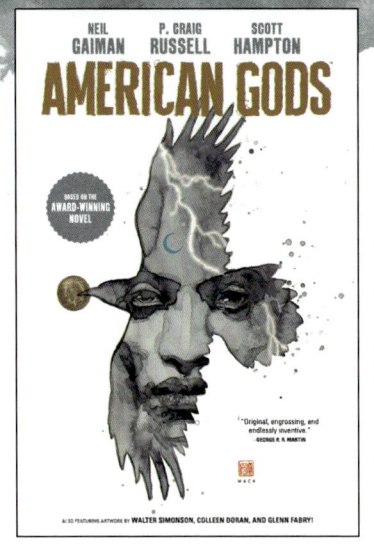

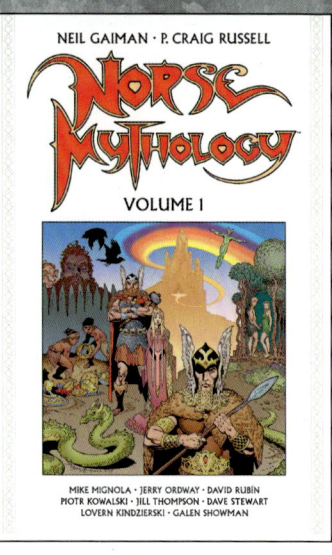

NEIL GAIMAN LIBRARY

VOLUME 1
Collects *A Study in Emerald, Murder Mysteries, How to Talk to Girls at Parties,* and *Forbidden Brides*
Neil Gaiman and various artists
$49.99 | ISBN 978-1-50671-593-3

VOLUME 2
Collects *The Facts in the Departure of Miss Finch, Likely Stories, Harlequin Valentine,* and *Troll Bridge*
Neil Gaiman and various artists
$49.99 | ISBN 978-1-50671-594-0

VOLUME 3
Collects *Snow, Glass, Apples; The Problem of Susan; Only the End of the World Again;* and *Creatures of the Night*
Neil Gaiman and various artists
$49.99 | ISBN 978-1-50671-595-7

AMERICAN GODS

SHADOWS
Neil Gaiman, P. Craig Russell, Scott Hampton, and others
HARDCOVER: $29.99 | ISBN 978-1-50670-386-2
$29.99 | ISBN 978-1-50673-499-6

MY AINSEL
Neil Gaiman, P. Craig Russell, Scott Hampton, and others
HARDCOVER: $29.99 | ISBN 978-1-50670-730-3
TPB: $24.99 | ISBN 978-1-50673-501-6

THE MOMENT OF THE STORM
Neil Gaiman, P. Craig Russell, Scott Hampton, and others
$29.99 | ISBN 978-1-50670-731-0

THE COMPLETE AMERICAN GODS
$124.99 | ISBN 978-1-50672-076-0

LIKELY STORIES
Neil Gaiman and Mark Buckingham
$17.99 | ISBN 978-1-50670-530-9

ONLY THE END OF THE WORLD AGAIN
Neil Gaiman, P. Craig Russell, and Troy Nixey
$19.99 | ISBN 978-1-50670-612-2

MURDER MYSTERIES
2ND EDITION
Neil Gaiman, P. Craig Russell, and Lovern Kinderski
$19.99 | ISBN 978-1-61655-330-2

THE FACTS IN THE CASE OF THE DEPARTURE OF MISS FINCH
2ND EDITION
Neil Gaiman and Michael Zulli
$13.99 | 978-1-61655-949-6

NEIL GAIMAN'S HOW TO TALK TO GIRLS AT PARTIES
Neil Gaiman, Fábio Moon, and Gabriel Bá
$17.99 | ISBN 978-1-61655-955-7

THE PROBLEM OF SUSAN AND OTHER STORIES
Neil Gaiman, P. Craig Russell, Paul Chadwick, and others
$17.99 | ISBN 978-1-50670-511-8

NEIL GAIMAN'S TROLL BRIDGE
Neil Gaiman and Colleen Doran
$14.99 | ISBN 978-1-50670-008-3

SIGNAL TO NOISE
Neil Gaiman and Dave McKean
$24.99 | ISBN 978-1-59307-752-5

CREATURES OF THE NIGHT
2ND EDITION
Neil Gaiman and Michael Zulli
$12.99 | ISBN 978-1-50670-025-0

FORBIDDEN BRIDES OF THE FACELESS SLAVES IN THE SECRET HOUSE OF THE NIGHT OF DREAD DESIRE
Neil Gaiman and Shane Oakley
$17.99 | ISBN 978-1-50670-140-0

HARLEQUIN VALENTINE
2ND EDITION
Neil Gaiman and John Bolton
$12.99 | ISBN 978-1-50670-087-8

NEIL GAIMAN'S A STUDY IN EMERALD
Neil Gaiman and Rafael Albuquerque
$17.99 | ISBN 978-1-50670-393-0

SNOW, GLASS, APPLES
Neil Gaiman and Colleen Doran
$17.99 | ISBN 978-1-50670-979-6

CHIVALRY
Neil Gaiman and Colleen Doran
$19.99 | ISBN 978-1-50671-911-5

NORSE MYTHOLOGY
VOLUME 1
Neil Gaiman, P. Craig Russell, Mike Mignola, and various artists
$29.99 | ISBN 978-1-50671-874-3

VOLUME 2
$29.99 | ISBN 978-1-50672-217-7

VOLUME 3
$29.99 | ISBN 978-1-50672-641-0

AVAILABLE AT YOUR LOCAL COMICS SHOP OR BOOKSTORE.
To find a comics shop in your area, visit comicshoplocator.com. For more information, visit DarkHorse.com

Likely Stories © 2018 Neil Gaiman. Text and illustrations of Only the End of the World Again™ © 2018 Neil Gaiman, P. Craig Russell, and Troy Nixey. Text of Murder Mysteries™ © 2014 Neil Gaiman. Adaptation and illustrations of Murder Mysteries™ © 2014 P. Craig Russell. Signal to Noise © 1989, 1992 Neil Gaiman & Dave McKean. Cover art © 1989, 1992 Dave McKean. Text of Harlequin Valentine™ © 2017 Neil Gaiman. Illustrations of Harlequin Valentine™ © 2017 John Bolton. The Facts in the Case of the Departure of Miss Finch™ text © 2008, 2016 Neil Gaiman, art © 2008, 2016 Michael Zulli. Miss Finch is a trademark of Neil Gaiman. How to Talk to Girls at Parties™ © 2016 Neil Gaiman. Artwork © 2016 Fábio Moon and Gabriel Bá. Neil Gaiman's Troll Bridge™ © 2016 Neil Gaiman, artwork © 2016 Colleen Doran. Forbidden Brides of the Faceless Slaves in the Nameless House of the Night of Dread Desire™ text © 2017 Neil Gaiman, art © 2017 Shane Ivan Oakley. Creatures of the Night is a trademark of Neil Gaiman. American Gods™ © 2017 Neil Gaiman. A Study In Emerald™ © 2018 Neil Gaiman. The Problem of Susan and Other Stories™ © 2019 Neil Gaiman. Snow, Glass, Apples™ © 2019 Neil Gaiman. Artwork © 2019 Colleen Doran. Norse Mythology™ © 2020 Neil Gaiman. Cover art of Norse Mythology © 2020 P. Craig Russell. Chivalry © 2022 Neil Gaiman. Artwork © 2022 Colleen Doran. Dark Horse Books® and the Dark Horse logo are registered trademarks of Dark Horse Comics LLC. All rights reserved. (BL 6043)

SPECULATIVE FICTION FROM

darkhorse originals

"Unique creators with unique visions."—**MIKE RICHARDSON, PUBLISHER**

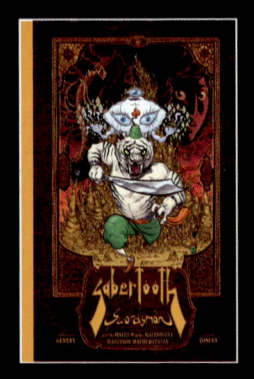

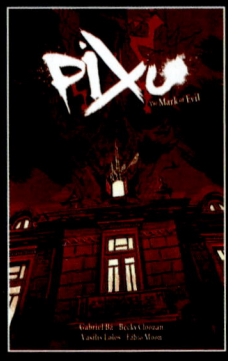

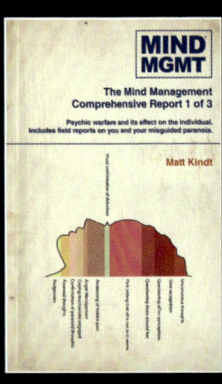

Sabertooth
Swordsman

SABERTOOTH SWORDSMAN

Damon Gentry and Aaron Conley

Granted the form of the Sabertooth Swordsman by the Cloud God of Sasquatch Mountain, a simple farmer embarks on a treacherous journey to the Mastodon's fortress!

ISBN 978-1-61655-176-6 | $17.99

Pixu
The Mark of Evil
Gabriel Bá · Becky Cloonan
Vasilis Lolos · Fábio Moon

PIXU: THE MARK OF EVIL

Gabriel Bá, Becky Cloonan, Vasilis Lolos, and Fábio Moon

This gripping tale of urban horror follows the lives of five lonely strangers who discover a dark mark scrawled on the walls of their building. As the walls come alive, everyone is slowly driven mad, stripped of free will, leaving only confusion, chaos, and eventual death.

ISBN 978-1-61655-813-0 | $14.99

SACRIFICE
SAM HUMPHRIES / DALTON ROSE

SACRIFICE

Sam Humphries, Dalton Rose, Bryan Lee O'Malley, and others

What happens when a troubled youth is plucked from modern society and sent on a psychedelic journey into the heart of the Aztec civilization—one of the greatest and most bloodthirsty times in human history?

ISBN 978-1-59582-985-6 | $19.99

DE:TALES

Fábio Moon and Gabriel Bá

Brimming with all the details of human life, Moon and Bá's charming stories move from the urban reality of their home in São Paulo to the magical realism of their Latin American background. Named by *Booklist* as one of the 10 Best Graphic Novels of 2010.

ISBN 978-1-59582-557-5 | $19.99

MIND MGMT
The Mind Management Comprehensive Report 1 of 3
Psychic warfare and its effect on the individual. Includes field reports on you and your misguided paranoia.
Matt Kindt

MIND MGMT OMNIBUS

Matt Kindt

This globe-spanning tale of espionage explores the adventures of a journalist investigating the mystery of a commercial flight where everyone aboard loses their memories. Each omnibus volume collects two volumes of the Eisner Award–winning series!

VOLUME 1: THE MANAGER AND THE FUTURIST
ISBN 978-1-50670-460-9 | $24.99

VOLUME 2: THE HOME MAKER AND THE MAGICIAN
ISBN 978-1-50670-461-6 | $24.99

VOLUME 3: THE ERASER AND THE IMMORTALS
ISBN 978-1-50670-462-3 | $24.99

DARK HORSE BOOKS

AVAILABLE AT YOUR LOCAL COMICS SHOP OR BOOKSTORE

To find a comics shop near you, visit comicshoplocator.com • For more information or to order direct, visit DarkHorse.com